Don't turn ~~que~~

Especially on Day One.

I rounded a corner and found her, kneeling in front of the burial tomb of a legendary voodoo queen. She stared at the stone slab as if she recognized it, as if it belonged to her; she was running her fingers through a fresh pile of Mardi Gras beads left by pilgrims seeking favors from the dead, a puzzled expression on her face.

I picked her up, checked her pulse, sheltered her in my arms for a moment while my head cleared. "She's fine," I said to myself, as if I needed some sort of reassurance.

But deep down inside I knew that wasn't true. There was something wrong here, too much information was trying to get through. Almost as if whoever did her jump didn't know what the hell they were doing.

I was too tired to care about another Newbie whose life just got mangled and torn in Fresh Start machinery. Too tired to realize that there might be more going on here than just a rugged jump.

It was the first mistake I would make on this case. But that didn't really matter. Because I was about to make plenty more.

AFTERLIFE

THE
RESURRECTION
CHRONICLES

MERRIE DESTEFANO

An Imprint of HarperCollinsPublishers

EOS
An Imprint of HarperCollins*Publishers*
10 East 53rd Street
New York, New York 10022-5299

Copyright © 2010 by Merrie Destefano
Cover art by Gordon Crabb
ISBN 978-0-06-199081-6
www.eosbooks.com

First Eos paperback printing: October 2010

Printed in the U.S.A.

10 9 8 7 6 5 4 3 2 1

For my husband, Tom

ACKNOWLEDGMENTS

The list of people who have influenced/helped/cheered/ca-joled me while writing this book is nearly as long as the book itself. People who helped transform the book into something much better than it was: my amazing agent, Kimberley Cameron; my awesome editors, Diana Gill and Ellen Leach; the brilliant cover designer, Amy Halperin, and illustrator, Gordon Crabb; Will Hinton and the rest of the HarperCollins staff—all of you deserve Warrior status. A heartfelt curtsy to both of my critique groups for performing red-pencil surgery on my behalf several times a month, whether I wanted it or not. Hugs and a round of applause for my husband, Tom, my son, Jesse, and our friend, Brad, for helping me understand the heart and soul of jazz. Kudos to the musicians who provided inspiration while I wrote every page: Coldplay, Jars of Clay, and Moby. And finally, to the person reading this book right now: Thank you. Really. I've wanted to write a story for you for a *very* long time now . . .

AFTERLIFE

AFTERLIFE

PART I

"*Remember, death is a choice.*
And I know you've all heard the latest rumor,
that One-Timers don't really exist.
They say that everybody's a First-Timer
and that when death comes, we all choose life.
I'm here to say that's just not true!"

—Reverend Josiah Byrd,
leader of the first pro-death rally

CHAPTER ONE

October 11

Chaz:

Jazz swirled through the room, competed with my heart-beat and pressed against my skin, sensuous as a lover's kiss, steamy as the bayou in mid-August. It stole my soul. It always did. For a few sweet moments I forgot about the world; I leaned forward and imagined another ending, one where I sat next to the bass player, nodding half asleep in a midnight mass of smoke and whiskey, saxophone reed thrust between my lips like the ultimate pacifier.

Bodies swayed and sagged, forever twined together with the music; it was a romantic symphony, it was worship for the weary.

And, in my mind, I was the worship leader.

I soared with the music to a land that didn't exist. Beyond time and space. Beyond the never-ending cycle of life and death, and hit-me-again, more life please.

Outside I could hear the ancient city of New Orleans whispering like a ghost down back alleys and twisted cobblestone streets, a rough, sultry memory of what she had once been, before the soul of the city had been stolen by urban regeneration; before the Cities of the Dead had been transformed into high-priced condos.

Is it too late for us, too late for redemption? That was my thought. But that wasn't what I said. Sometimes I get so caught up in the rhythms around me that I don't notice my own contribution to the white noise.

"Sterilization is the new death." That was what I really said.

"What?"

"Nothing." I nodded at a passing dark-skinned waitress, the one with the heart-shaped birthmark on her right cheek. Talking out loud was just one of the many unpredictable side effects of black-market whiskey. A moment later I had another crystal tumbler, two fingers full. I knew I should quit. At least for the night.

"What now, Chaz? You game?"

I blinked as I downed my second glass, felt the liquor sizzle down my throat all the way to my gut. Shadows moved through the club like disembodied spirits with lives of their own.

"Hey, yeah. We could, you know, go somewhere else. Dancing." A woman leaned into my line of vision, blue eyes, silver-blonde hair. Angelique. This was her first time. It had to be.

I chuckled. "I mean the first time at the second time."

"Huh?"

"Did I say that out loud? Well, it doesn't matter." I set down my glass, focused on her face. Smiled. "Yeah, dancing. Sure. That's what Babysitters are for, right?"

Angelique grinned, ear to diamond-studded ear. "Hey, yeah." She sucked down the last of her margarita.

I mentally focused on her speech patterns, a harmonic

convergence created in the Northeast, let's see, early twenty-first century—Norspeak, that's it. What I really couldn't figure out was, why do twenty-one-year-olds always drink margaritas? And why do they all want to be twenty-one? It didn't matter. A week out of the joint and this Newbie would be on her own; she'd be done downloading all her past lives and I'd be done playing chaperone.

I had six more days and nights with Little Miss Margarita. As far as I was concerned, that was seven days too long.

She stood up slowly, adjusted her dress. It was made out of one of those new synthetic fabrics that molded to her skin, whispering and rustling every time she moved. Very sensuous. Every goon in the bar was watching her, me included.

She was beautiful. More beautiful than I wanted to admit.

Maybe I was staring at her when I should have been watching the gutter punks who had sauntered in a few minutes earlier, all stitched up with black laces across their cheekbones. Just as we were about to leave, two of those underfed urchins broke into a fight. I saw the flash of knives and should have noticed that everything was too neat and clean, no blood, no torn flesh. Just the soft thud of knuckles against flesh and a few gruff moans.

But I didn't want to get involved in somebody else's mess, so I just hooked my right hand in Angelique's elbow and led the way toward the door.

"Time to leave," I said.

Right about then the shouts got louder and the bartender leaped over the bar, a baseball bat in one hand. While everyone else was focused on the brawling street thugs, a 220-pound genetic monster pushed his way through the crowd until he slid between the Newbie and me. He'd been staring at us from across the room, ever since we first walked through the door.

"Hey, sugah," he breathed, his words slamming together in Gutterspeak, that blue-collar dialect born in NOLA's Ninth Ward. "I'll takes ya dancin', baby. All night long."

He was high on stims. I could smell it, like the inside of a rusty tin can. But all I could see was the back of his metal-studded head and the muscles that rippled from his neck all the way down his oversized arms. Even his beefy fingers curved as if ready to strike.

"Back off, scumbag," I warned.

I mentally noted two gen dealers at five o'clock and a tattooed Nine-Timer cult gathering at two o'clock. Meanwhile, back in the corner, the gutter punks still rolled and tumbled, curses ringing out. Memories of the Newbie that went missing last week sparked through my mind, images of her mangled body on the freak show that posed as the ten-o'clock news.

At this point, I always wonder why I became a Babysitter. I mean, I had options.

The Neanderthal ran a meaty finger along Angelique's arm and pushed his bulldog face closer to hers. She stared up at him, mesmerized. Blasted Newbies. No mind of their own. Then he glanced over his shoulder as if noticing me for the first time. Sneered. White spittle caked his lips. "Get lost, puppy. This party's for two." A low growl rumbled in his throat and I stared into icy, soulless eyes.

"That's enough," I said as I grabbed his sweat-stained shirt and pulled.

Behind me I heard the inevitable scuffing of chairs as people backed up. A few of the regulars recognized me, so they knew what was going to happen.

My left hand slid into my pocket. I wrapped my fingers around my current weapon of choice, a soft chunk of liquid light. Molded it into a wad about the size of my thumb.

He was facing me now, muscles pumped, cord-like veins standing at attention.

I swallowed. It felt like I was in the Old West, challenging a gunslinger.

"This is your last chance," I warned him. I knew the stims had him going, had taken him to a land beyond logic. There was only one conclusion here. If that primate had half a brain, he would have known—

"The young lady, she stays with me, punk." His words slurred and his eyes narrowed. Angelique peered at me from behind his barrel-sized chest, like a teenager who'd been caught staying out after curfew.

"Move away from him, Angelique," I told her. She hesitantly obeyed, shoulders hunched. I gave her a nod and a soft smile. Good girl. Stay.

"You gots puppy written all over ya," he taunted. "Ya First-Timer!"

I've been called worse things. Doesn't mean that I like it. Or that it's true.

Then he lunged at me. There was a split second when I realized I may have misjudged him. I don't think he weighed 220; it was probably more like 250. I pulled my hand from my pocket and with a flick the liquid light ignited. A flash blasted from the palm of my left hand, shot toward him; electric current pulsed like jagged lightning, wrapping his arms and legs and chest in a sizzling blue-white anaconda. The force of it knocked him across the room, hissed while his limbs quivered. His eyes blinked in rapid succession, like he was trying to send us a message through Morse code.

Probably 250, not 220, I reminded myself as I waited for him to wake up. He got a lower charge than I expected. He convulsed on the floor.

All around me the room jolted to life.

"Somebody call the mugs! He gots liquid light—"

"He's gonna kill us—alls of us—"

I held up my hand, showed them the tattoo on the inside of my left palm.

A deadly quiet breezed through the club. Even the jazz stopped. I hate this part, the part where I kill the music. On the ground, the brute shuddered awake, lip twitching. He shook his head, struggled to fix one eye on me.

"I'm gonna gets the mugs on you, First-Timer," he choked out one word at a time.

I laughed. "No, you're not."

The Neanderthal forced his body to sit up, fought the storm that raged in his muscles. He pointed a quivering finger toward me. "Nobody pours liquid light on me and lives ta talk about it." He pushed one leg into position, then the second, grabbed a chair and used it to hoist himself to a shaky stand.

I turned my palm toward him. Showed him the tattoo. Watched his eyes widen, saw his gaze sweep the room as if one of the people there could help him. As if they would even consider it. "You see that woman over there?" I asked, nodding toward Angelique. He slid a nervous glance in her direction, not moving his head. "That's my baby, buddy. Nobody touches her—you got that? It's within my legal rights to send you all the way back to your own miserable beginning. You want to start all over as a single-celled zygote?"

He shook his head, his jaw slack. His lip was still quivering.

I reached into my right pocket, pulled out a tag, walked toward him.

He started to move backward, ran into a table, knocked it over.

I stopped. "Where do you think you're going?" I asked.

He froze, every muscle trembling now, but not from the liquid light.

I sighed. Reached over, clicked the tag on the back of his hand. A microscopic chip shot out, embedded itself in his skin. He flinched, but not from the pain. "That's my marker," I whispered. "You're my baby now."

He shook his head. "I didn't means nothin'. I didn't do nothin'."

"Well, then you just better pray that when you're my baby, nobody does nothin' to you, neither. Cause when your time comes, I'm gonna be your Babysitter. And sugah," I leaned dangerously close to his face, let my hot breath sink into his pores, switched my speech patterns to make sure he understood. "We's gonna haves lots of fun together. I promises."

CHAPTER TWO

Neville:

I stumbled out the door, my feet numb, my vision blurred. I slumped onto broken cobblestone, strains of jazz seeping into the alley around me as I landed facedown. Behind me, a high-pitched twitter mingled with the bright notes of a clarinet. One of my own boys was laughing at me.

"Boss, you shoulda seen yourself, you was tumblin' backward like a First-Timer with a mouthful of jive-sweet! Man, I wishes I had a VR of that pretty scene—"

I struggled to my feet, then grabbed the black-haired gutter punk by the throat and shook him until the change in his pocket jingled. The boy didn't fight back. He didn't dare. He sputtered and coughed, his lips turned blue.

Finally I dropped him to the ground, watched him gasp and flail.

"Was it pretty, like that?" I asked.

The boy cringed. Two other slender young men slid deeper into the shadows, their faces covered with fresh bruises from their recent mock battle inside the club.

I laughed until my voice echoed. "Good job, boys," I said.

Then I tossed each of them a token that spun through the evening gloom, engraved words catching the dim lamplight: FREE ADMISSION TO THE UNDERGROUND CIRCUS. Dangerous grins spread across their faces as they each pocketed their new favor.

"Was it her?" one of them asked.

I shrugged. Seven ladies downloaded in New Orleans today. I'd already discounted the two that had tumbled through the black market, a process that left their brains scorched and empty. Could be this one, but I didn't want to say yeah or nay, not yet. Still had three more to track down.

I sucked in a long, dark breath. My boys waited for a sign that it was time to move on.

I nodded. Slow, so they'd pay attention.

"We goes that way." I pointed toward the other end of the alley.

They all stared like they didn't believe me.

"But, boss," the punk on the ground finally coughed out a few words, his voice raspy, his neck still red from my grip. "That guy's a 'sitter. He's loaded with light. Nobody says he gonna be carryin' light or—"

"Or you woulda been too chicken to belly up for the job? Look, you gots a sister, right?"

The kid nodded, then looked away.

"And you wants yur sister to keep that pretty face. Or maybe ya don't cares no more."

"I cares." The boy shoved himself into a sitting position, then scrambled to his feet. "Let's go."

"Yeah." I punched him in the arm. "We follows the 'sitter."

The four of us headed down the alley. I rubbed my hand where that puppy had jammed a marker. I had to get this thing out, couldn't be on somebody's trackin' screen. The dark city stretched out before us like a maze, black-shadowed streets, yellow edges of light—all wrapped up

with knife-sharp corners. Only one safe path led across the
Big Easy once the sun went down. We lived in the belly of
the alley, gutter water ran through our veins, and the sewer
stench was our perfume.

I is the shadow, the fire that burns, the smoke that blinds.

I thrust another spike in my arm and then held my breath.

*F'true, I'll gets the marker out. Soon as my spike halo
fades.*

CHAPTER THREE

Chaz:

It was late, but an unrelenting crowd of bohemians, gutter punks and tourists still jostled their way through the Quarter, all of them carrying black-market imitations of Jamaican rum punch and Dixie Crimson Voodoo Ale. Musicians gathered on street corners, playing jazz improvisations to passersby, waiting for the steady waterfall of tips that jingled into open trumpet cases. Antiques shops and art galleries lured tourists toward brightly lit windows, and a pair of prostitutes strolled arm in arm, gossiping in French. The Newbie and I had walked from one blues club to another, watched the moon snake its way across the sky. My feet hurt and my head throbbed from my last glass of whiskey. A sure sign it was finally time to end the evening.

But now Miss Margarita was in the mood for adventure. As if her run-in with that genetic monster never even happened.

"I want to see the Cities of the Dead," she said.

"The Cities of the Dead are gone," I answered in my best

monotone. Nobody needed cemeteries anymore. The empty carcasses left over after resurrection were just piled into incinerators and toasted.

She shook her head. Waist-long platinum waves shimmered.

Why did they always look like Hollywood movie stars, when they should be sucking up worms and dirt? I sighed.

"I'm not stupid, you know. I used to be an attorney. I just, hey, yeah, didn't want to be one this time."

I wished I had another drink. Even a migraine would be better than this.

"I know they kept one graveyard—yeah, they did. For tourists. Saw it on the news, babe. You know, before."

"Before you went in the joint."

She nodded. She didn't want to talk about the joint. None of them ever did. I felt bad immediately. I should have let her bring it up first. Tears formed in the corners of black-mascara-rimmed eyes. Maybe she was remembering a husband and a kid that she left behind. Maybe there was a best friend, rotting away in a nursing facility somewhere, waiting for a phone call that would never come. Maybe there was a lifetime of memories crowding to the surface, all struggling to be part of the 50 percent that got to survive.

"Fine," I said, although it really wasn't. I shot a pulse beam into the night sky and signaled a taxi. "We'll go see the last City of the Dead."

Her eyes darkened when the cab pulled down from a nearby rooftop, gliding through the misty evening fog to stop beside us. I thought she would be happy. Thought she would smile at least—I mean, I did exactly what she wanted. But she just climbed inside the taxi and turned away from me, then stared out the window, hands rolled in tight little balls on her lap.

The cemetery appeared a few moments later, a gothic land of stone and skeleton, hard edges softened by moonlight and transformed into something mythic. We stepped from the taxi, both of us hesitating. The wrought-iron gates screeched when I pulled them open. I wanted to laugh, but for some reason I couldn't. This was a place where bones marked the transition from life to whatever lay on the other side.

No matter what the Stringers say, this was still a sacred place.

I watched as Angelique moved silently through moonbeams, shadowy fog clinging to her feet. It followed her like a living, breathing creature as she walked from one tomb to the next, poised beside her as she read rusted bronze placards. Names of the dead dripped from her lips. *Christophe. Marguerite. Francois.* She shook her head, moved on. I realized that she was crying. Something was wrong; some of her circuits weren't firing right. Tears slipped down pubescent-perfect cheeks. Movie-star lips quivered.

Suddenly I couldn't focus my eyes anymore. I staggered and grabbed on to a towering stone angel, almost lost my balance. Whiskey jitters were finally catching up with me.

"You shouldn't drink that black-market crap," she said. Her speech patterns were changing. I detected a faint Scottish brogue, a late twentieth-century accent. I had to watch out. She could collapse if the memories came back too rapidly. "I worked on all the synthetic alcohol patents. Whiskey's probably the worst."

I nodded. We finally had something in common. Standing in the middle of a cemetery beneath a silvery moon, we both agreed that contraband liquor was bad news. A whispering breeze passed between us, stirred the mists into curving rococo eddies. Just then I turned away and leaned against my angel friend again. Vertigo forced me to wobbly knees.

"Drink tequila next time," she said.

I held up my hand to silence her. Even a Babysitter deserves a moment of peace. Especially when he's curled over with jitters. The world seemed to be all mist and shadow, everything in soft focus, like I was looking through a camera fitted with the wrong lens. I wiped my face on my shirtsleeve, then caught my breath and stood up.

"Angelique?" Dead leaves rustled and tumbled through a narrow courtyard.

She was gone.

"Hey, yeah! Angelique. Where are you?" Stone met stone, shadows changed from gray to purple to black.

Babysitting 101: Never turn your back on a Newbie. Especially on Day One.

There were no sounds except my own footsteps as I stumbled through uncharted darkness; my own heartbeat, as it chugged along like a train on rickety tracks. I began to jog between temple-tombs, moved through what looked like a black-and-white vampire-movie set. I imagined Dracula, arms open wide, imagined Angelique welcomed into a land of the undead. A hundred dangers lurked in the shadows: thieves, murderers, kidnappers, hiding in the neat and narrow spaces between the tombs, waiting for tourists, hoping someone would pass by, someone unarmed and innocent.

Someone like my Newbie. Memories rose to the surface, stories of half-baked Newbies, caught and sold into slavery. They were so easy to program during the first week. I was running faster now. Thought I saw someone, watching me from a dark corridor between the tombs.

"Angelique—where are you?"

That was when I rounded a corner and found her, kneeling in front of the burial tomb of a legendary voodoo queen.

She stared at the stone slab as if it belonged to her; she was running her fingers through a fresh pile of Mardi Gras beads left by pilgrims seeking favors from the dead, a puzzled expression on her face. She must have heard me, but for the longest time she didn't move. She just continued to stare down at the tokens, mumbling to herself. Finally she turned and looked at me.

"Did you see him?" she asked.

"Who?" I glanced behind us.

"He's running away, he's free now." She tried to stand up, a ghostly smile on her lips, a long-dead memory. But then she blinked, her eyes rolled back, and she collapsed, disappearing beneath the mist.

I picked her up, checked her pulse, sheltered her in my arms for a moment while my head cleared. "She's fine," I said to myself, as if I needed some sort of reassurance. I struggled to forget about all the things that could go wrong, about the hidden clauses in the Fresh Start contract that protected me from scenarios just like this. I was tired of being the one that always came out on top of every bad situation. "You're going to be okay. Hang in there, kid," I mumbled as I carried Angelique toward the street. "We'll get you straightened out. Some jumps are just rougher than others."

But deep down inside I knew that wasn't true. There was something wrong here: too much information was trying to get through. Almost as if whoever did her jump didn't know what the hell they were doing. Fortunately the cab was waiting exactly where I left it. I signaled the driver.

Then I used two Master Keys, preprogrammed commands hardwired into every Newbie at start-up, and I whispered into Angelique's ear. "Wake up. Focus."

She instantly opened her eyes, stood up and climbed into the cab, one hand holding mine for support.

We drove away.

I was too tired to care about another Newbie whose life just got mangled and torn in Fresh Start machinery. Too tired to realize that there might be more going on here than just a rugged jump.

It was the first mistake I would make on this case. But that didn't really matter. Because I was about to make plenty more.

CHAPTER FOUR

October 12 • 1:16 A.M.

Chaz:

Angelique leaned against my shoulder, babbling softly, staring into space. The city melted around us as one narrow fog-drenched street bled into another. We swung through that section of the Quarter where the streets changed names; St. Charles Avenue veered off into downtown and turned into Royal Street, leaving the nineteenth-century millionaire's row behind.

I tapped the Plexiglas that separated us from the taxi driver. A row of colorful tarot cards clung to the barrier with a hand-written sign: FREE READINGS WITH A TOUR OF THE CITY.

"The Carrington. Bourbon Street."

He nodded. At least, I think it was a he. Long dreadlocks, black lipstick, massive biceps. I saw him studying me in the rearview.

"Newbie?" the he/she asked a few moments later, heavy-lidded eyes confronting mine in the mirror.

I nodded.

"You the Babysitter?"

Another nod. Followed by a yawn.

"Mind if I see some ID?"

I flashed my palm.

The driver shrugged. "Ever since that incident over in Barcelona last year, I always check."

"Yeah." I yawned again. "What can I say? The laws are different in Spain. You should be glad you live here." Just then the Carrington Hotel loomed into view, a tall brick-and-mortar Baroque masterpiece. For seven days and nights I have no life. I eat, drink and sleep with my assigned Newbie. I don't mean sleep in the biblical sense—nobody touches my baby like that, not even me.

Sometimes we stay in a hotel; sometimes we go to my place. On rare occasions, we go to the Newbie's home, but there are usually too many memory pegs there, even after it's been sterilized. My main requirement is that wherever we stay, I need my own room and a VR room. Once in a while a customer balks and says that's too expensive. I usually raise an eyebrow and tell them to take their business elsewhere. Right about then I laugh. Not hysterically. It's more like a well-planned "ha."

There is nowhere else. We're the only ice-cream store in town.

Angelique and I made it through the hotel lobby without incident. I take that back. There was a brief moment when she became disoriented, right about when I was getting the room key.

She looked up at me through half-closed eyes. "William?" she asked, confused. A tormented pause. "Jim?" She shook her head. I made eye contact with the concierge, then silently showed him my ID.

"Who are you?" Angelique asked.

"Chaz. Chaz Domingue. Your Babysitter." I briefly debated which of the five Master Keys to use. "Recognize."

She squinted her eyes, looked me up and down. "My *Baby-sitter*?"

"Focus," I said, pulling another key phrase from my limited bag of tricks. "This is Day One."

"Day One." She looked at the ground, shoulders sagging as the weight of the world came rushing back. "Then William is really gone." Her voice faded below a whisper. "And that means I must be dead."

"No, Angelique," I guided her toward the elevator, away from the concierge, who looked concerned. Few people see or remember the anguish of a Newbie's first week. If they did, they might not be so eager to jump.

"You're alive," I told her as the elevator took us almost instantly to the thirty-third floor.

But she just shook her head and kept mumbling the same dark phrase over and over.

"That means I must be dead."

Sometimes this job is enough to break your heart, if you've still got one.

1:58 A.M.

Fresh Start keeps its word when we say we give our clients a new beginning. I may be part of the family, but I don't have access to any "secret files." I honestly didn't know who the hell she was or who she used to be, any more than she did. And I didn't care.

Like I always say, I don't make the rules.

So, I tucked Angelique into bed, made sure she was safe and sound and asleep; then I locked all the doors and windows. It's habit, of course—no one has wandered into a Babysitter's suite, even by accident, in more than twenty years. Still, it makes me feel better, so I do it. Lots of things make me feel better. Like black-market whiskey. Like jazz clubs. Like a midnight session alone in a VR room.

The moon had all but forgotten about us. It disappeared behind the rugged skyline, and headed off to seduce other countries with silver shadows. I was long past tired. But I needed absolution.

I shut the door to the room, slipped into a VR suit, then snuggled down in the sensory chair and closed my eyes while it morphed to fit my body. With a thought command I switched on the Grid. Narrow bands of red, blue and green light shot across the room, sought and defined its dimensions, creating a chart of horizontal lines. The light quickly formed a graph of horizontal and vertical bands.

The Grid was up.

I went to my home page, a glittering seascape where waves crashed against a mountainous shore. Sandpipers waddled across the narrow beach, following the tides like tiny Charlie Chaplin impressionists. I took a deep breath, sucked in the smell of saltwater, felt the charge of negative ions.

I always have a hard time leaving my home page.

It was well past midnight in my tiny corner of the universe, sometime between rest for the weary and insomnia for the troubled. And yet—elsewhere on earth's canvas— dawn painted gray skies; sherbet colors layered the horizon; and the earth waited to run a rough tongue over the flavors of tomorrow. I spun a VR globe with my right hand, looking for places where the sun still cast long shadows, where the inhabitants had reached that point in the day where they could pause and catch their breath.

I have ten preselected locations around the world, ten different time zones, places I can visit whenever I have a chance.

Not everybody has a regular nine-to-five. I've learned over the years to find my solace where and when I can. Tonight it waited for me in a tiny stucco building in George, South Africa. I always start on the outside, on the dusty street. I know I stand out from most of the regulars, me in my glittering VR suit, them in their brightly colored caftans and turbans. But there will be others like me, visitors from around the globe. One man comes from China; his almond eyes watch me as we stand beside each other. I've never actually talked to him, but he nods and smiles, glances down at my right hand.

I'm carrying my sax.

The building glows from within, the glimmer of a thousand candles. I've come to fill up all my empty spaces, to patch the holes in my heart, to revive my ever-dull, ever-disobedient soul.

I sit in a back pew, my eyes closed, letting the song wash over me, cleansing me. Already I can hear her voice. Beulah. An old black woman, frail and tall, her nubby hair cropped close to her head, her neck long: her wide lips lift praise in a velvet-rich tone, her lungs an instrument as pure and clear as mountain sky. Then I lift the saxophone to my lips, joining the song. Somehow we always manage to stop at exactly the same moment. There is a hush, an expectant *selah*-pause as angels themselves draw nearer, eager to know more about this thing called salvation.

Sometimes I wish I fully understood it, how my part is going to add up to anything of significance in the end. Most of the time I think I'm fooling myself, trying to convince myself that I really matter at all.

But for now I just have to take it like every other One-Timer does.

Like credit in the bank. Invisible, but there when you need it.

Like faith.

CHAPTER FIVE

Chaz:

Night brings peace for some, for those who can sleep. Personally I think it's all a ruse. Go ahead, close your eyes. Tomorrow will be better than today. Go ahead. I dare you. Well, I'm not taking any bets. When I stand and look out at the night sky, I have a hard time believing that the sun is really going to rise again.

The landscape of George faded away, faster than I wanted. I was alone. Remembering that freak in the jazz club. He left a bad taste in my mouth. Almost like I'd swallowed a glass of his jive-sweet take-me-to-the-sky high, and now his snake-in-the-skin was going to rub off on me.

I've never liked gen-spike addicts, the way their skin ripples and shivers, like it's crawling with a hundred snakes. There's something primeval about them, as if evolution somehow reversed, imploded in upon itself; maybe Darwin stood up in the middle of the night and pushed a cosmic button and then suddenly all his clever theories began to unwind. Not that I ever believed in them in the first place, but somehow the gen freaks have his name tattooed on their souls.

And I hate to say it because it sounds so déjà vu, but I felt like I had seen this guy somewhere before.

A bad feeling slipped up my tailbone, lodged itself in the center of my chest and then twisted.

Had we been followed tonight? I thought I'd seen that guy earlier in the evening, outside the museum. He had turned around, watched Angelique when we got in the taxi and headed for the jazz club. And then in the cemetery, a flash of eyes watched me, between the crypts.

Was my imagination working overtime just because my Newbie collapsed and went off-line? Or—this one was even worse—was somebody after the Newbie?

Her identity was a secret: even she didn't know for sure who she had been in her previous life yet. That was all part of the deal. Fresh Start. Nobody knew who you were or what you'd done. Even the mugs couldn't come after you for a past crime, as long as you hadn't committed a capital. It was a little bit like redemption. I know that sounds corny, but it was true. Sign on the dotted line and then when the time comes, everything gets washed away. Your family can't find you, your creditors can't find you, even your best friend won't know where you went. A brand-new beginning. And if you planned everything right, there should be a nice little sum of money waiting, investments accrued over lifetimes.

Still, people have cracked the system before.

We pretend to be this omnipotent organization, but we've got our weak points.

"Run a track on marker number"—I paused and checked my log—"sixteen-point-four-three-eight-eight. Check to see where it's been tonight."

I tried my best to settle back and relax while the Grid ran a search on the gen freak I'd tagged a few hours ago. I knew he wouldn't keep the marker long. Within a few days he'd find somebody in a back alley with barely enough techno-skills to take it out. I just hoped that they would accidentally yank out some muscle and nerve at the same time. Our markers have tentacles that lace for at least five inches on either side of the insertion point. Not many black-market geeks have the talent to remove one. Or the guts.

The search paused and skittered, jammed to a stop sooner than I expected.

"Parameters?" a silver voice asked.

"Where and when. Give it to me on a satellite map, include street names. Make it 'up close and personal.'"

It flashed across the VR screen. Shorter than it should have been, both in distance and time. Either the jerk went home and fell asleep, or he had already found someone to remove the marker.

"Closer. Zoom in on the street names."

The map sizzled, then jumped, razor-sharp exact. I immediately recognized the beginning of the glowing yellow trail. I smiled. The brute must have taken a while to catch his breath. He didn't leave the alley behind the club for about half an hour, long after the Newbie and I left. Nice. I wish I could have put him down for longer. It's illegal, but with some of these Mongoloid jerks, I feel like the limits need to be stretched.

Nobody tells me yes or no. Nobody but me. And that little voice, almost too quiet to hear sometimes.

I stood up and walked closer to the screen. Read the street names out loud as I followed the trail with my finger. Something strange about the way he traveled. Stop and go. Almost made me think he wasn't alone, like he was with somebody else.

"You got any real satellite shots of this?"

A duplicate map, sans the yellow tracking line, shot up on the far wall. I walked over, examined it. I was right, there were four goons down there.

I went back to the first map, continued the trail. Stopped. That bad feeling was back. His trail led to the City of the Dead. The same time the Newbie and I were there.

He had followed us.

And as far as I could tell, there was only one way he could have found us.

That was as much evidence as I needed, but for some reason I continued to follow his trail. He didn't track us after the cemetery, didn't come here. I paused. Maybe I was wrong. Maybe it was a one-in-a-million fluke, like winning a lottery ticket. Maybe he hadn't followed us.

I took his trail to the end.

It had to be wrong.

"Is this data corrupted? Any chance somebody tampered with the marker?"

A long, reflective whirring pause. "No. The data is correct."

That Neanderthal's trail ended at Fresh Start, at our main headquarters.

This was beginning to look like an inside job.

CHAPTER SIX

Neville:

The Mississippi churned with froth and mud, and here, on the Toulouse Street Wharf, the wind blew chill. A steam whistle sounded in the near distance as the *Natchez* slugged closer and the river echoed with the captain's voice, calling through a vintage megaphone. Ambiance. It was all about mystique and how to charm tourists out of another fistful of cash.

I turned up my collar, shivering in the damp cold as I glared at the three-deck steamboat edging its way toward the dock. Somewhere, hidden in a private room, a steam calliope sang a thirty-two-note forbidden song.

Luring me and my boys.

The laughter of children, innocence bought and sold.

"Has you been inside before, boss?" one of my gutter punks asked.

I nodded, then flashed a dark grin. My spike halo was fading, and with it, the world was coming back into focus. The crowd began to shuffle up the ramp toward the boat, river water sloshing onto the first deck. Hidden in my pockets, my fists curled in anger at what I had seen less than an hour ago, a laboratory filled with empty cages—just like my boss expected.

We had been betrayed. The dog and the research were missing.

But for now, I followed the crowd, one step at a time, ignoring the stench of sweat and the press of flesh, forgetting about the near impossible task set before me by the latest turn of events. I vowed to push it out of my mind for the next two hours.

Instead I listened for the strains of calliope music.

And waited for the decadent pleasures that could only be found in the Underground Circus.

CHAPTER SEVEN

Chaz:

Angelique slept on her right side, curled in a tangled fetal position, legs tight to her chest, head buried in a pillow. One fist pressed against her mouth. Her eyelids twitched. She must have been dreaming.

I slipped into her room as quietly as I could. I'm always a bit clumsy when I'm tired, but right now exhaustion had been replaced by a jagged adrenaline rush. Fear isn't one of my favorite highs.

I took her left hand in mine as gently as I could. Ran a scanner over it. Nothing.

I wanted to feel good, I wanted to say, hey, one out of two. Chances are high that I was mistaken. But I've never been an optimist.

I reached for her other hand, twisted beneath the pillow. Tried to pull it forward. She moaned, tossed her head, stretched both arms and then repositioned herself. I waited. We each took a deep breath and sighed at the same time, one of those odd in-sync moments that catch you by surprise. I blinked and reminded myself that this was another human being lying here, with as many rights as I have. One of them being violated by Yours Truly right now.

She settled back into a deep sleep, her right hand draped over her thigh.

I ran the scanner again. A pulse of red light flashed.

She had a marker.

I gave myself a couple of minutes to think, paced back and forth in front of her bedroom window. Stared down at the almost empty street, then up at the starless sky. If I was waiting for a flash of brilliance, it didn't come. The only thing I got was a nagging list of questions, one that cried for attention louder than the others.

I was her Babysitter, so how and when did she get somebody else's marker? Messing with a Newbie is a capital, and none of the morons who run the kidnapping rings have access to this kind of hardware.

I decided to take a break, went out into the kitchen. Made myself some café au lait with chickory, then found a couple of cookies. I sauntered back into the VR room, rested in the chair and waited for my home page to boot up again, munched on something that tasted like chocolate chips but was probably a soy-based, lactose-free imitation.

Waves washed back and forth. Each one clean, fresh, new. White foam curling. Gulls complaining overhead. The sandpipers were gone. Now a baby seal and its mother glistened in the afternoon sun, sliding over the sand, chasing each other, barking like dogs with sore throats.

I wished my father was still alive. He understood this business like nobody else, had a way of explaining how it never compromised his faith, how he was more like a watcher on the wall, making sure Stringers kept their rights, while at the same time the One-Timers kept theirs. He believed that one day our family might be the only ones left with enough political power to stand up for the One-Timers.

Of course, the other One-Timers never saw it that way.

Dad wouldn't think twice about all this, I know. He'd confront my brother, Russell, in a heartbeat, ask him what the hell was going on. Why did this Stringer have a marker? Why had that goon been following me? And who did he know over at Fresh Start?

But underneath all of it, I still had a feeling, one of those stupid gut-intuition things. I couldn't believe Russ was involved in this. I mean, he'd made a few bad business decisions in the past several years, but he'd never actually crossed the line, never broken the law.

I was the one who always got stuck with the dirty work.

The café au lait was gone and I wiped cookie crumbs from my face as I stood in the doorway to Angelique's bedroom. I was going to have to use a couple of Keys I usually avoid. And do something that could get me thrown in jail.

"Sleep, Angelique," I said. "Deep sleep."

She sighed, rolled over on her back. She lay perfectly still, almost not breathing. It was creepy.

I took her right hand.

"No Pain." My words were clear, loud, firm.

She smiled.

I ran a tracker over the back of her hand, made a mental note of where the marker was. Swabbed her skin with disinfectant. Held my breath while I made a small laser incision, then carefully removed a tiny metal and plastic chip with tweezers. Fortunately, it didn't have long tentacles like Fresh Start markers, but there was more blood than I expected. I wrapped her hand in one of the hotel towels, pressed it tight enough to stop the bleeding.

She just continued to smile.

Once the bleeding stopped, I put a flesh patch on top of the incision. Then I cursed softly. The color wasn't quite right. Well, I hadn't planned on doing minor surgery tonight.

It made perfect sense to me that the skin patch wasn't the right shade. I just hoped that Angelique didn't freak out and decide to press charges in the morning.

I slipped the marker into a plastic bag and stuffed it in my jacket pocket.

I honestly had no idea what to do next. I was too hyped up on caffeine, sugar and adrenaline to sleep. So I decided to do what came naturally.

I went out on the balcony and played my sax.

CHAPTER EIGHT

Chaz:

I was eleven years old the first time I saw a Newbie, the first time I saw life and death trade places. I guess my life had been pretty sheltered up to that point.

A state-appointed teacher came to our cell, wearing one of those government suits with the high collar, his breath a mixture of coffee and mint. My brother Russell and I, we sat in the back and pretended to pay attention while the guy peddled the Ideal Plan, we even made faces at each other behind his back. We only had seven kids in our cell, but we could tell that we made him nervous. Seven kids in one room was enough to unnerve almost anyone. I'd heard of cells with as many as sixteen kids, but personally, I don't know if I really believe it.

We each had two bodyguards inside the room, armed and able to kill with their bare hands in less than three seconds if necessary. And outside the room there were at least fifteen more. A crackle of handset communications buzzed continuously between the teacher's sentences, a hoarse whisper of monotone voices.

"—Sadie took her medicine, yes, I will get her there in time—"

"—piano lessons at three. Of course—"

"—Jeffrey is listening to the teacher, Mrs. Damotta—"

The Ideal Plan had been enforced for the past fifteen years, so I had to study it just like everybody else, whether I wanted to or not. The teacher did his best to explain everything, all the way from Life Number One to Life Number Nine, covering everything from sterilization to college to the legal procedures involved in fighting a death cert case; then he gave us each a contract. My best friend, Pete Laskin, signed his that same day. I heard that his mother cried for a week when she found out, but it didn't matter. They kept us separated from our parents for a full month, so we could think about it without their influence. Sadie Thompson, a twelve-year-old dream come true who barely knew my name, laughed and signed hers almost immediately, dotting the "i" in her name with a heart. Russell, who was thirteen and of an age to make his own decision, immediately folded his contract into quarters and handed it back. Unsigned. No thank you, Mr. Government Man. Can I go home now, please?

At eleven years old, I was the youngest in our cell. Everyone else had to make up his mind within our month of isolation. But I had a full year to make my decision.

So that was when Dad started taking me to work, on the pretext that it was time for me to learn about the family business. I'll never forget that first day. Mid-October. Dry leaves whisked across the streets, crackled beneath my feet and turned to dust. The sky burned blue and bright overhead. A cool breeze poured between the buildings like fresh water, a welcome respite after the unending summer. People had been dying all over New Orleans from an abnormally long heat spell. Mostly old people, but a few babies had passed too.

Fresh Start had been busy, everyone working double shifts. Two extra crews had been flown in from Los Angeles. I'm sure that's why it happened. Somebody was too tired and the out-of-state crews didn't know our procedures.

I have to believe it was a mistake. The other possibility, that my father let it happen on purpose to teach me a lesson—well, I just can't go for that. Russell, in one of his dark moments, said that Dad did it to show us that life is, and should be, unpredictable, that we never should have pretended to be God.

Mom refuses to talk about it. I have to admit I admire her for not taking sides. I know she had an opinion about all of it, she always did. But for whatever reason, she let Russell and me make our own decisions, about Fresh Start, about the Ideal Plan, about what happened to the Newbie on that October day.

The inside of the plant was everything I'd hoped it would be. All stainless steel and molded plastic in the industrial sections; all luxurious leather and ceramic tile in the public areas. Not that anyone would want to, but you could eat your lunch on the floor anywhere in that 200,000-square-foot facility back then. It was that clean. And the smell was a bizarre mixture of dentist-office-scary and new-car-exciting.

For years, whenever anyone found out that I was Chaz Domingue, of the Fresh Start Domingues, a hush would sweep through the room almost as if something just sucked out all the oxygen. A long quiet would follow. And then when people started to talk again they would be ever so polite, opening doors for me, asking me if I would like some candy, asking my opinion about the weather. I liked the attention at first, but by the time I was a teenager I realized it was based on a combination of fear and envy. So I quit telling people my last name. Sometimes I pretended to be someone else entirely. When I got older I even pretended to be a Stringer, just because I wanted to fit in.

But on that October afternoon, when the sunlight was slicing through the warehouse at a steep angle, when the sounds of the city seemed muted because so many people had died, on that day I decided that I never wanted to jump. No matter how much I wanted to be like other people. No matter how much I wanted to live.

That day, one of the Newbies got stuck in between lives. In some nether world, where dark, swirling creatures spin traps like spiders. She got caught. Her old body, withered and white with decay, lay discarded on the other side of the frost-etched glass. Her new-cloned body, as beautiful as Eve herself, lay expectant on a metal gurney, modestly covered in white linen. Neither body breathed, neither had life. All the equipment was suspiciously silent, no beeps to register heartbeat or brainwave patterns. Too much time had passed. The technicians began to get nervous, but Dad just raised one hand to quiet them.

"Give her a minute," he said, a tone of assurance in his voice.

But several more minutes passed and the clone continued to stare, sightless, at the ceiling.

And then, like it was straight out of a nightmare, she started to talk. The machines refused to admit there was life in either body, yet some alien consciousness caused the clone's mouth to move and a hollow voice to speak.

The things she said have haunted my dreams, might just follow me all the way past Judgment Day into the great beyond. Might bring torment with me, like shackles, into God's kingdom, whether he likes it or not.

"I can't . . . I can't break free," she said, still staring up at the concourse of pipes and ducts that traversed the warehouse ceiling. "I'm tangled in something. It feels like a web." Tears streaked her face. Slow, glycerin-like streams. "They've been chasing me and I'm so tired of running, of trying to hide. Oh, please get me out of here! I don't know where I am. There's no light, just a dark glowing horizon, like fire in the distance. And these creatures—" She moaned, a heartbreaking cry, long and low and inhuman. I found myself wondering if we were really listening to a woman or if some spirit from beyond had commanded an audience. "They're like spiders, but much bigger. I saw one of them eat a man. It ripped his head right off." Her eyes closed.

Meanwhile, my father ran around the room, fiddling with dials, gesturing to the other workers to try and save her.

"It's so dark. So cold," she whispered, her voice hoarse. "And I'm so alone."

Most of them stood frozen, like me. Listening.

Then she turned toward one of them, looked right at him. Allen was his name. She reached one arm out, then shrieked. And she was gone.

To this day I still imagine her trapped in a twilight world, waiting for someone to rescue her. But I know now that no one ever will. God wouldn't have left her there if she were one of His. Even if we had messed with His plan, with His order laid down from the beginning, He still wouldn't have abandoned one of His chosen.

That's the only way I can rationalize all of it.

CHAPTER NINE

Chaz:

Pete Laskin leaned over his laptop, thick bangs tousled on his forehead, his pale skin blue from the monitor's glow. He cleared his throat, typed in a few more keys, long fingers looking almost ghostly as they flew in a blur. He glanced over at me, dark circles beneath haunted eyes.

"Where'd ya gets this?" he asked.

We both focused on the marker, still inside the plastic bag. I shrugged.

He shook his head, then leaned back. "No, man. You gots ta tell me. I gots—I mean, this here—we's in way too deep here."

I peered over his narrow shoulders, tried to figure out what all the numbers on his screen meant.

"Look, Chaz. I promises I won't tells nobody, but you gots to be honest with me."

"I took it off one of the Stringers," I said finally.

"It was your Newbie, wasn't it?"

I just stared at him. The less he knew, the safer he was.

"This here's a government job, boss."

I frowned. "What do you mean? Since when does the government put markers in Stringers?"

"Is she in there?" he asked, gesturing toward Angelique's room. The door was closed.

Outside, New Orleans fought against the inevitable. Fringes of black clung to the horizon, stale fluorescent light sputtered from spindly streetlights, and a steamy haze hung over the broken skyline. Somewhere in the invisible distance daylight crouched, like a golden panther ready to leap across the heavens.

Angelique would be waking up soon.

I nodded. I didn't say anything but I couldn't help wondering how he knew my Newbie was a woman.

Pete's mouth slid into a short-lived, sardonic grin. "Okay, so you don't wants to talk about your current assignment, but it seems likes somebody is pretty interested in her. Or him. Or whoever they was before they jumped."

"We were followed last night." I took a sip of coffee, glanced at Pete from the corner of my eye. We'd been best friends since we were nine, but I still wasn't sure how much I should tell him.

I could almost see the gears shifting in his blue eyes, thoughts processing through the motherboard in his brain. "Has you been tailed before?"

I shook my head.

Just then I realized that Pete wasn't looking at me anymore. He was staring at something behind me. I turned and saw Angelique standing in the doorway, wearing a T-shirt that barely covered her thighs. Her long hair hung in a Rapunzel tangle, a glittering mass of gold and silver. Somehow she was even more beautiful without makeup. She yawned.

"Do I smell coffee?" she asked.

"In the kitchen." I pointed toward a short hallway.

She ambled away on long sinuous legs. Poetry in slow motion.

Pete raised his eyebrows. "Man, I don't ever wants to hear you complaining abouts your job again," he whispered.

"It's not what you think."

"Trust me," he said as he stood up. "You gots no idea what I'm thinking. And you should probably puts that thing away." He gestured toward the marker. "My opinion is ya gots ta tell Russell. Forget about all the crap you two gots going on in your personal life for a few minutes and deals with this."

He paused at the door, ready to leave, laptop folded up like a sheet of paper and tucked into his shirt pocket. "I don't wanna scares you, boss, but that thing is trouble. The government's been wanting to gets their paws on your company for ages." He lowered his voice, forcing me to lean closer to hear him. "And it looks like they finally gots a way to do it."

CHAPTER TEN

Angelique:

Chaz said that I should start writing things down, that it will help me remember my past lives. He says that everybody keeps a journal now—even One-Timers. A secret collection of memories that no one else ever reads. It's supposed to help me remember what I don't want to forget. But I'm afraid of the past and the future. And I'm worried about what I might find out about myself.

There was blood on my sheets when I woke up. My hand hurts but I don't know why, and a heavy pain has settled in my chest, like my lungs are made of rock. We went to a jazz club last night, I think. I ran into a bald man there—his face, his voice—he seemed familiar. But then a fight broke out and in the midst of it, a picture flashed in my head: a stone crypt.

The City of the Dead.

Chaz took me there, but it didn't help. The picture got louder and heavier, like the pain in my chest. I ran away from him through the misty fog, feet pounding against cement while the mist hung heavy and wet, almost like rain.

I thought I heard a howling death, felt white fangs ripping my skin and I knew that I never wanted to fall in love again. Ever. That was when I saw it. The place that had called me. But I was too weak. Too afraid.

I felt the same way now.

I sat down with a stylus and a VR tablet, with trembling hands I began to write down random thoughts and words. Then it started to come back to me. Images. Sounds. Voices. The black holes in my memory dissolved into shocking memories; they thundered awake, sudden, immediate, demanding. My emotions were ripped and shredded.

A familiar face floated before me, a moment of joy and hope.

Then I remembered. It wasn't clear at first, but after a minute I could see.

My first life . . .

We lived on a farm in Scotland, William and I, on a parcel of hilly land near the River Esk. During the day we tended our herd of Hampshire sheep, watched as the wind ruffled the long grass, commented on how each blade enticed the sheep to linger, to fill their bellies. In the evenings after dinner we would sit before the fire, I playing my clarsach harp, he singing the old Celtic songs.

We were a strange pair, I know. Both of us willing to give up the modern city life to herd sheep, but you have to remember that the government gave incentives back then, trying so hard to get folks back to the farms. We were the lucky ones, that's for sure. Got our little piece of property for almost nothing.

He was ten years older than I was, and quite dashing, with his rugged, country-squire looks. Not at all the sort of man I'd hoped to meet when I went off to university in Glasgow. Not the sort of man I'd planned to marry, but there it is. You don't often end up doing what you have in mind in the first place.

I was going to change the world with my new ideas. I'd wanted to sail across the ocean and marry an American, leave this dull land of brilliant blue skies and emerald hills behind. Wash my hands of it, once and for all. Catherine MacKinnon, I said to myself more than once, you need to break with your clan and make a difference in the world.

Of course, I didn't know then the things I know today, but I still don't think I would have lived my life any different. It was time for one of us to stop the madness, to take a bold step into the future.

William never saw it the same way I did. And I don't know if I can ever forgive him for it.

He was the true love of my life. The love of every life I've ever had, and I don't like the counting of lives anymore. It makes me weary. But this was my first one, so it was different. It was special. It was the time I made my first decision to jump.

We were Catholics, both of us, but I never really took it to heart the way William did. He rose up in the morning and went to bed in the evening with his prayers. Granted, everything around us was changing. The Pope had made some radical changes recently, and the one before him was maybe even more liberal, if that was possible. So what we had wasn't the same as what our parents before us had.

It all started when the Pope took the ban off resurrection. "It's not the unpardonable sin," I think that was how he phrased it in the beginning. It took a few years, but then pretty soon almost everyone I knew got the implant. Even my mom. Two of my sisters, Kelly and Coleen, decided against it, which didn't surprise me since they made all their bad decisions together.

But my husband, William, he wouldn't even talk about it. If we were ever divided about anything, this was it.

"One life was all God gave us," he told me one day when we were herding the sheep into a different pasture. "It's all I want."

"But we could be together for almost five hundred years," I argued. I had calculated it all out, from Life One to Life Nine, carefully reading between the lines of the contract. I knew each of the resurrected lives began in a body about twenty-one years old and that you would live to be about seventy-two. So with no accidents or major illnesses, a person could live to be around four hundred eighty-eight years old.

It wasn't forever, but it was damn close.

I'll never forget the look he gave me right then. The sunlight came down through the trees, touched him on the face, set his hair on fire and made his eyes glow. It was like the Almighty had taken residence inside him for a few moments.

"We can be together for all of eternity," he said. "It doesn't take a blasted Fresh Start implant to give us what God already promised."

"But—but that's not the same," I said. "This is guaranteed—"

Another stony glance. He looked like Moses just after he stepped down from the mountain, when he had the Shekinah glory of God shining all around him. I wished the sun would set.

"Guaranteed? You don't think Jesus rising from the dead was a guarantee?" he asked. "Not a promise from God: 'Look here, this is what I can do for you'?"

"I don't know," I answered.

"Since when don't you know?"

"Since always. I never knew for sure."

"Catherine, my love, you're swimming in treacherous waters." He paused for a long moment. "Are you having doubts about your faith, or are you telling me that you never really believed?"

I took a deep breath, afraid of what I was going to say next.

"What I've been trying to tell you—" I stopped to lick my lips nervously. "What I'm telling you is that I got the implant. Yesterday. I just signed up for resurrection."

"Did you now."

A silence hung between us then, like the distance between two continents.

CHAPTER ELEVEN

Chaz:

Sun splattered the near empty streets. Only a few drowsy commuters passed us, all yawning and sipping coffee from paper cups. Apparently everyone in the Big Easy had a rough time last night, me included. Angelique and I stopped at a French bakery and picked up a couple of *beignets* drenched in powdered sugar. Her mood lightened and she laughed while she licked her fingers. Most of the city was still asleep when we got back in the car and drove over to the head office.

So I wasn't expecting the voice memo that came blasting through my Verse.

"Stand by for the latest Nine-Timer Report—"

Felt like I'd been standing by my entire life. Right now I was waiting for India to self-destruct. I was glad Angelique didn't have her smartphone implant yet. Explaining the end of the world wasn't on my to-do list today.

"Explosions rocked the suburbs of Jaipur, India, a few hours ago," the newscaster said.

Jaipur. We've got a Fresh Start plant there—it was probably the target of a local pro-death demonstration.

"Our sources are limited," she continued in a bright, cheery voice. "But apparently the explosions triggered a Nine-Timer scenario that spread for about ten blocks—"

I'd bet right now Russell and his board were scrambling to cover all this up.

"Almost all clones within that radius froze up and went off-line—"

Went off-line. The PC term for "died."

"—but as far as we can tell, this was a pocket of Six-Timers. Obviously, the mechanical breakdowns we've been hearing rumors about are no longer restricted to the Ninth Generation clones—"

There was a dramatic pause.

"Remember to stay tuned for our next Nine-Timer Report at noon," she said. "And may your afterlife be even better than your life today."

I pulled into the Fresh Start parking lot just as the broadcast concluded. Angelique's mood changed again when she stared at the building. Almost every Newbie has some sort of reaction when they see one of our plants, based on some hidden memory of when they first got their chip, so I didn't really pay too much attention.

I was still thinking about the report.

When I was younger, the end of the world always seemed a bit poetic. In between gigs, my jazz buddies and I would sit around and talk about it for hours, sipping coffee or whiskey, cigarettes burning, taking bets on the future.

But the bottom line was that the end was coming, whether we believed in it or not. Folks have been talking about this afterlife time bomb for the past fifty years.

I should know.

After all, it was my family that lit the fuse in the first place.

CHAPTER TWELVE

Chaz:

Sometimes my arguments with Russ were universal, no different from those that brothers have had throughout history. You got a bigger slice of pie, all the girls like you better, you always think you're right. But lately our words carried a sharper edge, a growing hostility that was pushing us apart.

And despite the increasing tension, I still saw myself in his shadow, following in his oversized footprints.

I hated those moments. Like now. When I knew that I needed to confront him, but I also knew that somehow he was going to make me feel like I had messed up; I was the one tracking mud through the house; I was the one leaving dirty fingerprints behind that would let the rest of the world know, once and for all, that the Domingues were to blame for everything.

Majestic cedars stood outside the window, a patient audience dressed in shades of mossy green and burnt sienna. Their rich fragrance drifted through an open door, a woodsy incense that made me think of childhood. Then the VR projection flickered. Probably a power surge somewhere in the city. For an instant, the large vaulted room filled with wooden desks and spiraling dust motes temporarily faded away to reveal the plant warehouse.

Meanwhile, the debate continued, like it always had. I'd heard this dispute before. I knew there was no conclusion. No happy ending.

"What are we going to do if the media gets hold of this? Nobody expected the problems we had with the Ninth Generation clones to show up in the Sixth Generation. Almost any amount of stress will cause them to freeze up—"

"—you're worried about the media? Have you thought about what the UN might do? Did you see what happened to that hot pocket of Six-Timers in Jaipur this morning? We weren't able to cover it up because one of our nearby plants was bombed. All of our resources were focused there. Just like last year in Tehran and Bangalore. These pro-death organizations are out for blood—"

"—I keep telling you, the pro-death committee is not behind this. Somebody else is pulling all the strings—"

"—the experts said this wouldn't happen for another century. The problem that was supposed to surface first was infertility. We never anticipated that the host DNA would break down this quickly—"

It was a corporate board meeting with all the Fresh Start top-level executives. All wearing their pretty-boy monkey suits and their we're-so-very-important scowls.

Just then, Russell filled my vision, larger than life as always. Big brothers always seem too big to put into words, especially when a sizable portion of their life has been spent playing the role of father. I stood in the shadows, arms crossed.

"Look, it's not like we were blindsided here," he said. "We tried to make changes, to give people incentives to stop jumping so often, especially in India. But the Hindu population has taken a personal interest in resurrection. Something about their search for Nirvana, some quest for a higher rung on the caste-system ladder—"

"Why does this always come back to religion? Why do you One-Timers always have to make this an argument about God?"

Russ held his own for several minutes, arguing with Aditya Khan, the guy with the unfortunate job of overseeing our business in the Middle East and Asia, where the lion-tiger-and-elephant share of our problems was currently taking place. Then Russ glanced over his shoulder and realized that I had walked into his VR conference call.

"Well, look who decided to get his little hands dirty and pay us a visit." He paused, then turned back to the board members. "We'll continue this later." Aditya started to protest, but Russ ignored him. He hit the DISCONNECT button on his wristband and slipped out of his VR suit. Instantly the conference room vista, replete with rustic nineteenth-century woodland ambiance, sizzled and faded. We were back in the plant warehouse now: concrete floors, a buzz of activity in distant office cubicles, the clatter of hospital-grade carts rolling down hallways, and a vague sterile odor hanging over everything.

And somewhere behind us, Angelique was running through a battery of hand-eye coordination tests in a sound-proof booth.

A fine layer of dust seemed to hang in the air. Like guilt.

"You really must be some sort of idiot," Russ said, his dark-eyed gaze sifting through the dust. He seemed out of place, dressed in an evening suit, one of the latest designer-from-China things, the top buttons hanging open. There was a cut on his forehead and a few drops of blood stained his

white collar. "What kind of game were you playing in that
bar last night?"

As much as I had tried to be prepared, he still caught me
off guard.

"Do you realize we could have a major lawsuit on our
hands," he continued, "if that brute you tangled with decides
to press charges?"

"Trust me, there's no way that Neanderthal's gonna slam
us with a lawsuit—"

"You didn't identify yourself, bruh." He sighed, then
glanced over my shoulder at Angelique. "One of the mugs in
the French Quarter sent me a VR report, minutes after you
sauntered out of that club."

I paused. Mentally re-enacted the events in the club last
night. "I told that goon who I was," I countered, but all of
sudden I wasn't sure.

"You showed him your tattoo, all right. *After* you blasted
him with light. Look, I'm not in the mood to fight," he said
wearily. "I got yanked out of a dinner with the mayor last
night by another board meeting, came in here and had to
fight my way through a pro-death rally—"

"Is this one of your infamous 'my job is tougher than
yours' speeches?" I glanced back at Angelique and noticed
that she had stopped her tests. She was staring at Russ, a
guarded expression on her face.

"—then I got in here," he continued, "and found out that
an e-bomb had crashed our computer system. We almost lost
a Newbie in transit."

"Okay, okay, you win. Your job really is tougher than
mine." I pulled the plastic bag with the marker out of my
pocket and slammed it on the table in between us. "Just tell
me one thing, what the hell is this?"

Russ looked at the bag, then back up at me. "It's a marker.

Apparently taken out of a Stringer, since there's blood on it."
He shrugged.

"It's not one of ours."

I saw something flash in his eyes, something I couldn't quite pinpoint. Anger, maybe. Or fear. His face seemed to shift in the descending dust, like he was changing into someone I didn't know anymore.

Like the old Russell was gone.

CHAPTER THIRTEEN

Angelique:

The tests looked easy at first. And they were. Then I glanced through the window and saw another man across the warehouse floor. He was talking to Chaz. I pretended not to notice him, but the back of my neck started to prickle. A strange feeling settled in my stomach, like I had a blender inside me and somebody turned it on real slow. Just fast enough to make me sick, but not fast enough to kill me.

All of a sudden I couldn't figure out the answers, my hands wouldn't do what I told them and my words wouldn't come out right. I hovered there, alone inside the booth, somewhere between nausea and death, wondering what was wrong with me.

They were arguing.

The other man looked a little bit like Chaz. Taller, darker, maybe a little more handsome. Maybe not. I tilted my head and stared at him, caught him looking back at me.

My hands started to sweat and I couldn't grip the controls properly.

I was done. I didn't care about the tests anymore. I just wanted to get out of there.

Wanted to get out *now*.

CHAPTER FOURTEEN

Chaz:

The marker lay on the table between us, a small chunk of glittering hardware that suddenly seemed more important than the trillion-dollar resurrection monopoly that surrounded us. For some reason I flashed on a Babysitter mantra that one of my teachers had drilled into me years ago.

Trust nobody during Week One.

I watched Angelique from the corner of my eye, saw her fumble at the controls, her hands slipping and her eyes blinking. I could already tell that she was going to fail this test—the easiest of the bunch. Last night she had almost wandered off with a meathead stranger who probably would have sold her before the sun came up. This was beginning to look almost as bad as a black-market jump. I wondered if she might have been involved in one of those suicide cults in her previous life—those bottom-feeder freaks who loved dancing on the knife edge between death and resurrection.

Meanwhile, my brother frowned and pulled the marker closer. He put on a pair of glasses. "What do you mean this marker isn't one of ours?" he said. "We've got a patent, nobody else is allowed to—"

"It was made by the government."

I continued to watch his face, saw his brow furrow, saw something resolute in the angle of his jaw.

"Where did you get this?" Russ demanded. "Chaz, you're not involved in something illegal, are you?"

"Are you crazy? I got it off my Newbie. I thought these clones were supposed to be wiped clean before your boys turned them over to me."

He studied me for a long, silent moment. "They are."

"Well, this one's on Day Two and she had government hardware jammed neat and pretty in her hand. On top of that, that jughead from the bar followed us last night, like he was after something." I paused, leaning closer. "And believe it or not, his trail ended right here. At Fresh Start. So why is the government suddenly interested in what we're doing?"

Russ crossed his arms, let a slow grin slide over his cheeks, brought his I-should-have-been-a-politician dimples out of hiding. "Do you seriously think this is the first time that the government, or any of the myriad resurrection cults, have tried to get a piece of what we have?"

"Not like this," I said. I decided to toss in a wild card, see if it would shake him up. "Is there some sort of secret project going on here? Something I should know about?"

He shook his head, then laughed. For a brief, surreal moment all my fears bobbed to the surface like dead bodies after a shipwreck. I wondered if he had sold us all out, if everything Mom and Dad had worked for was going to vanish in an instant, if the Feds were going to walk in.

If life and death as we knew it was going to change. Forever.

But that was ridiculous. I mean, Russ cared as much

about Fresh Start as Dad ever did. At least, that was what I'd always thought.

"Where y'at, Russ?" I said finally. Then I repeated my question. "Is there something you want to tell me?" I tried to read between the lines, tried to figure out if his deep, dark secret was life threatening.

"No." His eyes met mine. "I mean, we're knee-deep in a senate investigation about that Nine-Timer claim that society is going to collapse in on itself in a few years. And we're getting pressure from the Right to Death committee— they want a census to track the success rate of jumpers. And there are a number of hot pockets in the Middle East, places where almost anything could trigger a Nine-Timer scenario if we can't get it contained in time. But it's really all just life-after-life business as usual." He paused, suddenly reflective. "What did your Newbie say about the chip?"

"Angelique. Her name's Angelique Baptiste, and I decided to ask you about it first."

"Good idea." He pursed his lips, then stared down at the marker again. "Why don't you leave this with me? I'll look into it."

I forced a grin, not quite ready to turn this over to him. I picked up the bag, stuffed it back in my pocket.

Then Russell took a sharp breath, as if he just remembered something. "Sorry, with everything going on the past couple of days, I almost forgot." He pulled something out of his pocket and tossed it on the table—an envelope with almost illegible printing.

To Uncle Chaz

"What's this?" I asked as I picked it up.

"An invitation to Isabelle's birthday party. She wanted to have it early this year, didn't want to share it with all the monsters on Halloween."

I hesitated. I loved my niece like she was my own kid,

but after last night I wasn't sure if my Newbie was ready for social gatherings.

"Go ahead and bring the Newbie—I mean, Angelique," Russ said with a flippant wave of his hand. "She may as well learn that families aren't as wonderful as everybody thinks. Maybe it'll even make her glad she doesn't have one."

"Maybe she does have one."

"Yeah, and maybe I have an island off the coast of India. Look, just be there tonight at six and let's not fight, okay?"

I could tell that there was more he wanted to say, saw a flash of emotion, heard his voice catch in his throat. I pretty much had it figured out, but I gave him some space. Let him say it.

"Mom's gonna be there," he said finally, "and I think she's bringing Dad with her."

CHAPTER FIFTEEN

Chaz:

I hadn't seen Mom for about a week. I guess I'm about as guilty as the next guy when it comes to staying in touch. Especially when I'm on a job, although that's really no excuse.

The last time I saw her was on Tuesday. Or maybe it was Monday.

It was about 6 P.M. I usually go right after dinner. Watching one of the attendants feed her is a little more than I can handle. As liberated and open-minded as I try to be, I have to confess that sickness and death still bother me, probably more than they should, considering I'm a One-Timer.

She was in bed, resting. I came in and sat beside her and waited. I knew she would open her eyes soon. As quiet as I was, I knew the smell would give me away. VR suits always give off an odor; some people say they smell like maple syrup, others say it's more like vanilla cake. Since I'm usually the one inside the suit I don't really have an opinion. Virtual reality caught on big-time a few years before my father passed away, and I'm sure that's why he did what he did. He got caught up in the craze and wanted to give Mom an anniversary present she wouldn't forget.

Well, none of us ever forgot that one.

Like I said, Mom was in bed, silver hair smoothed on the pillow, her skin pink and paper-soft with age. Her hands lay at her side, elegant long fingers wearing rings of wrinkles at each joint. She had lost some weight. The monitor over her headboard registered 101 LBS. in glowing red numbers. Her pulse, temperature, blood pressure, electrolytes and cholesterol were all readily visible, along with a few other numbers that I never could figure out. I glanced at the cheat sheet I had brought with me, compared the current numbers with what they had been last time.

She was fading away. Pretty soon she would just vanish. All her numbers would read zero and her spirit would sail away.

When I finally got the courage to lift my gaze from my mother's frail body, I saw him. Damn holo has uncanny timing. Right when I looked across the room to the corner, where I knew it was—this supernatural, super-spooky, three-dimensional rendition of my father when he was thirty-eight years old—it looked up and stared right back at me. And smiled.

A tear formed and slid down my cheek.

I hate that holo.

He looked just like he did right before he died. Dad never grew old. Never got gray hair or wrinkles. So this creature that occasionally flickers and skips with a hiss and a crackle actually looks a lot like me.

It's disconcerting to outlive your own father. To realize that every year after this one will be one more than he had.

Mom woke up right about then, when I was analyzing the miserable lack of accomplishment in my life, when I was silently cursing a technology that could keep a virtual ghost of my father alive forever but couldn't find a cure for what was slowly killing my mother.

"Hi, sweetheart."

She reached out and touched my VR arm with her hand, a caress as soft as velvet. That's as close as we're going to get, until her last few minutes and the doctors allow us to actually go inside her quarantined room. It's not so much that they're afraid we might catch what she has. It's more that what we have might kill her. A cold. A flu. Some random bacteria, happy to live innocuously on our skin, but much more excited to leap into her compromised immune system and develop into pneumonia or tuberculosis or tularemia. All deadly.

"Hi, Mom. How do you feel?"

Her eyes glittered, a pale blue sky filled with diamonds, like stars in the morning.

"Better now, honey. Always better when you are here."

She smiled.

My mother is dying and we are surrounded by a world filled with people who refuse to die. We are the ones who give them more life.

And yet, this is the only one she wants.

I return her smile. And I refuse to cry.

CHAPTER SIXTEEN

Angelique:

We drove through the mid-evening gloom, daylight clinging possessively to the hem of darkness, sparks of light glimmering around us as the City That Care Forgot remembered it was time to get up and play. Silence hung in the car, heavier than the impending darkness. Tension peered in, my own reflection staring back from the window, watching the reflection of Chaz, watching the rocky brittle silence, a new barrier I couldn't seem to cross.

Chaz was distracted about something. He'd been acting strange ever since we went to Fresh Start. Ever since he'd had an argument with his brother.

"I remembered something," I said, hoping to break through the suffocating quiet. My insides felt like a taffy pull: sticky, sugar-sweet pastel-colored emotions that didn't seem to connect, fears and hopes that stretched off into an invisible distance. "This morning I remembered my first life."

"That's good," Chaz answered, his face turned away from me.

We were riding in one of the company cars, heading over to his niece's birthday party. I wanted to go see a group of children—it was like being invited to the president's house for dinner—but I didn't want to see Chaz and his brother fight again.

"What's that?" Chaz asked as he pointed to the back of my right hand. "Did you cut yourself?"

I instinctively wrapped my left hand around my right one. I remembered the blood on my sheets last night, the sting on my hand in the bar.

"What's wrong?" he asked, looking at me now, his eyes dark, unreadable.

"I think I fell down in the City of the Dead. I must have cut my hand. I don't know."

"You don't remember?"

I shook my head. It was an accident, it had to be, I didn't mean to talk to that strange man in the bar, I didn't mean to run away from Chaz in the cemetery, I didn't mean to fall, I didn't mean to hurt the dog—

I flashed on a black dog, lying lifeless on the ground. Dead. Then it got back up again. Alive. A series of images looped through my head. Over and over. The dog was on its side, then it was on its back, then it was on its stomach. But it didn't matter how many times we killed it, the dog wouldn't stay dead.

I tried to roll down the window, I wanted to escape, I wanted to run away from all of this—

Just then Chaz tossed something in my lap. A plastic bag with a small metal-and-plastic chip inside. "Here," he said. "This is yours."

I stared down at it, a numb feeling in my hands. "What is this?"

"A government marker. It was in your hand."

Somehow I figured out how to make the window roll

down, a button on the armrest, almost hidden in the dark. The glass slid down instantly and cool air rushed in. A row of brightly colored shotgun cottages flew past. In one fluid movement I grabbed the bag, smashed the contents against the door, then threw the bag out the window. Chaz didn't have time to react, although I don't know what he could have done anyway.

He stared at me, a slight frown on his face. I had surprised him.

"Why are they tracking you, Angelique?"

I shrugged and looked away from him, ready to jump out if I had to. Somehow I had an entire escape route planned out in a millisecond, where I would go, how I would get there, what I would do when I got there. I could see a map of nearby city streets in my head, a vein of routes that would lead me to safety. A new strength flowed through my muscles, an ability to do whatever I needed to in order to survive. "I don't know," I answered as the car began to slow down. We must have been close to our destination, Russell's house.

I still didn't know what was going on, or anything about my most recent life.

But I had figured out how and when I got the marker. That man in the bar.

He'd run his fingers down my arm.

Then my hand stung.

He'd put that marker in me. Whoever he was, he was looking for me.

CHAPTER SEVENTEEN

Angelique:

I've been here before. A whisper memory rushed over me, made me feel weak, helpless. I shivered as we drove through wrought-iron gates covered with wisteria and wild bergamot, past lonely columns set like sentinels along the winding carriage road. Abandoned slave quarters stood to the left, a fleur-de-lis carved in the sagging door. Many considered the stylized iris to symbolize either the Virgin Mary or the holy trinity. But it didn't mean that here.

There was little, if anything, holy here.

Russell lived in one of those antebellum mansions built in the mid-1800s. Tucked away in a secret corner of the city, filled with all the magical beauty of the bayou. Here the Mississippi River branched into one of the countless slow-moving streams lined with crape myrtle and camellia, oleander and oak; Spanish moss dripped from the trees like syrup; yawning alligators slithered through the freshwater marshes. Legends say that the estate belonged to one of the first New Orleans' voodoo queens, a woman with an exotic blend of Haitian, French and African slave blood; that her mother was one of the *filles du roi*, mail-order brides sent by King Louis XIV for his settlers. She left a touch of gris-gris throughout the property that couldn't be erased. Carved in the trees were recipes for her renowned fetish bags—spells that would revive love, bring wealth, heal the sick.

Perhaps she left a curse behind as well.

My legs shook as Chaz led the way up wooden stairs. Plantation shutters stood open at the windows and incandescent light filtered through.

I wasn't going to survive the night. Something in me was going to die, some innocence, some part of me that I had been clinging to like a raft in a turbulent sea. It was going to wash away and drown, and at the same time something else would be born.

Inside the house, children laughed and danced, and their sounds echoed through the centuries.

I had a child once.

Joshua.

Chaz and I crossed the threshold and my past lives began to unwind, a spool of flesh-and-blood memories tangling around my feet and arms, a thread of images that turned serpentine, that coiled, ready to strike and bite. Each pierce of venomous fangs brought a visceral rush, an encyclopedic volume of smells and sounds.

I found myself pinned to the wall from the weight of it, unable to move or speak. Trapped in my own delight and horror, I was unable to stop its progression.

Around me, everyone began to dance to the slow-fast-slow rhythm of zydeco music.

Inside me, another dance began. The dance of life and death.

The dance of penance and pain.

The dance of remembering.

CHAPTER EIGHTEEN

Chaz:

She stood in front of a full-length VR mirror, adjusted the projection as she tried on one outfit after another. A rapid procession of glittering, shimmering pink and white concoctions melted into one another as she pushed the remote control faster and faster. Her entire wardrobe zipped by in a blur of silk and satin and sequins. When it finally came to a halt, she was wearing a Mardi Gras hat with gold beads and lavender feathers, a black body stocking and a pink tutu.

She stamped one foot, pouted, then said the line that every woman learns at birth.

"I don't have anything to wear."

My five-year-old, almost-six-year-old, niece glanced up at me.

"What you have on is perfect," I said, pretending to be serious.

Isabelle giggled then climbed up on her bed and started jumping like she was on a trampoline. "I know," she said breathlessly between bounces. "It's my favorite. I think I should wear this."

"I agree completely," I answered. I had been sent upstairs by Isabelle's parents, a delegate with the untoward duty of persuading Her Royal Highness into coming downstairs to her own party. I fell into that strange and temporary category of grown-up uncle/best-friend confidante. Isabelle wasn't old enough to know that one day soon she would only share her secrets with other little girls, women in training who would walk hand in hand through the forests of adolescence together. Right now I was the one she told everything to.

I wasn't looking forward to the future.

Angelique sat nervously in the corner, a silent observer. She hadn't said much since we got back from Fresh Start. Her tests, the ones she took while I argued with Russ, hadn't turned out very well. Just like I thought last night, there seemed to be something missing, like a connection between her lives wasn't firing properly, some sort of brain synapses thing. I couldn't quite figure it out. And I definitely didn't want to think about it now. I needed to get Isabelle downstairs before VR Grandma and Holo Grandpa arrived.

The house was already surrounded with a security team that rivaled the White House. All the children in Isabelle's cell had been invited, as well as the children of every Fresh Start employee in the country. Apparently Russell had debated whether to make the invitation to all our employees worldwide, but decided it wasn't right to put that kind of pressure on people who worked for him. They would have felt obligated to come, no matter the expense or danger involved in traveling with a child.

Funny. I didn't get my invitation until this morning. I had the feeling that the rest of the country had known about it for a month. Something was bothering Russ, something he obviously didn't want to talk about.

"Is it safe? Are you sure it's safe?" Angelique asked quietly when my niece ran into the bathroom to comb her hair.

"What?"

"This party. All the children. I think I saw at least seventeen children downstairs." She ran a finger along the hem of her skirt, her gaze lowered. "I honestly can't remember the last time I was around that many kids all at once. I just—it doesn't seem safe."

I had my doubts too. But this had been a family tradition for the past one hundred years. There was no way Russ would disappoint Mom, not now, not when she probably wouldn't live to see Isabelle's next birthday.

My niece danced back into the room just then, her hat on backward, her hair in messy pigtails. She smelled like apple blossoms, and when she smiled, she revealed two rows of tiny perfect teeth. Her skin was a dusky cappuccino-colored Creole blend, like mine. In fact, she looked like she could have been my daughter. But of course that was impossible.

Russ got Dad's death certificate, not me. And when the time was right, he had a TRS, the federally approved operation that temporarily reverses sterilization. And then, about a year later, *voilà*. Isabelle Eloise St. Marie Domingue. The most beautiful baby in the world. Ever. The fact that there were only 65 babies born that year didn't matter. Or the fact that 250 babies were born every minute back at the turn of the twenty-first century.

To most people, Isabelle was exquisite.

But to me, she was perfect.

CHAPTER NINETEEN

Chaz:

The spicy fragrance of crawfish gumbo and dirty rice steamed through the house. It was the sweet perfume of New Orleans, and jazz was its pulse. I paused at the foot of the stairs, not quite ready to join the party. People swirled past me, some familiar, some I'd never met. Everyone wore colorful costumes, gold masks, shiny beads and ostrich feathers: it was always Fat Tuesday here. If there was ever a city drunk with life, this was it.

And I was tired of trying to find fault with it.

Every corridor vibrated with the laughter and wild, untamed kinetic energy of children. Running. Jumping. Singing. A flash of light sizzled as Isabelle chased two of her friends through the living room, each child wearing a bright, slender BP collar. Beacon protectors were the latest child safeguard device, and Russ and I had fought hard to make them mandatory on children under the age of thirteen, just like seat belts and VR age controls were in the past. If a child's heart rate increased drastically, like it would during an abduction, the device would automatically emit a blast of light outward in a complete circle, a blast that would temporarily blind anyone within twenty feet—with the exception of anyone wearing a BP—and thereby give the child an opportunity to escape.

"They were a good idea," a familiar voice said next to me.

Cake. Definitely vanilla cake.

I looked to my left and saw a woman who looked quite a bit like Mom. A slight haze blurred her facial features and she was outlined in pale yellow light. Is that what I look like? It felt strange to be on the other side of a VR suit.

"The BPs," she continued. "I saw the statistics last week. So far they have prevented six kidnappings and helped locate two missing children. Did you know that flash of light can be seen from our satellites?"

I grinned. "No, I didn't." She meant the Fresh Start satellites, of course. The ones we use to track and transport dead bodies, the first stage in our regeneration process.

"I think there might be something wrong with your Newbie, honey."

Mom never wasted time.

"I talked to her for a few minutes when you were all singing 'Happy Birthday' to Isabelle." She paused and glanced over at the corner. She nodded and smiled at holo Dad right when he looked up at her. The two of them had this synchronicity that seemed to defy time and space and death. It really made it seem like that holo thing was alive. Sometimes I wonder what gave him the idea to have that blasted thing made just two weeks before he was killed.

Maybe he knew somehow. Maybe he wanted to leave a part of himself behind. Like we send prayers forward into heaven, maybe he wanted to leave one behind.

I felt a slight chill. Noticed that the front door was open. I could see out into the night, where a mass of faceless bodyguards hulked around the house perimeter. They were dark spots blotting out the light.

"Have you started her tests?"

I nodded, kept my attention focused outside. Did I see movement, somewhere between the black-on-black muscle men? The complexion of the party seemed to change. It was probably my imagination, but everyone suddenly looked a bit sinister. I never have liked Mardi Gras masks; tonight they went beyond irritating, all the way to ominous.

"Well, you'll probably attribute this to women's intuition." She glanced around the room, focused on Angelique, standing alone in between two groups of laughing people. "I have a feeling something went wrong during her jump. You need to make sure she pulls through okay."

"I always watch over my Newbies—"

"No, trust me, this one is different."

I wondered if she knew more than she was willing to admit. Mom had an almost supernatural gift for reading between the lines, for knowing things that couldn't be known. Like that time Dad lost his wedding ring down in the bayou and she knew exactly where it was.

Mom laughed and then changed the subject. "Now where's that crawfish gumbo? I heard that you can taste food in these VR suits, I want to give it a try—"

Just then the front yard erupted in a chaos of shouting and all the perimeter lights flashed on. I instinctively shut my eyes just in time. Four children in the living room went into a panic and their BPs sent out a shock wave of light. Now people were shouting all around us.

"I can't see!"

"What the hell happened? Jimmy, are you okay?"

"Where is he? Where is my son? Is this a kidnapping?"

"Somebody call the mugs—"

"We don't need the mugs," I yelled back. "Kids, come to me. Right now."

A line of children began to form obediently in front of me. They had been trained how to respond in an emergency like this and I needed to take control immediately. Before another one shot off a blast of light.

"Six, seven, eight—Isabelle, get over here—twelve, thirteen." I lifted my head. "Where's Deacon?"

"Here," a feeble voice answered as a little boy crawled out from beneath a nearby table.

"Okay, I have eighteen. That's right, isn't it?" I shouted to Russ. He nodded, an expression like relief in his gaze. For a brief moment I realized how much he trusted me, something he'd mentioned once or twice but I always managed to ignore. "Okay, all the kids and all the guards, up to Isabelle's room. Russ, you lead the way." My niece's bedroom was the most secure location in the building. "Russ, call me when you're all inside."

I waited a minute. Then the Verse implant in my ear buzzed.

"We're locked in," Russ said.

"Just a second." I saw Angelique, crouched on the floor. "Pete, take her upstairs with the kids. Two more coming up," I told my brother.

Then I grabbed a handful of liquid light from my pocket, enough to render an entire crowd helpless, if necessary.

And I headed outside.

CHAPTER TWENTY

Chaz:

I used to think I was special. Not walk-on-water special, but almost. Sometimes I relive my childhood in an instant, remember the way the entire universe seemed to revolve around me. Then I remember the moment that I realized I wasn't a magnificent literati, that I didn't actually encapsulate the sun, moon and stars. I learned that there were a thousand others like me scattered across the world, a thousand brighter than the sun and more precious than the moon.

Other children.

Not just the handful that I knew about in New Orleans. One thousand twenty-nine, to be exact, between the ages of one and twenty. Morbidly fascinated with this group of marauders, I learned everything I could about them, then put it all into organized categories. The government took all my statistics when I was done with my project—thank you very much for your hard work, young man—and to this day, that information is hidden away in a file somewhere.

Eighty-two percent of the children belonged to families

of One-Timers. One life, one child, one spin on the genetic roulette wheel. This group routinely passes their death certificates down to immediate family members.

Eleven percent came from Stringers, those who were at the end of their line. Usually these were Eight- or Nine-Timers, but a Stringer occasionally quit jumping at life Three or Four. Again, these death certs almost always pass to a spouse or family member.

Three percent were wards of the state. This was usually the result of a Stringer who left no will. In that case, death cert ownership was contested—maybe somebody in the dead Stringer's sous-terrain société claimed they had an agreement, or maybe a distant relative suddenly crawled out from hiding behind the Right to Privacy Act. Whatever caused it, the death cert became property of the state until proven otherwise. These certificates often ended up getting tied up in decade-long court battles and, in the end, were almost always doled out to high-ranking government employees.

That left four percent unaccounted for.

At first I thought I had made a huge error, that my numbers were wrong and it caused me to check and recheck my calculations.

Of course, I was only ten at the time, so I'd never heard of the Underground Circus.

I didn't know about the dark edges of society: how people longed for children but couldn't have them, or that the Worldwide Population and Family Planning Law enforced sterilization whenever someone entered puberty. I would learn more about this later, when one of my close friends went missing right before her thirteenth birthday, and consequently, right before she would have been sterilized.

There was much conjecture among my small group of friends as to whether Sadie Thompson had been taken to *become someone's daughter or whether she would be used as an illegal breeder of children herself.*

I never saw Sadie again.

But the day she went missing was the same day that Russell and Pete and I made a blood pact with one another. We all vowed that nobody would ever get close enough to touch one of our kids.

Because if they did, there would be a resurrection hell-on-earth to pay.

CHAPTER TWENTY-ONE

∞

Chaz:

Some moments freeze forever in your mind, turn into icicle daggers that cover the landscape. I will always remember the cold breeze that swept across the verandah that night, the way it wrapped itself around me and made me hunger for warmth as if heat was a long-forgotten memory, as if it was something that had been stolen from me, something that I would never feel again.

I stood on the porch, one hand in my pocket, shaping and reshaping the liquid light between my fingers; I faced the unknown, my back to the party, my thoughts still on that upstairs room filled with frightened children.

An unnatural chill bled into my soul and I pretended that it didn't matter, focused instead on the dark shapes that moved between wavering, steamy lights. I tried to sense where the danger was, tried to feel the pulse of evil that dared to beat within my family gates.

In my mind, it became a night of voodoo magic, dark and thick as incense. I could almost hear the gris-gris chants and the rattle of dry bones. Someone had invited a demon presence into our midst, and I knew that it hadn't been me.

Most of the guards had left their assigned posts to form a black shadow cluster on the right side of the front yard. Having no form or shape or substance, it parted as I approached. I unintentionally walked through a patch of night-blooming jasmine, crushing the plants beneath my boots, staining the air with the heavy perfume of death.

I saw a smaller shape emerge from the testosterone-charged troupe. Feminine and cat-like, it moved toward me, head down. It was a woman. Almost. A Newbie, still sparkling with the radiance that comes from resurrection.

"Chaz?" she spoke before anyone else, her velvet voice like a siren calling men to crash on the rocks. "Chaz, I'm so glad I found you."

One of the guards grabbed her by the arm and pulled her back.

I tried to focus on what was happening, but at the same time I knew something was wrong.

"She claims to know you, boss," another guard said. He laughed. "Says you two were kids together."

She leaned toward me, lifted her head, pointed a delicate chin in my direction. Dark eyes caught and held my attention. "Chaz," she whispered, her words so soft they forced me to come closer. "Don't you recognize me? I'm Sadie."

"Sadie?" I shook my head. "No, that's not possible."

"Isn't it?" she asked. A tear formed, then cascaded down her cheek, reflecting moonlight like a jewel. "You remember when I went missing, don't you? The cell, our cell, we were right in the middle of studying for our Algebra finals. You and I worked together that night. You explained it all to me. But then I left your house and I never saw you or my family again."

My heart thudded, a flame of guilt burned in my gut. I was the last person who had seen her. I'd always blamed myself for her disappearance. I'd had a crush on her and wanted to spend time alone with her, but maybe if we hadn't studied so long—

She lifted a hand to my face. "But it wasn't your fault. I know. I've played that night over and over in my mind for years. One of my bodyguards betrayed me, he sold me to a—to a slave trader." She paused, and looked out into the black night sky. It seemed as if she was watching a play and reciting the actions of the performers, like the pain of everything had gone so deep inside that she was numb. "At thirteen years old I became both daughter and wife. My first child was born when I was fourteen." Her voice became a flat monotone, a ribbon of silk with no ripples. "They let me keep my daughter for two months before she was sold. After that I lost count of the number of husbands and children that I had, of how many different homes I lived in, sometimes in chains, sometimes with as much freedom as I have now. Then finally I just couldn't take it anymore. So I bribed someone to help me and I jumped."

At that point the guard released his grip on her and she slid into my arms. She pressed her head against my chest. She didn't look like Sadie or sound like her, but nobody looked the same after resurrection.

And yet, as much as I believed her, something still lodged itself in the center of my spine, a premonition borne without reason. Like a shadowy gray incantation recited in a wooded glen, doubt whispered something in my heart, over and over, nudging me. But I couldn't understand the words. Couldn't hear them.

"I'm glad you're safe," I said, breathing in the fragrance of her dark hair.

She lifted her face, looked up at me, eyes filled with starlight. The essence of innocence reborn.

"How many memories did you keep?" I asked.

"As many as I could."

I touched her chin. "Do you remember that time we snuck away from our math tutor?"

She nodded, a half smile on her lips.

I bent down, cupped her face in my hands and kissed her. It was long and sensuous, nothing like the kiss of a teenager, nothing like any kiss in recent history. I pulled away with great reluctance.

"I remember," she said only loud enough for me to hear. "You were just a boy, but I will never forget that kiss."

I put my hands on her shoulders and pushed her away.

Already the alarms were ringing in my head.

"I was a year younger than Sadie," I told her. "We were friends, but never more than that. Who are you and why are you here?"

Then I could finally see through it, the deception that hung over all of us. There were too many guards in front of the house. Who was guarding the back?

"Jacques! Andre!" I shouted. "Around to the back, hurry!"

"It's too late," she said. A mocking grin broke through the kiss that still lingered on her lips.

Just then we all heard a sizzling crackle and I smelled the characteristic odor of liquid light. It was the smell of ash and fire and brimstone. A blast cracked through the upstairs windows and splattered out onto the lawn, a shower of glass and fire that fell all around us.

"Get inside!" I yelled to the rest of the guards. "Upstairs, to Isabelle's room!"

The woman who had pretended to be Sadie grabbed my arm, a grip almost supernaturally strong. She pulled me back toward her.

"Where is the dog?" she demanded, her voice hard as a knife.

I suddenly realized that she held a weapon in her other hand, something I had never seen before. I wrenched my arm free, but she struck me with a lightning kick to the groin. I knew then that she was dangerously different, some sort of genetically enhanced creature that could move faster than I could even think.

"What dog?" I asked as I struggled to catch my breath.

"Ellen and the dog," she answered. Then she danced backward, just out of reach when one of the remaining guards lunged toward her. "Where are they? What did you do with the research?"

"I don't know what you're talking about."

She punched a button on the cylinder she held, but I never could have anticipated what happened next.

Her eyelids fluttered and her body began to crumple to the ground. I grabbed her around the waist and tried to force her to stay, although I knew it was impossible. She was getting ready to jump, to download into another body, probably to an unknown safe house, one of the few that existed apart from Fresh Start.

She sagged in my arms, only a moment or two of life left.

"Consider this a warning," she breathed. "Next time we won't be so—gentle."

Then she died.

I dropped her body on the ground and ran toward the house, hoping that I wasn't already too late.

People huddled in self-protective swarms downstairs, some crying, a few screaming. But none of them made a move toward the stairs or the room on the second floor that held their children. The room that had just exploded.

I pushed my way through the ineffectual human mass that stood in my way, cursing them as I passed.

I dashed up the stairs, taking three at a time, only a heart-beat behind the guards I had ordered inside a moment ago. Smoke trickled down the stairs, a smell of ash, of singed hair.

It was the smell of death.

The door to Isabelle's room was shattered, but I didn't know if the guards had broken it on their way in or if some-one else had done it, some savage intruder.

I jumped over cracked boards—the shards of wood that had once been the door to my niece's bedroom—and then stopped, overwhelmed by what I saw.

Bodies lay strewn around the room, children immortally frozen in positions of fear. Arms and legs pummeling air, they had all been running for their lives when the burning light caught up with them. Like a macabre game invented in the pit of hell.

Tag, you're dead.

The smell of charred flesh hung in the room, oily and thick, and remnants of the liquid light still licked the corners of the room, sizzling and crackling and hissing. It sounded like the laughter of demons, a horde from hell that had just stolen everything we loved.

I saw Russ and Pete rise from the ashes. They struggled to stand, then fell, wobbled on weak legs, collapsed and tried to get up again.

Then I realized that whoever had done this had intended to kill the children. The blast was set high enough for them, but low enough to let the adults survive.

"Consider this a warning."

I scanned the room again, mentally sorting through the jigsaw puzzle of bodies that lay on the floor. I began to move through the room, hurrying from one lifeless form to an-other. I reached the window, picked my way through the shards of glass, forced myself to count the bodies again. It was almost impossible to recognize the children by their faces, but their clothes—

There was no sign of a black body stocking and pink tutu.

"Isabelle," I said softly.

Russ glanced up at me, a question in his eyes. He couldn't talk yet, his vocal cords were still immobilized.

I skimmed the room one last time.

Two children were missing. Two children and Angelique.

Then I lifted my head and saw the closed bathroom door, liquid light snarling and hissing around the edges. The door glowed like there was a fire trapped inside. It buckled and surged, as if breathing. Fighting against intense pressure.

Like it was about to explode off its hinges.

PART II

"Up until now, experts claimed
that only 50 percent of your memories would
survive from one life to the next. However, recent
studies have proven that journaling,
the daily writing of thoughts and feelings,
will keep your most important memories alive,
even if the journals themselves are lost."

—Roger W. Inglewood, Ph.D.,
author of *Journaling: A Method to Maintain Self Identity*

CHAPTER TWENTY-TWO

Angelique:

Nothing was the same after I walked through Russell's front door. Past and present fused, became liquid metal flowing through my veins; it turned me into an alien beast that stepped through time, from one life to the next. I couldn't stop the mad succession of images.

And through it all, I had to navigate in the present. I had to walk and talk and pretend like I didn't want to curl into a ball, my hands covering my head.

I pushed my way past dead husbands and forgotten friends, invisible hands that reached out from the grave. A haze of hallucinations hovered around me; they whispered and pawed at me, their slippery fingers tugging at the hem of my dress, latching onto the soles of my shoes. Suddenly I remembered my names from previous lives.

Catherine MacKinnon, Rebecca James . . .

Then I knew what was wrong.

There should have been one more name. One more life.

As far as I could remember, in my first life I had been

Catherine MacKinnon, and I had taken the resurrection chip when I was about sixty years old. Then that memory faded away, replaced by another: my second life as Rebecca James. In that life, I had been a lawyer and married a man named Jim. Then he got cancer and, even though I cared for him right up to the end, when he jumped, he deserted me. No matter how many lifetimes I have, I will never forget what he did. After that I wanted to change the way life plays out.

It was just a few months before my second death that I met him.

The bald man with the studs in his head, the man who put the marker in my hand.

He talked to me about the Nine-Timers, told me how they were working to solve the problems caused by resurrection. They were looking for faithful people to enlist. He recruited me, there and then, got me to agree to give up one of my lives for the cause, told me I'd get training, I'd get everything I needed. After I died, I was supposed to wake up in a fresh clone, custom-designed for the job I had to do. They were going to hook me up to their network, an underground mesh of agents working to change the world—

My lungs flattened as the last series of memories came back, too sudden, too strong. It felt like I was watching everything through a lung tunnel, images distorted, smells too strong. But it was me, I knew it had to be.

My name had been Ellen Witherspoon and I was reliving my death . . .

I worked late in the lab that night. Outside, thunder shocked the bayou and the world trembled beneath silver rain. The storm shook the windows, made me catch my breath. Everything was ending, sooner than I expected.

I turned in a quick circle, tried to think. I still didn't know if I was doing the right thing, but it was finally time to make amends. If that was even possible.

I heard whimpering in the corner. Omega. He was still alive. I walked over to his cage and stuck my hand between the bars. He licked my fingers. After everything we'd done to him, that dog still loved me.

I was beginning to think he was more human than I had ever been.

I opened the cage door and slipped a collar and leash on him. The collar almost disappeared beneath the German shepherd's thick black coat. I knelt beside the dog for a moment and nuzzled my face in his neck.

Chocolate eyes stared at me, a rough tongue licked my cheek. Then his lip curled and a low growl sounded in his throat.

We had to hurry. Somebody might be outside.

Together we headed out the side door of the lab, ready to run toward the bayou. Suddenly I realized that I had made a mistake. I bent down and unhooked his collar. Like everything else around here, it probably had a tracking device.

Then I ran, as fast as I could, the dog loping faithfully at my side.

Into the woods. Into the black, wet night. Into oblivion.

About an hour later, I returned, jogging through the dark as rain pelted my face, puddles growing deeper with every step. I paused at the edge of the parking lot, stared at the baptism of cement and stone that waited: the laboratory, a man-made technological fortress. Behind me an army of oak and cypress seemed to taunt, green demons that swayed in the wind.

I barely made it back in time for my shift. I had changed my clothes and washed all traces of mud from my shoes and hands. The storm still screamed overhead; its intensity seemed to drown out everything we'd been doing, making us seem insignificant. I felt like I had been playing a part from the movie Frankenstein, *but I couldn't remember if I was the monster or the doctor.*

I had switched sides so many times that I didn't know whose side I was on anymore.

Supposedly, there had been another undercover agent working in the plant, but I never found out who it was. And now, after what I had just done, he or she wouldn't back me up if I got pushed into a corner.

I had broken every rule, everything I ever believed in.

I wondered if Omega would make it, if he could push past his sense of duty and let survival take over. Duty would bring him back to the lab, to an unending series of horrific deaths. Survival would take him—well, there would still be an unending series of deaths. I couldn't undo that part of the equation. But he would be free. Alone, but free.

That was what I needed.

I entered through the front door. Only a few people here knew what projects I had been working on. I smiled at the anonymous faces I passed in the corridors. Along the way, I donned a white lab coat, joined the nameless crew that worked side-by-side in this factory of man-made horrors.

Just then the door to my lab swung open and a dark-haired man grabbed me by the arm.

"You're late," he said as he pulled me inside and closed the door. Then, when we were alone, he kissed me. It was an impatient and selfish kiss. I think that was the only kind he knew. He slid his hands inside my coat. "I told you to get here early. My wife is out of town. We can spend the night in that bed and breakfast in the French Quarter that you like."

"Yes," I answered. I didn't want to go, but it would look too suspicious if I ended the relationship now. I needed to give Omega time to get away. And I had to make plans for

my own escape. It wouldn't be easy, the people I worked for wouldn't appreciate one of their top-level executives just disappearing. But if I planned it right—

"You must think I'm a fool," he said, his touch suddenly turning rough. That was the first time that I noticed the fire in his eyes.

I pushed him away and feigned anger. "Well, yes, I do. I've thought that for a long time. Any married man who gets involved with one of his employees—"

He slapped me, slammed me across the room where I crashed into one of the empty cages. I could have fought back, but I needed to give Omega more time, if that was still possible.

It wasn't. That split second cost me a lot.

He jumped on me before I could get up.

"You're a government plant, a spy. You came here to steal my research—"

"I came to help you, to make sure you got it right. Finally."

He hit me again. Already one of my eyes was swelling shut, but I couldn't let the pain distract me. I slammed the palm of my hand upward, toward his nose. A fraction of an inch to the left and I would have killed him, would have sent a shard of bone up into his brain. But I missed. Jammed him in the cheek instead. Sent him sprawling backward like a crab on his hands and knees.

I climbed to my feet and started to run into the plant. He wouldn't dare hit me in front of his employees. But just then my foot slipped in something wet.

Urine. That gen-spike junkie had peed on the floor.

He grabbed me by the ankle and pulled me down. My right arm slammed against the cement floor and a shock wave of pain rocked through my body.

"You let the dog go, didn't you?" he said as he pinned me

down. *"You think that's going to stop me or my research? I still have all of our notes, all the files. I can just replicate the results—"*

I didn't have to answer him. The grin on my face said it all.

"You witch! What did you do with the files?"

His hands were around my throat then and I think some sort of madness took over. He didn't care that his research was missing or that the dog was gone. I knew that later he would look back on this moment and wish that he had done things differently, that he had interrogated me, tortured me, done whatever was necessary to get the information back.

But instead, he just continued to press against my windpipe while I flailed helplessly.

Until everything turned black and I stopped breathing.

The memory faded and left me disoriented, confused. I closed my eyes and tried to remember more. For some reason, it had all been in shadows, the bayou, the laboratory—even my lover's face. The only thing that really stood out was the dog.

Omega. I could smell his fur, felt the scratch of his tongue on my cheek.

I wondered where he was and if he was still safe.

CHAPTER TWENTY-THREE

∞

Angelique:

We went downstairs again, the three of us, Chaz, Isabelle
and I. That was when I realized that there was something
sinister in the air tonight, more than the apparitions that had
visited me. As bewildering as the transparent illusions were,
I knew that I deserved their torment. But there was something else.

It was like the sound of hooves clicking on pavement, like
an approaching danger.

Chaz sensed it too. I could see it on his face when he stared
out the door toward the black, shapeless night. I turned and
looked through one of the windows, but I couldn't see anything. Still I could feel it.

Fingernails scraping over brick, flesh ripping, teeth grinding.

It was like that slender breath of calm when the eye of a
hurricane passes overhead, that moment when you realize
your entire world is about to be destroyed.

I've heard that demons can disguise themselves as angels

of light. I don't know if it's true, don't know if demons even exist, but if they do, then one stood in our midst that night. It came in a shower of blinding light and it cast a spirit of confusion on all of us. Isn't that what William used to say?

Something happened outside. There were shouts—I thought I heard a woman's voice, but that was probably my imagination. A split second later, the outside of the house was bathed in light, bright and hot.

Then when I turned back around, I realized that the children were terrified. They wore thin, translucent collars, something that I had never seen before. One of the kids screamed. And then I didn't even have time to blink. A blinding surge of light blasted across the room—it started like a halo around one of the little girls, a pale amber that flashed and turned blue white. Then a radiant circle exploded outward, knocking people over.

I seem to remember that the light didn't affect any of the children, as if they had some sort of immunity to it.

But then my nanosecond of observation was over.

The blaze of brilliance hit me square in the chest, knocked me backward, cleaned my lungs of air, scorched my skin like an instant sunburn. And it blinded me. I've always thought blindness would be black and suffocating, but this was dazzling, almost sinfully addictive. I lay propped against the wall, numb and slightly aware of the fact that my skin burned. And I didn't care about anything else.

All coherent thought seemed to dissolve.

I took a deep breath, glad that I could still breathe. I blinked. Everything was white and luminous. I felt like I was glowing, like the burning sensation came from a fire deep inside of me.

Then somebody grabbed my arm, pulled me to my feet. I heard a man's voice and I tried to understand his words. We were going up the staircase and I was stumbling, my hand on the wall for support.

"You gots to blink your eyes. Quick," he said, whoever he was.

I did. My vision began to come back.

"Blinks 'em again. Hurry!"

I could almost see him now. It was that guy who came over to the hotel this morning. Pete. He had been talking to Chaz when I woke up.

"I think I know you," I said, my words tangling on my tongue.

"Yeah, ya do." He pulled me down the hallway, leaned me against the wall. "You gots to shake off the blast, Angelique. Come on, I needs ya awake, Ellen, come on!"

"What?"

"Look, I'm sorry—I done the best I could, but you was dead a long time when I gots there. Ya'll gots to come out of it, now—"

"Do you know what happened to me? How did I—"

"Not now," he said, guiding me toward a door. "You gots to trust your instincts. You been trained for situations like this. You knows what to do." He pulled the door open and I saw a bedroom filled with children. And Russ. A knife blade of terror pierced my chest when I saw him. "Whatever happens," Pete whispered in my ear as I crossed the threshold, "makes sure Isabelle is safe. Do you understand?"

I nodded. Suddenly my instincts kicked in. Just like he said they would.

For a moment I could see fear as it hung suspended in the air. Then it descended, like droplets of sweat, until it covered everything and everyone. It glittered on the skin of the children, it sparkled in their fawn-dark eyes, it moved like a frost around their blue-white lips. It followed in their foot-steps, leaned against them, pressed against their backs, bur-rowing like a parasite through their innocence, looking for a way inside their souls.

And across the room I saw it mirrored in Russell's hollow eyes.

He couldn't save them. He wouldn't even be able to save himself.

I lifted my head, then took a deep breath. The air held a winnowing blast. Chaff would be separated from the grain tonight. Men would remain men and the others, whatever they were, would be exposed.

Pete was watching me. I could feel it.

In an instant I saw everything in the room, the position of the furniture, the windows, the doors, the slow movement of the children, the static posture of the guards. I felt both alive and electric, every muscle ready to do exactly what was necessary. I could kill—if I had to.

A tremor ran across the floor, brushed against my feet. I glanced at Pete. He felt it too.

It was time to pretend, to play another role.

"Isabelle," I said, a soft smile on my lips. "Your pigtails have come undone. Let's go into the bathroom and I'll fix your hair."

Russell glanced backward, toward the window.

Something was moving toward us; something heavy and dangerous.

Isabelle looked up at me, wanting to believe that she was safe, seeing the promise in my eyes. Together, we headed toward the open door, the bathroom. Another little girl qui-etly followed us, slipped inside before I could close the door. She tried to hide her fear, but I could hear it, like a bird trapped in her chest, wings fluttering.

I didn't know what was coming, but I could guess. I locked

the door. I lifted the children off the floor and held them by the waist, one in each arm, then set them on the counter.

"Take those off," I whispered, pointing to the slender plastic rings they wore around their necks. "Hurry!" I couldn't risk another explosion of blinding light.

They did as they were told.

And then the nightmare we had been dreading shocked into the room. First, a blast of broken glass, an almost musical destruction, and then a flash of fire that we could see in the narrow space between the door and floor. After that: screams, too many screams.

Liquid light. I had never seen it before last night when Chaz threw it in the bar, and yet, somehow, I knew everything about it.

I grabbed some towels and a rug, crammed them in the space beneath the door.

But I was a second too late.

I managed to plug the holes, but my hands were pressed against the towel when the light hit. It sizzled through the fabric and shocked up my arm, all the way through my body. I couldn't breathe and I couldn't let go.

And I became a conduit, pulling the liquid light into the room.

PART III

*With our Silver Package you get free
downloads and all the latest software,
including Verse and VR banking.
Whether you're on the top of the Himalayan
Mountains or at the bottom of the Mariana
Trench, our satellites
will locate
your body in a matter of minutes*

—Fresh Start brochure, page 16

CHAPTER TWENTY-FOUR

Neville:

The bayou shivered at my back and the house fell still, all cries and laughter inside quelled. Lights flooded the front lawn, but here in the back, shadows reigned. Just like I'd planned.

I climbed up the side of the house, then yanked open a pair of weathered plantation shutters. With a grin, I peered in the window—I was the last monster these kids would see. I waited until one of them looked me right in the eyes before I smashed the glass and tossed in a fistful of liquid light. Then I slid down the rope and dropped to the ground. If both the Domingue boys had been in the room, I probably would have lingered longer than I should have. I knew my boss wasn't going to approve of my methods on this one, but that Domingue *krewe* needed to be taught a lesson. Apparently they had all forgotten about what had happened thirteen years ago, that night when the three of them, father and both sons, wandered out of that Fresh Start plant late at night.

Well, I never forgets.

I was still running through tall grass toward the shelter of

the bayou when a blast of light sizzled and cracked out all
the upstairs windows. A heartbeat later, a battalion of trees
surrounded me and I heard the soft call of my boys, waiting
for me in a boat. I was jogging then, knee-deep, through
Louisiana mud, all of my muscles feeding off a sweet-as-
sugar gen-spike high. With a leap, I tumbled into the boat
and we were speeding away, carving a path toward the Mississippi.

*We flies through river mud and swamp water, and I is
remembering—*

Those Domingues all thought it had been just another pro-
death rally outside their plant that night. They had probably
hoped that the barrage of catcalls would fade away and the
protestors would go home to their perfect little One-Timer
families in their perfect little One-Timer houses.

They was wrong.

That was when rocks had started to fly through the night
sky. Invisible and lethal. Followed by a rough growling
thunder as the rally changed, turned savage, almost bestial.

"Death is a choice," one man had cried, leading others to
join him in a chant.

"Your clones don't have souls!"

"Repent, Domingue! One life, one death!"

Stones hit flesh, then cement, then bone. Tears mixed with
blood.

My *krewe* had laughed between the blows.

In the midst of it all, a rock hit Old Man Domingue
square in the temple and, without a sound, he slumped to the
ground. He never got back up again.

Dead by my command. Just likes I wanted.

And now, the wind was rushing over us, cold and wet.
I shivered as one of my gutter punks wrapped a blanket
around my shoulders. Those Domingues had no idea what
it was like on my side of the gutter, or how many back-alley

knife fights it had taken to earn my first black-market jump. I'd shuffled along from one miserable and maimed clone to another, until finally I proved I could lead my own ragtag battalion of misfits.

Soon we were all going to get our reward. That fountain of eternal life was going to pour out, free and strong for me and my boys.

Or I was going to make those Domingues wish they'd never invented resurrection.

CHAPTER TWENTY-FIVE

∞

Russell:

I was standing right beside my father the night he was murdered, his blood wet on my hands as he slid to the ground. By the time the mugs got there, the lynch mob had melted away: turned into faceless, nameless voices that scattered in the misty New Orleans midnight. On the surface it looked like just another violent pro-death rally, spurred by radical activists. That was the way the mugs saw it. They said that people like to commit their evil acts in the dark—it works like an eraser, covers your tracks, destroys the evidence. When the world hides in black velvet, good people forget what separates them from the monsters.

Problem is we're all really monsters. And it doesn't matter if it's day or night. Evil flows through the streets of this city like a tidal wave, steady and constant.

But I didn't know that back then. I was only seventeen.

I was too young to see the irony behind a family of One-Timers holding the key to resurrection. Didn't realize that one of my ancestors passed down a legacy that none of us wanted—a trillion-dollar empire that went against every-thing we believed in.

Chaz was convinced that the leader of the rally was one of the elders down at First United Baptist. But the guy had an alibi. Supposedly, he and half the church attended a baptism that night, over at Lake Pontchartrain. Somehow it never seemed strange to the mugs that the water in the bay was about fifty-five degrees that October, or that there were toxic warnings posted all up and down the polluted beachfront.

I guess if you have enough people to stand up for you, it doesn't matter if you're guilty or innocent.

The bottom line is my father's murderers were never caught.

That was the year my father had started training me to take over the business when he was gone. Neither one of us had expected it to happen so soon, although he had gotten plenty of death threats over the years. Sometimes he would laugh and mention one at the dinner table. "You won't believe the latest 'Your Life Is History' letter I got today," he would say casually, right in between "Would you pass the rice?" and, "Did you boys remember to wash the isolation chamber?" But I could always tell by the look on Mom's face that it wasn't a joke, that there really were people out there who hated us enough to kill us. People who pretended to be our friends when they saw us on the street, who smiled and waved during Mardi Gras.

And then, a month before Dad was killed, I saw one of our accusers for myself, up close and all-too-personal. A man wandered into the warehouse one night, after everyone else was gone, when shadows covered the streets and the seduc-tive music from the French Quarter beckoned. I thought he was lost at first, this strange-looking man, his fleshy bald head covered with metal studs, his heavy lidded eyes cloudy and unfocused. He wore a long dark coat, so I couldn't see him very well, although I sensed a growing tension within him, like expanding muscles were rippling beneath transparent skin. I wondered if he was a suicide cult member, one of those miscreants who gets high on rapid death and resurrection.

Then I overheard him talking to Dad. I guess I shouldn't say overheard. He wanted me to hear him, looked right at me with those lizard-green eyes, then licked his lips, slow and deliberate.

That's what I see at night when I can't sleep. His eyes on me, his slow tongue. A combination of evil and ecstasy flickering on his face like a pornographic movie.

At first he spoke too fast for me to understand, but when he saw me in the doorway he slowed down, enunciated every syllable like he was the teacher and I was the student.

"We gots a problem, Domingue," he said, using Dad's surname, like he had a right to talk to him with disrespect. "Resurrection, it ain't working. Nine times ain't enough." His voice sounded like tires rolling over gravel.

"Nine times is all there is," Dad answered, smooth and calm, as if a soft answer could turn away this demon's wrath.

"No, there's always a way to gets more. No matter what ya wants." Lizard Man shook his head. He leaned forward into the light. Shadows played war games on the crevices in his face. "Tell me, One-Timer, what does ya wants?"

Dad stood silent. Finally he answered, "I've got everything I want."

"Maybe ya does," the other man said. "But can ya keeps it?"

"Are you threatening me?"

The stranger shrugged.

Dad didn't say anything. But I had a feeling that he knew what the scumbag was going to say next.

"Nine times, it just ain't enough for the rest of us—" He paused to smile, to run his tongue over his lips one last time. "But maybe for you, one time ain't gonna be enough."

He slid back into the shadows then, a quiet liquid movement, like a poisonous snake slithering off through grassy rocks. He became as invisible as the black night, but the stench of his presence remained. Thick, oily, rancid, the smell of unwashed hair and decaying flesh.

It was the smell of death, and from that day it never left me.

He became my nemesis, this dark creature of the night. I learned later that his name was Neville Saturno and he was addicted to genetic engineering. It was his Achilles heel, the bit in his donkey mouth that some other unknown monster used to move him across the chessboard of my life.

It was too dark, so I couldn't see him the night my father was killed. But I could smell him. That sugar-sweet smell of rotting flesh filled my senses and blinded me with fear. I know Chaz thought I was brave because I cursed our attackers and cried for help.

But I was only trying to save myself. I didn't care about Dad or Chaz. I was trying to run away when my father collapsed, when one of his arms got tangled around my feet.

I couldn't break free.

I panicked in the suffocating black night. I screamed and kicked and cursed until my voice faded to a whisper, until I was the only person left in my collapsing universe.

And sometimes I feel like I'm still trying to break free.

CHAPTER TWENTY-SIX

Russell:

That lizard monster, that human-esque creature that stalks my nightmares, came back years later, just like I knew he would. It was the last week in May, about four years ago, and I was just leaving our West Coast headquarters—the very first Fresh Start laboratory—when I decided to go for a walk. I needed to clear my head. Lately every meeting with our top-level executives spawned something dark. Things had gotten increasingly complicated in the past several years, ever since that Stringer rejected his new body and accidentally downloaded into someone else's clone. Problem was, it was already occupied. Two Newbies in one body. And we didn't figure it out for five months. By that time both Newbies had gone insane. The media crucified us when they got hold of the story, and all the major governments were demanding to see our records, to make sure that it didn't happen again.

Nobody cared about the poor clowns that got fried in the process. They just wanted to make sure that it never happened to them.

So, I wasn't paying attention to where I was going and I

should have kept one of the company guards with me. Hindsight is all about wishing that you could change the past. I don't care about that. I wish I could change the future, that I could rewrite the bloodstain splatter on the wall that I know is coming.

Neville found me in Costa Mesa, on the corner of Harbor and Adams. It was even more horrific to see him on a sun-drenched street than in the darkened caverns of my memory. His muscles were carved from a fresh trip to a gen lab, his breath as sour as the pit of hell, and his smile was exactly the same as the night he threatened my father.

"I gots something for ya, puppy." The lizard monster stood in my path, beefy reptilian arms crossed. I could see liquid movement beneath his skin as sinew and bone refolded, regenerated. A snappy tension hung in the air, seemed to surround him like a crackling halo, a vortex that could pull me in if I got too close. He tossed me a translucent plastic chip about the size of my fingernail. Some sort of computer file. "It's a project ya needs to finish for me."

"What makes you think I would help you?"

"I hears yur mama, she ain't feeling too good."

I shrugged. "So?"

"Ya thinks it's an accident, yur mama beings so sick?"

I paused, trying to figure out the connection between the chip in my hand and the mysterious illness that had recently incapacitated my mother. I didn't notice his hand sweeping toward me. Don't think I could have moved fast enough anyway.

He grabbed me and yanked me into a nearby alley, into blue-black shadows, where he shoved me down on the ground and held me with a knee to my chest. I gasped, tried to fight back, to break free, but it was over before I knew it.

"I hads a feelin' ya would needs some convincin'," Neville breathed in my ear.

Then he jammed a two-inch gen-spike in my left forearm. I shuddered and gasped again, sharp pain shredding down my arm, then throughout my body. A second later I got the adrenaline kick and I shrugged Lizard Boy off me like he was a piece of paper. He flew across the alley and landed with a dull thud, his back against a distant brick wall, legs splayed out beneath him, and a wicked grin on his primitive face.

The genetic cocktail rushed through me, bringing waves of delirious ecstasy. Like some sort of superhero, I could feel the muscles in my arms and chest expand like bands of steel. I could have wrapped that monster's legs around his head, and I moved toward him, ready to crush his skull with my fist.

But he simply held his hand in front of me, palm up.

He had my mother in his hand: a tiny VR projection, a three-dimensional, real-time recording. She was talking to a doctor dressed in something like a space suit.

"I'm sorry, but we don't know what's wrong with you, Mrs. Domingue. We've never encountered these symptoms before," the miniature faceless doctor said. "We're going to have to quarantine you, for your own safety—"

Mom sat on an examining table, silent.

"Of course, that is, until we can figure out how to treat your illness."

"I can't go home." It was a statement, a resignation.

The doctor shook his head.

My mother lowered her face into her hands and began to weep. It was quiet and heartbreaking, a devastating scene that she never would have wanted me to see.

"You're a demon," I said. I wanted to kill this creature sprawled on the ground in front of me.

"Yeah, and yur gonna helps me. Or yur mama, she dies."

Nemesis is too small a word for what this beast was or what our relationship would become.

I staggered backward then, as the second wave of the genetic cocktail hit me. It was better than euphoric. It was heavenly. Suddenly I didn't care about our corporate image or my dying mother. I was caught in the middle of an inconceivable high, muscles growing, endorphins roaring, and I was already wondering how I could get my next fix.

Then I understood.

This reptilian beast had me exactly where he wanted.

The little plastic disk explained it all. The secret government experiments. The doctors and scientists with the yard-long credentials who would be oh-so-happy to work with me. The current state of the research process.

They were close, but not close enough. They needed access to my grandfather's research, the original resurrection formula—before it was altered for clone bodies. They needed my laboratory and my equipment.

They needed me.

I sat in front of my computer, deciding which of their experts would be best to work with, scrolling through curricula vitae that read like scientific encyclopedias. At the same time I clutched a handful of gen-spikes—my precious thirty pieces of silver, for which I was ready to betray my family, to destroy everything they had worked so hard to preserve.

I took hours to select the members of my team. When I got down to the final person, I debated for a long time, torn between four different applicants. I toggled back and forth from one list of credentials to another. At last I opened their photos. That was when I made my choice.

She had long glossy black hair, green eyes, olive skin—

she was gorgeous. Her credentials weren't quite as impressive as the other three, but if I was going to sell my soul to the devil, then I may as well enjoy the trip to hell.

Ellen Witherspoon. That was her name.

And I was right. It was an incredibly wonderful journey to hell.

CHAPTER TWENTY-SEVEN

Russell:

Sunlight poured through the lab windows, casting stark black-and-white patterns on the far wall. Cages. Bars. The long soundproof room was lined with crates, like tiny jail cells. In the beginning the animals barked whenever we entered the room, eager for attention. Now they whimpered, withdrew into shadowy corners and tried to look invisible. Ellen and I worked a late shift, after the rest of the crew had gone home. I could tell the stress of the project was beginning to get to her.

Of course, she didn't have a shoebox full of gen-spikes to help her forget what we were doing. So I guess I could understand the circles under her eyes. The hollow way her cheekbones stood out, like she didn't eat, or maybe couldn't.

She knelt beside one of the open cages, running her fingers through the fur of a golden retriever. It was dead.

"Can you tell me again why we agreed to experiment on dogs?" she asked.

I shrugged. "It was in the research done by Smith and Clarksburg—"

She stood up. "You don't mean Clarkson? Immanuel Clarkson?"

"I guess."

"That Nazi? I can't believe we're using his notes—"

"He wasn't a Nazi, he was just—well, I guess he was just about as bad."

Ellen shook her head. "Tell me about the research." She paced the long room, glancing in on the dogs that she passed.

"The government started it, years ago—"

"The U.S. government?"

"Yeah, about fifteen years ago somebody discovered that dogs could recognize their owners, even after resurrection."

"I thought that was an old wives' tale."

"Apparently some old wives' tales are true. So the government started running experiments, behind our backs of course. Nobody at Fresh Start knew what they were doing. After resurrection, one of their operatives would go to a neutral location, someplace they had never been in their previous life. Somebody else would bring their dog, the dog that had belonged to them before, see, and kind of 'accidentally' let the dog off the leash. About seventy-five percent of the time, the dog would run to its previous owner. Even though the dog and the resurrected person had never met. I guess certain dogs tested higher. German shepherds, Doberman pinschers, poodles, golden retrievers. So those were the breeds that Clarksburg—I mean Clarkson—decided to work with."

Ellen was kneeling beside a cage at the end of the room, petting one of the dogs through the bars. I think it was the black German shepherd. Omega. I kept telling her not to name them, that it made it harder to do the experiments if you got too close to the animals, but it was almost impossible to say no to her.

She had a way of getting whatever she wanted.

I cleared my throat, suddenly feeling awkward. Sometimes she made me wish that I had never met my wife, that maybe Ellen and I could have had a chance at something more permanent—although I never knew for sure if she felt the same way.

"We need to record the data," I reminded her.

She nodded, and lifted the tag that hung on the shepherd's cage. "Omega," she said while I wrote down the information. "Life Fifteen: last death sequence on August third. Formula T3-a." She moved to the next cage, where a Doberman cowered, unable to look her in the eyes. "Theta. Life Seven: last death sequence—" Ellen paused. When she spoke again, her voice was heavy with emotion. "—yesterday. That would be August fourth. Formula T3-b." She walked to the next cage, to the open door where the dead golden retriever lay. "Epsilon. Life Ten: last death sequence this morning. August fifth at one A.M. Formula T6-a."

"Still no signs of life?"

"No."

"What's the longest period so far between death and resurrection?" I asked as I flipped through the log.

She stared off into space. "That would be Tau. The time between her last death and resurrection was three hours. After that she only lived for about twenty minutes, and then she was gone for good."

"Three hours." I was trying to be objective, to avoid thinking about the golden retriever, the smiling dog that my little girl would have loved. "So Epsilon has been dead for almost nine hours . . . Do you think there's any chance—"

"No." Ellen shook her head. "But I'd still like to give her a little more time. Just in case."

I nodded. Like I said, I would do almost anything for Ellen.

* * *

It was an ever-twisting road, this quest for immortality. It was a journey with no clear beginning or end. I felt like a pawn, a dead marionette hanging on tangled strings, and I could feel my conscience bleeding out with every injection I squeezed into a patch of coarse dog fur, with every gen-spike I slammed into my own muscle-weary flesh. I had to hide the stench of my addiction. The heavy fragrance of flesh decaying from within, the atrophy of muscles stretched past their natural limit followed me everywhere I went. I started wearing loose clothing so no one would notice the bodybuilder physique that came and went on a regular basis. I took four showers a day. I began to avoid intimacy with my wife, so she wouldn't see the obvious evidence of genetic restructuring, and at the same time I opened my bed willingly to Ellen.

I think a part of me wanted to get caught. I wanted an end to the horror.

I just never expected the ending to come the way it did.

Like a crash of lightning. Immediate and irreversible. Like the death of my father.

With blood on my hands. Again.

She dropped by in the middle of the night once. I thought I was alone. This section of the lab was off-limits to the general staff. Not even Chaz was allowed back here.

They were all dying. Our experiments were failing. We lost three dogs in the middle of the night. One more that morning. Only one was left—the German shepherd, and he was pretending to be asleep. But I knew he was watching me.

He was always watching me. I was always the one who killed him.

I'd reached a limit, I guess, some line that I drew in the sand and dared myself to cross. I didn't know what to do. We were one step away from losing everything, from failing.

And if I failed, they would kill my mother.

I got ready to euthanize the last dog, prepared the injection, set it on the counter and then stared at it. After a long quiet moment, I picked up the syringe, rolled it between my fingers. It would be so simple to just slide the needle into my own skin, let the drug flow through my veins until my heart stopped. The pain would disappear, all of this would just fade away. I pulled up my sleeve, stretched out my arm. At that moment, images of my mother, sick and dying, flooded my mind. Without realizing it, I began to weep. The syringe slipped from my fingers, I crumpled to the floor and buried my head in my hands.

I think Ellen must have been standing in the door, watching.

She picked up the syringe, tossed it in the wastebasket, and then knelt beside me.

She started to cry and I thought that she understood. It seemed like we were one person that night, one mind, one soul. But I was wrong.

She had no idea what was truly in my heart. No one did. Not even me.

I couldn't sleep. For two days I lived in a twilight world of caffeine and tequila, my thoughts rising and falling through the depths of a murky, wave-tossed sea. I had moments when I thought we would somehow make it. That our last dog would survive and we would finally conquer immortality. We would succeed where the gods had failed.

And then I would sink—stony weights fastened about my wrists and ankles—plummeting through blue-and-green despair. The dog would die. It would stay dead. My mother would die.

But I knew it wouldn't end there. My mother was only today's pawn. Tomorrow they would burrow their talons into someone I loved even more. They hadn't whispered their plans yet, but I could feel them, could see them written in a black scrawl across stormy clouds.

Isabelle. My daughter. My reason for living.

She would wear the stain of my failure like a butcher's apron.

As much as I feared for her life, I knew that there were things they could do to her that would be much worse than death. At times, the vile imagination of man far exceeds any demon dream, any scene in hell with scorching flames.

Images of the Underground Circus danced like the lake of fire in my mind.

I downed another glass of tequila—the real stuff, not the synthetic crap. And then another. When I caught my breath, I slammed a gen-spike into my arm, sucked in the swirling moonlight, black and gold, cloud and shadow, filled my lungs with the sour and the sweet. Closed my eyes. Said a prayer, something I rarely did anymore.

Then I went to the lab. To check on my last hope. Omega. I wanted to bury my head in his fur, to believe in the loyalty that flashed in his dark eyes.

I wanted to believe in something again. *Anything.*

CHAPTER TWENTY-EIGHT

∞

Russell:

I thought I saw black shadows running toward the bayou, running through the shifting rain. There were only a few lights on inside the plant, an early shift that started at 5 A.M. Puddles glittered and shivered in the half-light of early dawn, while rivulets of dark water forged a brave course, daring to band together to form tiny streams that thickened, broad cold veins that pushed toward freedom. I darted through the grumbling storm, reached the side doors and punched in my code.

A second later I breezed across the threshold, wet, a chill spreading over my shoulders.

My vision blurred, focused, blurred again. I stumbled through shadows toward the lab, legs and arms stiff from my genetic cocktail. I got lost once, turned down an empty, darkened corridor and tripped over a rolling cart that someone had left out.

A lifeless clone stared up at me. Eyes open, mouth parted. It lay on the cart, draped in a white linen sheet, waiting—

for life, for someone to claim it and make it real, to fill it with emotion and thought and purpose.

As if any of us really has purpose.

I shrugged it off, shook my head, felt the cold seeping through my clothes. *I shouldn't be here*, I thought, as I stumbled away. I should have stayed at home and let the dark night pass. I should have curled at the foot of my daughter's bed, glad that she was still safe.

But here I was, blundering my way through an echoing darkness, ignoring the occasional employee that darted across my path.

I was at the door to the lab now. *Maybe I should just go home. Wait until my head clears. Let my flesh take one more step toward complete decomposition.* Then I saw something. Light flooding out from beneath the door.

I forced the door open.

Companionship was something that I craved, an antidote to the space that flowed between me and everyone else. They were only lab animals, subjected to the worst treatment imaginable. But they were living creatures and I craved life.

I pushed my way across the room: my legs wooden now, all elasticity gone. The euphoric high would dissipate in a moment, my vision would clear. But the cages were empty. I snarled as I passed each one, growling uncontrollably, searching for some beast to meet me in this place of the animal that I inhabited. But there was no one.

I was the only beast here.

I knew then what I had seen outside. Ellen had been here, she had taken Omega and together they had run toward the bayou.

I felt a growl, deep inside my chest, reverberating, resonating. It ebbed and flowed, like river water through a tide of delta mud. I sucked in each breath, my lips hot, and my hands clenched at my sides. The muscles in my chest stretched and expanded in one last band of steel and I could feel the buttons on my shirt strain. I closed my eyes. Red flames roared somewhere in the back of my mind.

I heard footsteps coming closer, gentle and soft. It was her.

She had just murdered my mother and here she was coming, ready to kill my daughter too. The door opened and I grabbed her by the arm, pulled her inside, closed the door so no one could see us together. She was wet, fragrant from the lightning and the thunder. I know now that it was probably rain on her face and hands.

But to me she was drenched in blood.

My vision blurred.

Focused.

Ellen was on the floor, my hands around her neck. And then she was lying limp. Crooked. Her legs and arms twisted and unnatural. Something was wrong.

The dog was gone. The research, all the files were missing.

And now she was dead.

I sat in a chair, stared out the window. Saw the sun crest the distant trees, push its way through clouds. It wouldn't win. Darkness and rain would prevail. It was the season of storms. I drummed my hand on the counter. Fingertips making patterns of blood on the ceramic tile.

Sorrow filtered through, remorse for what I'd done—emotions I hadn't felt in years. Ellen was the only person I had been able to confide in, the only one who really understood. And now she was gone. I looked back at the floor. She was so still, so quiet. Suddenly something snapped inside of me.

What if she resurrects? What if she remembers that I murdered her?

I had to get her into an isolation chamber and make sure she didn't download. Then I realized that I was going to need help.

I rinsed my hands in the sink, then tapped the Verse jack in my left ear. Commanded it to contact a familiar number. Heard a sleepy voice, a voice I'd known since childhood.

"I need you—I need you to help me with something." My voice cracked, something I hadn't expected. "How soon can you be at the lab?"

"Boss? What's wrong?"

"I can't, not now. Just hurry, Pete. Meet me in the isolation chamber up on the third floor, the one that's right above my lab."

"Russ, is you—"

"Just hurry."

I couldn't talk anymore. I had to dispose of Ellen's body. I knelt beside her, this altar of flesh and bone that I had knelt before countless times when passion surged through me. But tonight the wrong passion had conquered.

And now my altar was gone.

CHAPTER TWENTY-NINE

Omega:

The dog ran through the rain, paws striking pavement, then dirt, and then finally river water. He was swimming. Across a steady slow-moving current, then up a shallow bank. Away. He was running away.

The woman was running beside him at first, talking to him, her hand on his head. At one point she knelt beside him, buried her face in his thick black coat. He thought he heard something in her voice, a choking sound.

He paused, laid his head in her lap.

She ran her fingers through the thick mane of golden-tipped fur around his neck. She understood. She always did. That was why she was sad. Why she was crying.

He glanced backward. Lifted his head and sniffed. She seemed to sense the danger too, began to run again, leading him deeper into the bayou.

"Come on," she said. "Run, hurry! You can't stop. You can never stop, do you hear me?"

He looked up at her.

"They'll come after you. You have to hide."

They continued to run, but her pace was slowing.

"Keep going! Never come back, never. Do you hear me? Never!"

Then she wasn't running with him anymore. He was alone in the thick, dark morning, swimming through brackish water, paws scraping against stone and bark and earth. Running. Faster. In between trees and black sky. Above him the dull heavens growled and sharp white fangs shot down; they splintered the ground with hot light.

But Omega kept running.

He wouldn't stop. And he wouldn't go back.

The rain stopped. Daylight teased the bayou with narrow beams of light. Steam rose in puffs from the river, a haze that hung between shifting shadows. Day and night merged, neither one strong enough to own this place. Omega crouched beneath a low bush. Hiding. Listening.

He burrowed his nose in the moss, closed his eyes. He took a deep breath, a sigh.

The woman was gone now. The woman who smelled like sunshine. He would never see her again.

He heard the Others in the distance, had heard them for a long time. Sniffing. Hunting. Howling. They had come to him before, when he lived in the cage, when life was divided into those who are trapped and those who are free. They sniffed around the edges of his world at night when no one else was there. He could hear their claws scratching on the other side of the wall, he could smell them. He knew when their females were in heat and when they had just killed a rabbit; he knew the deep growl of their leader.

Sometimes they howled just outside the door. Like they were waiting for him. Calling him.

And they were here now. The wild dogs. He sniffed the

black air. Two females. Four males. The Others knew he was here, somewhere. He could tell they were looking for him.

And they were hungry.

Five dogs made a circle around him. The leader lowered her head, pulled her lips back to show massive canines, then let out a long, snarling growl.

She tried to get him to back up. Run away. Roll over and submit.

Omega refused.

She took a step closer, eyes reflecting the dark afternoon light. She had a wild look, long bushy tail, silver fur. Wolf blood. Her muzzle opened wide, then snapped shut. Another long growl, another step nearer. The rest of the pack followed her lead, each one taking another step closer, the circle grew smaller.

Omega lowered his head. He wouldn't run.

She charged forward, in that instant when he bared his teeth. She latched onto his throat, dug her teeth in. The entire pack erupted in a low wolf-lion growl, a rumbling roar. They all attacked at the same time. Fur ripped. Bones crunched.

Omega squealed, a high-pitched whine, a death cry.

The female leader lifted her head and snapped at the air.

The Others backed away. It was her kill. It was her right.

Omega cried, took a last breath, blood flowing. He trembled.

Then he was still.

Dead.

The female stood guard over her kill, turned and snapped at the submissive female behind her. The other female backed up, lowered her head. Whimpered. The rest of the pack pulled away. Moved over by the edge of the river. Watching.

The female lowered her muzzle, pushed it against Omega's chest. Cold. Lifeless. She sniffed. Then she opened her jaws, ready to rip flesh, ready to eat.

Darkness flowed over him like a river, all light disappeared. Black ice. Cold. Silent and numb. His blood—the dark, cold river was his blood. He couldn't see.

Omega fell backward into the arms of Death, those familiar arms that tried to hold him down.

For one brief second he could smell sunshine. And he remembered an eternal moment when he was loved. Once. A forever long time ago.

Then the earth cracked beneath him. The sky changed color. The air turned to smoke.

And he shocked back to life. Again.

His bones mended, his wounds closed. Lifeblood flowed through his veins.

He opened his eyes, saw the female lunge for his soft belly, for his entrails.

He grabbed her by the throat, a vise-like grip, his teeth pressing against the vein that held her life. In that instant, she was his. To kill or not kill.

He jumped to his feet, twisted his body, pinned her to the ground.

She bellowed, whimpered, a loud, high, whining yelp.

The Others could have helped her. But they didn't. This was the battle for leadership.

To kill or not kill.

She looked away, the whites of her eyes showing. She couldn't look him in the eye, didn't dare. She rolled on her back. Submissive. Tucked her tail between her legs. The Others crouched low, afraid.

Omega growled. Held her down. Held her life in his mouth. He could taste her death. Sweet and warm.

She whined again. Twisted her head to lick one of his healing wounds. Then she laid her head back on the ground. Waiting.

He opened his jaws, slowly. A low, rumbling snarl. He lifted his head. Looked at the Others. None of them would look him in the eye. The female was the only one who dared to move.

She licked his wound again.

His decision came easier than he expected.

Not kill.

PART IV

Start building the family you want
today, one person at a time.
Complete anonymity,
relationships guaranteed up to five
lifetimes—an investment in your own
sous-terrain société *is priceless.*

—Advertisement for Happy Life,
Grid Chatter Bar 0087-PL2

CHAPTER THIRTY

October 12

Chaz:

Flames sizzled and flickered, the bathroom door buckled and groaned. A bitter stillness hung in Isabelle's bedroom as I focused on the door; heat radiated in waves, embers burning, following the wood grain, popping in concentric patterns. Any second now, the fire could spread into the walls and the whole room could burst into flame. I still wasn't sure, but it was possible that the peron I loved more than any other was trapped inside.

Isabelle.

The perfect, innocent child that I always wished had been mine.

I froze in front of the bathroom door, surrounded by a graveyard of children, their singed bodies an Escher puzzle of death. Guilt settled in my throat, like I had swallowed a mouthful of ash. My fault. All my fault.

And beneath it all, I heard a voice hissing, a dark taunting undercurrent, a voice I instantly recognized.

You can't save your niece. You're already too late.

"Isabelle!" I cried, ignoring my inner demon. I leaned toward the door, tried to figure out what to do. "Isabelle, are you in there?"

My mind filled with doubt. Then a voice echoed mine; pitifully weak, it strained through the whipping crackle and the snarling fire. I almost didn't hear it.

"Uncle Chaz! Help, the fire—"

The door buckled toward me and smoke burned my eyes.

Just then an automatic fire extinguisher snapped on, a filmy foam that covered everything in the room. It slid over my skin, stung when it hit my eyes. I blinked it away. Liquid light isn't like regular fire. It can't be quenched like this. It feeds off the electrical impulses that flow through humans and animals, and right now it was feasting on something. A body had to be on the other side of the door, a body that, hopefully, was still alive.

"The beacon protectors," a voice whispered behind me. I turned and saw Pete leaning against the wall, his legs trembling. He pointed to the dead children on the floor. "They catches the liquid light."

I cursed under my breath. How had we missed this? No one at Fresh Start had tested the BPs with liquid light; we never anticipated that anyone would use it on kids. I reached down and snapped a collar off the nearest child, switched it on, then tossed it to a far corner. Almost instantly a thin line of snarling fire darted away from the bathroom door, zapped into the collar and stayed there.

Pete and Russ were both beside me then, struggling to stand, peeling the collars off the dead children, turning them on and hastily flinging them away. Each time, a portion of the liquid light shot out hungrily, a bleeding trail of fire and light that latched onto a collar, then zapped inside, instantly imprisoned.

The pressure on the door was lessening. It sagged on weary hinges now, flames reduced to fading embers.

"Move away from the door!" I yelled to whoever was on the other side.

"Uncle Chaz, wait—"

I heard a scuffling, thought I heard another little girl crying, "No, I can't, I'm afraid."

Then Isabelle spoke again, her brave voice quivering, "Okay, we moved."

"Cover your face," I said, then I grabbed a chair, swung it against the door. It cracked down the middle, shivered and splintered, a shower of sparks and firefly light. My shoulders and hands burned from the heat.

Let them be okay, please let them be okay, I pleaded, afraid to see who was on the other side, grateful that at least Isabelle sounded safe.

Another swing. Broken chair against broken door. Hinges snapped. Beside me Russ began to pull the wood away with his bare hands; he yanked half the door back and tossed it behind us, a smoldering birthday-party memento.

"Isabelle, baby," he said, his voice a hoarse whispering growl. Tears coursed his face, ran between the veil of dusky ash and silky foam.

My brother spent so much of his life hiding his emotions that I was shocked by the raw panic I saw in his shaking hands. This wasn't the after-effects of liquid light. It was the combination of love and fear, that deep well of courage we draw from when we have to win the battle. It was the first time I realized how much he loved his daughter.

We could see inside the small room then, all three of us.

Half the door had been ripped off, the other half was crumbling and charred.

Isabelle stood against a far wall. Wide-eyed and scared, but alive.

She held hands with another little girl, a delicate redhaired child with almost elfish features. Both of them were safe, unharmed.

Then I saw the body on the floor, lying facedown, arms outstretched and blackened. *Angelique.* Somehow she had saved the girls, had put herself in between them and the liquid light. Her body must have absorbed the electric fire; the current must have run up one of her arms and then back down the other, a continuous circuit.

Isabelle must have pulled her away from the door just a moment ago. I could see the palms of my niece's hands now, blackened by the lingering fire.

I let Russ shoulder his way through the door first, let him scoop his daughter into his trembling arms. Pete staggered into the room next and carried out the little redhead. After they had both made their way out, I went inside, knelt down beside the Newbie that I had vowed to protect, pressed my fingers against the jugular vein in her neck, praying for a heartbeat, some lingering sign of life.

A faint pulse. Or maybe it was just my own heartbeat that I felt.

"Angelique."

I gently turned her body over, winced when her muscles hung limp. I couldn't tell if she was breathing.

"Angelique." I cupped her face in my hand. "Wake up. Focus."

The mugs were in the house now, charging up the stairs, heavy voices barking orders. In a few minutes a VR station would be set up and the rest of the world would watch as the investigation began. We would be judged before any evidence was even gathered.

Angelique. Don't jump. Stay.

Her eyes fluttered, then her mouth opened and she sucked in a deep breath, coughed black ash from her lungs. She shuddered and I turned her on her side. She coughed again.

Angelique. Live, please.

She braced one hand on the floor, lifted her head and looked through the door into the bedroom. I followed her gaze and saw the labyrinth of dead children, arms and legs twisted. Black death everywhere.

Tears welled in her eyes.

With an expression of horror, she glanced down at her hands, scorched from the liquid light. It looked like she was wearing black evening gloves that went up to her elbows. "What happened?" She turned back and stared at the makeshift cemetery that used to be Isabelle's bedroom. "Who would do this?"

Obviously she didn't remember risking her life to save my niece, didn't know that she had just crossed over into the exalted territory of hero.

"Angelique," I said, trying to calm her. "Recognize. I'm your Babysitter—"

"Babysitter?" She cocked her head, facing me now. "But, but . . . I'm not a Newbie—"

"Focus." She didn't even remember who she was. "Recognize—"

"I'm not a Newbie—I'm a lawyer. I've got a case this afternoon. I've got to get out of here—"

But I didn't have time to break through the roadblocks her brain was putting up, the natural defense mechanism Fresh Start installed to prevent her circuits from getting fried in a situation like this. A mug suddenly materialized in the doorway behind us, a hulking silhouette against the bright lights that now swept through the bedroom.

"Just hold on there, both of ya. Stay right where ya are." His face was invisible, masked in black shadow, but I recognized him immediately. Lieutenant Skellar.

"You know the drill, Domingue," he said. "Come on, hands out and don't try nothin' stupid. As far as I'm concerned, your Babysitter status is gone."

CHAPTER THIRTY-ONE

Chaz:

Everything went black for a long, awful moment. Like the universe had been dipped in tar. I was coming out of it, swimming to the top, arms burning, like the bodies, like the smudged blue-black horizon of tiny bodies. I caught a breath when my head came above the resin-dark surface, thought I felt the heat of a coal-burning furnace.

"Hey! You can't do that"—Angelique seemed upset— "this is his crime scene—"

"Really?" Some nameless mug came over and held her down. Poured liquidmetal cuffs around her wrists. Paused a heartbeat while the nano-alloy hardened.

"This is against the law," she protested. "You morons have no jurisdiction here—"

She was right, of course. Apparently everything she had learned in a previous life as a lawyer was bubbling up to the surface of the pitch, smoke-filled bubbles that burst when they crested the tar skin.

I was on fire.

A second mug pulled a laser from the holster on his hip,

then flashed a red-hot beam on my palm, burned off the top layer of skin, erasing my tattoo. I yelled and jammed my knee in Mug Number Two's gut.

"Stop it!" My voice wasn't loud enough. No one heard me.

Through the doorway I could see Russ and Pete on their knees, hands behind their backs while Skellar read them their rights. Meanwhile, a group of distraught parents stood in the hallway, some crying, some trying to push their way through the crime scene barriers. A VR camera scanned the scene, beams of white light scorching the room, white arrows that pierced swirling ash. Any minute now we would go live with the rest of world. Film at 11. Look, everybody, the Domingues are going down.

"Your badge is on the line," Angelique said to the mug who held me down. She was standing now, hands braced against the counter, a glazed expression on her face.

"What the hell's goin' on here?" Skellar growled when he walked back in the doorway. "Drop that laser, Broussard! We haven't even processed him yet. And Domingue, tell your Newbie to settle down."

The other mugs took a half step backward. Meanwhile, Angelique threatened to charge the police department with her bill—a thousand dollars an hour—when this was all over. She promised to make sure the lieutenant's supervisor got a detailed account of his incompetence.

Skellar glanced at me, raised an eyebrow. I was as confused as he was, but I tried to hide it.

"In the case of a murder that takes place in a private residence"—she stared at the floor, frowned as if trying to figure out what to do next—"a Babysitter has seniority over a police lieutenant."

Skellar narrowed his eyes, seemed to remember some piece of information, probably buried away in a back file cabinet inside his dusty brain. "Okay, that's enough with the client-lawyer routine." An unexpected grin revealed teeth stained by years of jive-sweet. We all have our addictions, some legal, some not. "I'd fancy up, if I was you, Domingue. It's time to walk the gauntlet."

"You aren't seriously going to make him walk through all those—" Angelique tried to stop him, but he and his crew of brainless musclemen were already dragging me out the door.

"In the case of a capital," he said, leaning toward her as he paraphrased as best he could, "where the crime involves a minor, where the crime takes place in the home of a 'sitter—or a home that belongs to anyone in the 'sitter's ugly family—then the 'sitter may as well pack his bags and move into an eight-by-ten cell, custom decorated just for him."

His jack-o'-lantern grin was fixed in place.

"Get the Newbie too," the lieutenant said then, almost as if he'd been planning it all along.

I didn't see it of course. Not until all the excitement had worn off and nobody really cared anymore. But I heard that our exit from the crime scene got the highest viewer rating in almost twenty years, that it ranked higher than that Super Bowl incident where a Chicago Bears quarterback blew himself up to protest the war. Russell, Pete, Angelique and I were all dragged out, hands cuffed behind our backs like villains.

The gauntlet.

A special scenario reserved for top-notch terrorists and serial killers, those who had already lost all their civil rights and were one short step away from conviction.

Virtual-reality recording beams sizzled through the darkness like serpentine strobe lights; they caught and captured our every nuance, memorized our movements in 3-D. We got in-your-face-and-then-some exposure as we were hauled past the parents of the dead children.

This same group of people, who had cowered downstairs only moments before, now demonstrated a callous bravado. They spat, cursed and clawed as we passed. One woman yanked a handful of Angelique's hair. One man swung the broken chair I had used to open the bathroom door. Pete stumbled beneath the blow.

"Murderers!" another man bellowed.

"That's enough!" Skellar said as he pushed the man out of the way.

The screams deafened and assaulted. The blows weakened us with every step.

Still there was something else, something much more sinister, which ran beneath the surface. Something that the video technicians quickly edited out.

It stood at the edges of the wild crowd. Passive and cold and calculating.

While some of the parents reacted with violent, out-of-control anger, a larger majority of them stood back, silent, almost numb. A familiar expression on their faces. One I immediately recognized.

Apathy.

These children hadn't been kidnapped: they were dead. There would be a legal death certificate in the mail in a few days.

These children could be replaced.

CHAPTER THIRTY-TWO

∞

Angelique:

In typical mug fashion, I got slammed together with all the suspects in the case. Didn't matter that I was probably innocent. The fact that my arms had been burned from the liquid light should have branded me as a victim here. And although I still couldn't remember exactly what happened, I had a vague memory of pulling two of those kids into the bathroom and blocking the door. Just chalk it up to another good deed that went awry.

New body. Same old story.

Skellar shoved us single file down a narrow passage, hands cuffed behind our backs. For a few harrowing moments I was blinded by the VR strobe lights; in that instant the surrounding catcalls grew louder, more oppressive; the gauntlet corridor narrowed, transformed into a Mephistophelian birth canal that didn't want us to survive.

Meanwhile, the parents of the dead children loomed over us, arms waving, faces red with fury, shrill voices barking and howling and shrieking as we stumbled forward, step by step. Suddenly somebody grabbed me by the hair. I screamed and fell backward, staggered to catch my balance.

I collapsed on top of someone else, my body pressed against his, my face against his chest. I felt it immediately—a horrible familiarity: his smell, the touch of his skin, his voice when he spoke to me, softly, beneath the cacophonous layers of the crowd. When I struggled to lift my head, my lips accidentally brushed against his cheek and his eyes met mine.

Russell.

In that moment I remembered everything. How he loved me. How he killed me. How his hands knew every inch of my body. How those same hands had closed around my throat in a death grip, pressed against my windpipe, crushed my bones—

"Russ." His name came out like a hiss. I blinked, tried to pull away, couldn't breathe.

An electric shock flowed between us, an instant, silent, deadly communication.

He whispered. So soft no one else heard it. Maybe he didn't even realize he said it out loud.

"Ellen?"

He recognized me. He knows who I am. That murdering monster saw through my disguise before I even had the sense to hide.

I pulled away, forced my legs to stop trembling, turned my gaze away.

"Move along there, sister!" one of the mugs shouted as he pressed his palm against my back.

I ducked my head instinctively as someone swung a chair over our heads and slammed it down on Pete with a blood-soaked thud. He fell to his knees, cried out. Chaz tried to shelter him, managed to push him to the end of the corridor, then he turned back.

I could see Chaz looking at me through dark, twisted shadows. His mouth was moving, but I couldn't hear him. I nodded. Pretended I understood.

"I'm coming," I said as I tried to push my way through.

But all I could hear was Russ calling me Ellen and I knew. It was time for me to get out of here. Time for me to run.

CHAPTER THIRTY-THREE

October 13 • 5:35 A.M.

Chaz:

Shadows melted; clouds shattered; stars fell from the sky. The world became a barren landscape, painted in muted shades of gray and brown, a scorched horizon of broken glass and barbed wire. An invisible minefield surrounded by a poisonous moat. My throat felt like I'd been drinking fire, while my left hand melted and evaporated in the lava-bright heat.

Gone. Everything recognizable was gone.

I was empty. Tired. My blood had been drained out by some vampire and now there were ten more lining up, waiting for a drink. I couldn't remember the last time I'd been able to sleep longer than five hours. I wanted to close my eyes and lose my identity. Plunge headfirst into a Rip Van Winkle coma.

More than anything, I wanted to sleep without that nightmare.

"What nightmare?"

I lifted my head, stared unblinking into Skellar's Mongoloid face. I grinned. He was so ugly he was an insult to Mongoloids worldwide.

"You think I'm a Mongoloid, do ya? You want to spend the rest of the week inside? I got a sweet little cell with your name written all over the urine-stained walls."

I glanced over my shoulder. Sensed a shadow there. Angelique. She nodded.

I rubbed my face. They must have given me something to make me talk. I was probably babbling like a teenage girl with her first smartphone implant.

Skellar chuckled. "What do ya know about teenage girls?"

"That's enough, he's clean and you know it," Angelique said. "The Fresh Start lawyers already gave you the surveillance tapes from the Domingue security team. Chaz was outside when some nutcase climbed up the side of the house and doused Isabelle's bedroom with liquid light—"

"And you both know that all his fancy lawyers got no jurisdiction here, not when it comes to a capital involving a minor." Skellar leaned against the wall, slid a cigarette out of his pocket and lit it. A cloud of sulfur and smoke circled his face, made him look even more demonic than before. He picked a sliver of jive-sweet off his lip before he spoke again. "So, what about you, sweetcakes? Why did you take those kids in the bathroom right before the blast? You were in on it, weren't ya?"

"Look," she snapped. "If I had known that somebody was going to blow up that room, I would have gotten *all* those kids out. I wouldn't have grabbed just two. How heartless do you think I am?"

He shrugged. "You tell me."

"Sugar, I've got whatever it takes to play this game with

you." She braced her hands—now neatly bandaged with
synthetic flesh—on a long, low table and leaned toward him.
"We can go on like this all day and all night long. We can
do it in here," she waved at the interrogation room, "or in the
courtroom. Your choice. Just remember. The meter is running and your dollar pays for it all."

He shook his head. "Not if you lose."

"I've never lost a case."

I rubbed my temples. I felt like I had just swallowed a rat
and it was trying to claw its way back up my throat. I could
feel it, one paw at a time. I closed my eyes. I was going to
lose it, at any moment—

"Here, use this." Angelique shoved a wastebasket in front
of me.

There's no pretty way to say it. I puked. Rat and all. I
knew it was there, somewhere. An invisible ball of fur and
claws and teeth.

"Would you shut up already? There's no stinkin' rat."
Skellar crushed his cigarette out with his heel. "You're going
down, Domingue. You and your whole family. And you
better believe your brother, Russell, is spilling his guts in
the next room." He laughed at his unintentional joke. "Well,
probably not like you just did. But we got some inside info
that claims he might be behind this."

Angelique avoided his gaze as her lips curved in a slow,
dangerous smile. She nodded.

"What do you know about all this?" Skellar asked, his
eyes hooded in shadow.

She ignored him. Stared across the room as if she could
see things we couldn't.

He came closer, predatory head lowering, voice soft as a
silken noose. "Why did he do it? Was he testing resurrection
on those kids?"

She ran her fingers through her hair. A deafening silence followed.

"She just downloaded two days ago," I said. "Her memories haven't stabilized yet."

"Leave her alone, Domingue. And don't pull any of your Babysitter mumbo jumbo," Skellar said. "If she has information about this investigation—"

"All I know is, it's not right to kill someone," she said then, as if she needed to justify something, "even if they resurrect, it's still murder—"

"Is your Newbie nuts, or did your brother kill somebody?" Skellar was in my face now.

I paused. Russell could never kill anybody, he didn't have what it took—something I'd had to do more often than I wanted to admit. Anytime there was a really dirty job, I got stuck with it. That was why I was the Babysitter and he was the one sitting pretty in the CEO chair all day long—

"Look, I don't need to hear your friggin' family history, Domingue. I'm tryin' to figure out if we got another homicide here. You two know something about this and you're gonna tell me, if I have to keep ya here for—"

Angelique turned toward him, all the curves in her face melting into sharp angles, her spine turned to steel and her eyes diamond bright. "This interrogation is over, Skellar," she said. "End of your miserable mug story. Go ahead and investigate Russell until the hybrid cows come home, for all I care. Maybe he's guilty and maybe he's not. But you've got nothing to implicate either one of us in the murder of those kids. So, hey, yeah, you're going to let us out. Now. Or I promise you, you won't be able to buy your jive-sweet next month because my expenses will be coming out of your paycheck."

Skellar stopped.

Apparently Angelique had finally found his hot button.

He made a weak effort at maintaining control, pulled an-other cigarette out of his pocket, lit it, watched us through billowing smoke. Then he made a slight, almost insignifi-cant gesture with his left hand. A second later the door to the interrogation room breezed open.

We were free to go.

CHAPTER THIRTY-FOUR

Chaz:

Sometimes the big, tough-guy image shatters. Like a fragile, handblown glass Christmas ornament, it slips through your fingers and tumbles to the floor; and suddenly everything is in slow motion. There's a second when you still see the world the way it should have been, the way it was just a moment ago. Then you see the destruction. Fragments of glass spray in every direction and you realize that it's never going to be the same again. Ever. It doesn't matter if it's your fault or not, doesn't matter if everyone in the whole world knows what happened or if you're the only one.

At that point you just can't pretend anymore.

For me it happened at about four o'clock in the morning, after a grueling night with Skellar, where we played party games with one of his latest interrogation drugs. That was when I learned that Russell and his wife, Marguerite, were still in custody. And I just about ripped the arms off a mug who said my niece would have to stay in some "safe house" until the authorities straightened everything out.

Lucky for him, he changed his mind.

I took Isabelle home with Angelique and me. I gave my niece my room, and tucked her into my bed. I planned on sleeping out in the living room, but when I headed out the door, Isabelle started to cry.

"Don't leave me, Uncle Chaz, please—"

A tiny glass reindeer started to spin, tumbling down.

"I won't go, sweetheart." I went back inside, knelt beside her.

It hit the ground; fragments of light and shards of glass shot up.

She curled into my arms, pressed her head against my chest; her sobbing grew stronger and I suddenly realized how hard all of this had been on her. Up to this point all I had been able to think about was the fact that she was alive, that she was safe, I hadn't realized that to her, she wasn't safe. And maybe she never would be again.

A roomful of blackened, burned children. Dead on the ground. All of them her friends. Dead because they came to her party.

"Is he going to come back, Uncle Chaz? Is that bad man going to burn me too?"

"No, baby. No one is ever going to hurt you. I promise."

But I could feel the world spinning even as I said the words, felt the pain in my chest tighten, felt my eyes sting as tears came. For the first time, I could actually imagine a world without Isabelle, a place where some evil monster could climb up a wall in the middle of the night. I didn't know if I was really going to be able to protect her from the people who had done this.

And the ache made me feel like I was being turned inside out.

* * *

I stood at the edge of the patio door, staring down at the street.

"Is she going to be all right?"

I turned, saw Angelique curled on the sofa, wrapped in shadows.

"Yeah," I answered, trying not to think about the synthetic skin that now bandaged my niece's hands. This was one of those times when everything had to be interpreted in black and white. No gray. "Maybe not today or tomorrow. But yeah."

"Good. I mean, I wouldn't want anything to happen to her, she's a good kid."

I ran my hand along the door frame, finally settled on the handle, pulled the door open and let the cool, misty air inside. I didn't look at her. Didn't want to see her face, a chiaroscuro version of someone that I thought I knew yesterday.

"You saved her life," I said when the air shifted around me. The silence between us turned heavy. "You might not remember it, but I won't forget. Ever."

Outside the music of another day was already beginning. Cars shuddered down crowded streets and a helicopter flew in the distance, silver-and-black choppy noise that brooded over smoggy midnight blue.

"My memory's coming back," she admitted, her voice soft, almost as if she regretted the things that were swimming to the surface.

I turned to face her. This was one of the things I hated most about working with Newbies—they could be your best friend one minute and they could forget they even knew you the next. But it didn't matter. I had no right letting my emotions get tangled up in this mess.

At this point I just had to trust her and she had to trust me.

Because I had a feeling that if we didn't, neither one of us was going to make it.

"Did I say anything about a dog?" I asked. "When Skellar was interrogating me?"

She frowned. Searched her damaged memory banks. Shook her head. "No, you were talking some nonsense about an invisible rat." A smile flickered. "By the way, if you pulled that rat thing to irritate Skellar, it worked. But no, you never mentioned a dog. Why?"

I avoided her question. "Why did you act like Russ might have killed somebody?"

"It was a red herring," she said, flipping back to her lawyer persona, that safe zone where she knew all the answers, her matter-of-fact voice solid and sure, cutting like a knife through the fractured morning darkness. "I just wanted to give Skellar reasonable doubt. So he would let you go."

She sounded like she was telling the truth, but there was something in her posture that said otherwise. Her lip quivered slightly and she kept her gaze on her lap.

"You're lying," I said, challenging her to defend herself.

"Am I?"

I sat in a chair across from her, waited for her to look up at me, so I could see her eyes. I'd know if she was telling the truth or not if I could only see her eyes. But she didn't look up. Instead she stood, headed toward her bedroom. Left me alone in the living room. Enveloped in a muggy, uncomfortable silence.

I knew I should get some sleep. That drug of Skellar's was still coursing my veins and part of me wanted to rip the skin off my face. It felt like my skull had suddenly grown too big, like my flesh had stretched beyond its capacity. I wished I could pound Skellar's face through the wall.

Instead I lay on the sofa, my legs hanging off the end. Before I had a chance to analyze how uncomfortable I was, I fell asleep. For some reason my familiar nightmare gave me the night off. Probably for good behavior—after all, I hadn't flattened Skellar's nose, like I wanted.

Instead I dreamed I was in the bayou, wearing waist-high boots, wading through murky swamp water. I was looking for something lost, something important.

At the same time, I was wondering how many alligator eyes were watching me from the darkness.

CHAPTER THIRTY-FIVE

Angelique:

In my mind I'm walking through a foreign city, following a lifeline that drifts through thick, choking clouds, each step leading me closer to some new understanding. Sometimes I unconsciously go too fast, and everything begins to spin out of control. Too much information tries to process at the same time.

Then, in the midst of it all, I suddenly realize that the missing pieces have been erased by me. On purpose. Apparently it's all part of the picking and choosing of our afterlife memories.

But I got rid of the wrong things.

One image flashes before me, beautiful and fleeting and incomplete.

My son, Joshua.

It's immediately followed by an emptiness that I can't quite grasp. Pain settles in my bones like a long-forgotten war wound, something that causes me to limp when the weather gets cold. But I can no longer distinguish it from the myriad shards of shrapnel still buried somewhere, waiting to be discovered like a carefully planned minefield.

Maybe I did something wrong, made him angry. Maybe we disagreed about something important, and he stormed away to a far corner of the universe. I'll never know because I tried to wipe it away.

Isabelle reminds me of him. I didn't realize it until now. I can't quite figure out if it's her eyes or her smile, maybe it's everything put together. But right now I can see his face superimposed on top of hers. His life taped to hers like a paper-doll cutout.

I lie on the bed and wish I could sleep. The morning will come too quickly. The world will tip on its side, daylight will pour in the window and all my past sins will be revealed, like evidence beneath a microscope.

My body forces me to rest. But it is the uneasy rest of a convict, waiting for the verdict. Waiting for the moment when the executioner is going to walk through the door and demand payment.

CHAPTER THIRTY-SIX

Chaz:

I have a theory that we all carry a secret pain. Like a tattoo that you got back when you were a teenager, you hide it away beneath layers of baggy clothes and you only show it to someone you really trust, someone you know won't laugh because they probably have one too.

I don't tell very many people about my tattoo.

It started out like a beautiful drawing, a black intertwined gothic outline of two young people in love, with similar beliefs and goals. We were working on it together, filling in the hollow spaces with color. I wasn't going to hide this one away. I was going to wear it on my forearm, with my sleeve rolled up so everyone could see.

I wanted the whole world to know how much I loved Jeannie. We were going to get married, do the whole family routine; as soon as we got married we were going to use Dad's death cert and have a kid.

"What do you want?"

Jeannie and I stood on a hill, overlooking the Loire Valley, a sinuous river somewhere down below, winding its way through the castle-dotted landscape. This was the story-book phase of my life, when every thought still had a happy ending and I still believed that I was the master of my own fate. I was twenty-three and had just finished studying music at Juilliard. Next month I was going to start basic training to become a Babysitter. My first courses would involve advanced weapons training, hostage rescue and counterterrorism, but I was trying not to think about it.

Because that was next month.

She turned to face me, her curly dark hair blowing in the wind. The afternoon sky held the fragrance of lavender, the colors of a Monet painting.

"What do you want?" she asked again.

I've heard that question countless times throughout my life, and it's always sounded like an accusation. I mean, what could I want that I didn't already have?

"Besides you?" I asked. She didn't smile. It's always been hard for me to understand women. They seem to come wrapped in mystery, like layers of fine gauze. You think you can see through it, that you finally understand, but then you discover that you've only peeled away another layer and there are about a thousand more left.

I realized later that there was a subtext here. That she was really asking something else. She crossed her arms and tilted her head. I was taking too long to figure out the secret meaning of life.

"I want what everybody else wants," I said finally, deciding to tell the truth.

She shook her head. "No. Everybody else wants what you have."

"I mean, I want the right to choose."

"Choose what?"

This was where the subtext got as loud as a roaring lion, just seconds before it snaps off your head. But I still didn't realize it.

"Life," I said. "Death. What I do for a living. I never signed up for any of this, Jeannie. It just got dumped in my lap."

"Nobody's forcing you to stay at Fresh Start. Your family can't make you . . . they can't keep you from—"

Suddenly I could hear the words within the words. One more layer of invisible gauze peeled off like a snakeskin and blew away on the wind.

"They can't force me to be a One-Timer, is that what you're saying?" I asked. She didn't answer. She didn't have to, but for the first time I realized that her eyes were the color of gunmetal, a cool liquid gray. "You're right. No one can make me choose death over life, although I've been preached to enough over the years." I didn't want to look at her anymore, didn't want to see eyes the color of my future. "I thought we both decided that one life was enough."

"That was what you decided."

"Look, I just want to live the best life I can," I confessed, my back to her, my words soaring like birds over this valley of forgotten French kings. "And then when it's all over, I want to die and leave all this behind. I want to see my father again. I want to step through that door into heaven and I don't ever want to come back."

She was quiet. For a moment I thought she was gone, that she had headed back down the grassy knoll toward our rented car. But when I turned around, she was still there, and the wind had turned cold.

She gave me a half smile. "I just wanted to make sure," she said. "I mean, if we're getting married, it's important, isn't it? That we understand what we each believe."

Her words felt like a balm as I took her in my arms. I had revealed my secret heart, something I don't do very often, and I felt a moment of complete peace. Maybe we disagreed about this small thing called resurrection, but we could still make it work. Somehow.

Together we headed back down, through mossy meadows.

It was probably the last chance I would have at a normal life and I didn't even realize that it was already gone. There was no way either of us could know that the rest of her life would be measured in hours. A slippery mountain road lurked up ahead with her name on it, written in blood.

Within twenty-four hours her body would shudder to a stop and she would jump.

She already had her next life preplanned.

And it didn't include me.

There was a time when I thought that she'd look me up, at least to say hi or "Guess what, I never really loved you." But no. She just disappeared in the vast ethos of Stringers.

Like everything else in my One-Timer life.

Gone, but not forgotten.

CHAPTER THIRTY-SEVEN

Russell:

Somebody was pounding on my head with a jackhammer. Another second and I was going to grab the idiot sitting across from me and drag him around the room in a choke-hold. Crack his lazy skull against the cement wall. Watch his blood pool on the floor. And laugh. I was going to laugh.

"Hey, this guy hasn't stopped laughing since we gave him that injection."

Funny. This was all just too funny. My house was full of dead children, so instead of trying to catch whoever did it, the mugs decided to drag me in for questioning. As if I had any idea who did it. Or why. Like I would want to hurt my own little girl.

"I don't like the look on his face. You think we should give him another dose?"

Did they really think I was crazy enough to hurt any little kid? I started to laugh until tears ran down my face.

"That drug isn't supposed to have this effect. You guys said he would answer our questions. But it ain't workin'. Hey, I'm talking to you! Can anybody hear me out there?"

I was done waiting for this human fungus to let me go, I was going to yank his ugly head off his double-ugly body, use it for a soccer ball, bounce it against the walls until somebody told me where Isabelle was and whether she was okay . . .

"Get this monster off me! I think he's taking spikes— somebody get in here, *now*, this guy's as strong as a moose!"

Soccer ball bounce, dead man talk, get me outta here, get me outta here, or you're gonna die, you ugly mug, I'm gonna peel your arms off one at a time, then I'm gonna snap your legs like breadsticks, and then I'll twist off your head. Bounce it around until all your teeth are gone. I'm gonna laugh and you're gonna be dead if you don't let me see my daughter, let me know she's okay . . .

"Hey! Domingue. Look!"

I lifted my head, loosened my grip on that lousy toad-eating mug, let him fall limp to the floor.

She was standing in the doorway. Tired, long hair still in tousled pig tails. Still wearing that tutu and black body stocking. My laughter melted into tears.

Isabelle. She was okay.

I fell to my knees. Somebody tackled me, pulled my arms behind my back, poured liquidmetal cuffs on my wrists. I rolled on my side so I could see her for one more second.

"Daddy." A tiny smile curved on her perfect face. She held her arms out to me. But they wouldn't let her come any closer.

The bloodsuckers wouldn't let her come in.

The door closed and Isabelle was gone. A dream that never existed. The one good thing in my life. Gone.

Now there were five mugs in the room, all dressed in black. Two had some kind of hoods over their faces. As if it mattered whether I knew who they were or not.

"Ya gonna talk to us now, Domingue? Ya gonna tell us

about that break-in that ya orchestrated?" one of them asked.

I grinned. That drug of theirs was like candy compared to what I was used to. They could ask all the questions they wanted. I was innocent and I knew it, and that was all they were gonna get out of me.

I closed my eyes and rode the wave. Like an expert surfer that knew how to navigate this opiate ocean, I could handle the swells and the curls, avoid the hidden shoals.

Because I had to survive.

For Isabelle.

I didn't know if it was day or night. It felt like I'd been in this room for a week. I think I fell asleep curled in a corner and then when I woke up, every inch, every muscle ached. I wondered how much of that rotten interrogation drug they had given me and whether they would give me another go-round when they realized that I was awake.

But I was glad for the absence of my interrogators. Figured that they had all gone to sleep. I pressed my skin against the cold cement wall. The rough chill scratched my face, made me realize I was still alive.

I had to remember what I saw. I locked it deep within my brain where no drug could ever steal it. *Isabelle. Safe.* I hated to admit it, especially in this dark snake pit where the mugs had found a way to make my every thought known, but the fact of the matter was that I didn't care about the other kids. The ones that were dead. I only cared about one.

Mine.

It was my secret just how shallow my heart was. My secret cross to bear.

I could hear a symphony playing inside my soul. A bittersweet serenade. The battle between light and dark would be over soon. A crashing, thundering crescendo of violins and drums and wind instruments. Beautiful and sad. I could almost see my heart curling at the edges, burning, folding up into something hard. Like coal, it almost glistened.

Black and brittle and broken.

And dead.

The door flew open with a crash. I jerked awake. Didn't even know I had fallen asleep. Realized someone had removed my liquidmetal cuffs. I licked my lips and wondered how long it had been since I'd had anything to drink.

"You got a visitor, Domingue." A mug stood just outside the doorway. I couldn't see more than a dim outline of features, closely cropped hair, broad shoulders. "Fancy up, pal. It's your lawyer."

A tall, slender man gingerly walked into the room, his features slightly feminine, long hair pulled back in a neat ponytail. He was some sort of hybrid. I'd seen that model before, in the illegal chop shops that competed with Fresh Start on the black market. He had fair coloring, blonde hair and blue eyes combined with Asian bone structure. It was one of the latest prototypes that wed the exotic with the mundane.

He grimaced as he sat across from me.

This guy wasn't my lawyer, I'd never seen him before.

The door closed.

"They can't hear us," he said, his words precise as he looked me up and down. "This conversation is completely private."

I leaned forward. I could break this pretty boy in half if I had to. I thought about telling him that, but decided to wait and see what his game was.

He folded his hands neatly in front of him on the table. I could see that he had something tucked inside his right palm. Some sort of device. Maybe he was one of those new messenger models I'd heard about, disposable clones built for one-way missions followed by a quick download.

"You're a Newbie," I said, recognizing the unmistakable glitter. "A month old, maybe." It was my turn to look him up and down. "East Coast chop shop. My guess is you came from Harry Kim."

"Yes, of course. East Coast. You now have four minutes." His eyes turned cold, his speech pattern skipped a beat, slipped into something almost foreign. He said a couple of words I couldn't understand, then he returned to English. "If we waste time, you will regret it."

I shrugged.

"Where is Ellen?"

I felt the hair on the back of my skull stand up. I glanced around the room, tried to figure out if there were any cameras or recording devices that I couldn't see.

"I need to know the research progress," he continued. "You haven't turned in any reports for several days and my sources have informed me that the last dog, Omega, is missing."

"Okay, you wanna know what happened? She split, that's what happened," I said, trying to sound angry and betrayed, trying to keep my thoughts in check. "That mediocre research assistant your boss pawned off on me just disappeared. She ran off when the last dog died, that's how much she cares about your little project. And this research is all a pile of crap, I haven't had anything to report because it all failed—"

"That's a lie. This model," he made a sweeping gesture that referred to himself, "is equipped with many modern conveniences that Fresh Start does not offer. You are lying about—" He paused and looked up to the right. "The dog, he is not dead; the research, it did not fail. And Ellen." He took a deep breath. "You are at least telling a partial truth. She ran away."

He glanced at his watch. "You have one minute. I have to tell you, this is your second warning."

"What are you talking about?"

"We gave you a clear warning just before the break-in. We told your brother that we needed the dog. And the research. But now the stakes have gotten higher. For you."

"You monsters almost killed my daughter last night! How much higher can the stakes get than that?"

He smiled: a thin decadent crescent that revealed dimples. "Do you really think that death is the worst thing that can happen to a young girl? Just how naive are you, Domingue?" He flashed long eyelashes at me, lowered his gaze flirtatiously. "I, myself, grew up in the Underground Circus, back in my first life. It would be delicious to teach your daughter a few of my own special tricks—"

I flew at him then, lunged across the table and grabbed him around the throat. We crashed to the floor and tumbled. But he didn't fight back. Instead, I saw a faint light flash in his hand—the device he had hidden in his palm.

His limbs fell limp, his features waxen. His eyes met mine.

"Second warning," he whispered.

Then he died.

I stood up and screamed, then I started to kick the weasel. Bones cracked in his chest and blood seeped onto the floor.

"Get in here and pick up your rubbish!" I shouted as I continued to beat his worthless carcass. "Hurry up and get your garbage before I make a mess!"

The door opened quietly and two mugs dressed in black, wearing hoods again, came in and carried out the dead Newbie.

Then another man walked in, someone I'd never seen before. There was a weariness in his features, but his eyes were dangerously bright.

"You're free to go, Domingue. Apparently your brother threatened the jumps for every mug in the station if we didn't let you go," he said. "So go ahead. Get outta here. But if I was you, I'd use the back door. There's a mob waiting for you out front."

The sun splintered through the darkness. Black sky changed to indigo.

I hovered in the doorway, an intruder in my own home. Black boot marks stained the floor; like a dotted line they led upstairs, where the investigation continued. Strange voices murmured. Someone was talking with a French accent, someone else was slipping through the bayou mud in Gutterspeak.

"I don't sees how they gots liquid light. It's illegal for anyone 'cept the lawmakers and the 'sitters—"

"That was the idea. This stinks like a setup."

"So ya still thinks they're innocent, those Domingues?"

"I didn't say that. But we need to forget whose house this is or we're gonna miss the important clues."

"I'll tells ya the important clues. Them dead kids. Them sixteen babies that was burned alive. That's what ya needs to remember."

I couldn't face the mugs that had taken residence in my daughter's room. Instead I turned down a hallway, followed a path of polished wood and painted wainscoting. I could hear a faint hum in the distance, felt a slight electric buzz in the air. Saw a pale blue glow beneath the door as I came around the corner. Heard the whisper of voices.

The hallway smelled like a bakery: shelves lined with cookies and cakes, walls smeared with vanilla frosting.

I hate that smell. Virtual reality. The candy shop that never closes.

I heard crying, so I opened the door. My wife, Marguerite, stood in the middle of the VR room, wearing a VR suit, sur-rounded by about a dozen faceless, shapeless creatures that looked just like her. All sobbing and sniveling. It was her *sous-terrain société:* her flesh-and-blood surrogate family, grafted and stitched together from serendipitous encounters. They usually met in Grid chatter bars and, after several months of friendship and a brief civil ceremony, they chose assigned familial roles. Brother, sister, mother, cousin. Like children playing with blocks, they built their own fragile ancestry.

Weeping and wailing and gnashing of teeth. That's about all the *sous-terrain société* was good for. This group of Stringers didn't even notice when a real live human walked in the door.

"Hey, I thought you were going to wait for me at the station," I said, then watched as startled VR heads turned.

Marguerite swiveled to face me. Even with her suit on, I could see the tears glistening on her cheeks. Her voice wavered when she spoke, "I was—I did, but the mugs made me leave."

For a moment I realized how vulnerable she was, how our lives were never going to be the same after last night. I thought about the first time we met, that red dress she wore, the sound of her laugh. Then I did something I hadn't done in months.

I put my arms around her, held her for a long, quiet moment.

"Why don't you turn that thing off and go take a nap," I whispered. "You'll feel better—"

"But the funeral is this afternoon. I need to invite my family—"

"Marguerite, you're a Stringer—" She didn't have any family. They were all dust in the wind and had been for years.

"You've never understood what it's like to be *les enfants sans sourire*," she said as she pulled away from me. All the

VR heads around her nodded, murmured in agreement. "To be one of the children of no joy—"

For a second I thought I saw sixteen children, dead on the floor. Their ghosts seemed to surround us, filled the room. "Where's Isabelle?"

"Chaz wouldn't let me take her. He said I'll need at least seven guards before he'll let her leave his hotel suite."

I paused, frustrated. Felt tension building in my chest. I needed another gen-spike, but my stash was upstairs. And so were the mugs. "Okay, why don't you round up ten or twelve guards. We'll pick her up after the funeral."

"I don't—I don't know who to—"

"Just call Pete. He'll take care of it!" I snapped. I wanted the tension and the pain to stop, wanted her to shut up, to quit being weak. "And I told you to turn this off! I have a conference call with Aditya Khan in a couple of minutes." I hit the DISCONNECT button and the glittering crowd around Marguerite faded away.

"I wasn't finished!" She pulled off her face mask and threw it on the floor. "You don't care about anybody but yourself. For the past two years all you've done is humiliate me!" She paused, narrowed her eyes. "Do you think I don't know what you've been doing, staying late at the office every night—"

I grabbed her by the arm and pulled her close. She winced in pain.

"What do you know?" I asked, my voice low.

"That you've been having an affair with that dark-haired research assistant of yours, that Ellen." Her eyes blazed, a smoldering combination of fear and anger. "And apparently she's had more than enough of you and your gen-spike Jekyll-and-Hyde routine, because she split. I don't know what happened between the two of you and I don't care, but the mugs are pretty hot to find her—"

I gripped both of her arms now. She cried out and her knees buckled.

"They're here now," she gasped. "Upstairs."

"What did you tell them?"

"Just what I said. She's gone. You two were having an affair. And I don't care. About either one of you."

I released her and she collapsed on the ground.

"Bastard." She rubbed her arms, then glared up at me. "As soon as Isabelle gets back, I'm taking her and leaving—"

"I don't think so."

She stood up and stumbled backward, away from me. "I'm her mother."

"And that death certificate we used came from my father. Legally she's *my* daughter and you're nothing more than a surrogate."

Marguerite watched me like a caged tiger, all bristle and claws and dagger-sharp teeth, and all of it useless. "You won't be able to stop me."

I walked over and held the door shut so she couldn't leave. Crossed my arms. Flexed my muscles. Felt a left-over surge of gen-spike rush through my veins. When I spoke, my voice sounded like something out of a nightmare.

"Do you want to disappear like Ellen?" I asked.

She cocked her head, then her eyes slowly opened wider. She moved her mouth, but no sound came out.

I opened the door.

It took a long time, but she finally got the courage to walk past me.

Out of the room and away.

CHAPTER THIRTY-EIGHT

Russell:

I hate watching the news. Hate watching the world shrivel up and die. Especially hate it when the End of the World interrupts my VR transmission. I was trying to patch a transmission through to Aditya, but I was having problems. Probably because of the thick cloud cover left behind by that volcanic eruption in the Andaman Islands last month.

Then a special news bulletin jammed its way through.

A 3-D holographic map of the world rolled out across the screen. A horrific patchwork quilt of the inevitable, colors that marked the boundaries between tomorrow and yesterday.

A man's voice played over the scene, silver words framing enameled images.

"We interrupt your VR transmission for an update on the Nine-Timer Report," he said in a bright artificial tone. "Last night a tour bus crashed in the city of New Delhi, already a known hot pocket chiefly inhabitated by Five-Timers. After the accident occurred, a large crowd of tourists and bystanders died almost immediately, their circuits on overload from the shock—"

Photos flashed larger-than-life on the screen. Like the aftermath of a medieval civil war. A portion of the once colorful city of New Delhi had disintegrated into brown and gray rubble; the once noble land that had competed with Japan as a leader in technology was crumpling like a handmade paper kite. Cars were stalled in city streets and dead bodies were strewn everywhere. In the distance, a river of dark water was thick with bloating bodies. The Ganges, once a holy river, had become a river of the dead.

"—this caused a panic, which then spread throughout several city blocks, within which both Six- and Five-Timers froze up as well."

The newscaster stared into the camera. This was big news. *Pay attention, world. Somebody Important is telling you Something Really Important. Maybe you'd better go check your records and figure out what life you're on. Right now.*

"They stopped breathing," he said after a long dramatic pause. "Wherever they were, whatever they were doing, they just fell over. Dead. This is a new turn of events, something we've never seen before in the Fifth Generation clones—"

They hadn't seen it before, but I had. I'd even seen it take place in Third-Timers, when the stress factor was high enough. It was just one of the many elements that played into this bizarre end-times scenario.

"Riots and looting began soon afterward and, as you can see from our satellite photos, the panic is spreading," the newscaster continued. "Right now, power is out throughout most of the state of Delhi—"

I switched off the Grid, rubbed my temples, glad that there were no children in the photos. No starving babies, no abandoned toddlers, no homeless adolescents. Although that truly was our greatest problem here—all the clones after the Sixth Generation were infertile. The DNA broke down sooner than we had anticipated and, on top of that, with each successive generation there were fewer and fewer One-Timers. Before long, there wouldn't be enough sources of pure DNA left to go around. The Nine-Timer scenario that everyone had been fearing, a sort of New Dark Ages, could happen anytime. We used to think it would happen in another two hundred years, but we underestimated the popularity of resurrection, underestimated the possibility that large population segments might jump from one life to the next at a rapid rate.

We never guessed that stress alone could short-circuit a cluster of Three- or Four- or Five-Timer clones, or that once it started it could sweep like a blanket of darkness, knocking out several city blocks at a time. Eventually, even whole provinces could topple over like a row of dominoes, cascading into one another, turning off the lights for each other, shutting down farms and factories, cutting off communication and transportation. The Nine-Timer lifespan for resurrection was winding down, slamming to a rapid glue-in-the-machinery halt. We didn't even have a system in place to dispose of all the dead bodies. And there would be nobody left to take their place when the last set of clones died.

From its onset, people had advocated that resurrection would improve our world, that we would now have the opportunity to achieve long-range goals.

But those of us who stood behind the steering wheel knew the truth.

Resurrection had almost single-handedly undermined every major religion. We all just pretended to believe in an afterlife anymore. All our tomorrows were man-made, granted and blessed by man. We'd finally found a way to take the Big Guy out of the picture.

Today it was the state of Delhi.
Tomorrow it would be the Middle East.
Immortality. Resurrection. Death.
In the end, only a handful of One-Timers would survive.
And I planned on being one of them.

CHAPTER THIRTY-NINE

∞

Chaz:

There are moments that echo with beauty, like notes in a piano solo. They stir the soul, and then, like pebbles dropped in a pool, they ripple ever outward. The memory of one perfect moment can make you spend the rest of your life trying to recapture it, to reinvent it, to prove it really happened.

I slept. I don't know how long. At times it felt like my head would explode from Skellar's psychotropic cocktail, but somehow I managed to sleep through the pain, aware of it in some helpless nightmarish way, unable to stop it or wake up.

And then autumn sunlight poured into the living room, beams of honey, thick and sticky sweet with humidity. I woke slowly, with a sense of heat centered in my chest. And an unusual feeling of peace.

My eyes flicked open, blinded for a moment by the cascading light. Then I saw her—my niece—curled up beside me on the narrow sofa, her head resting on my chest. Her mouth was open and she was snoring softly. A slow, steady purring sound, almost like a kitten. My right arm ached, but I knew if I moved, it would wake her.

It would destroy this perfect moment.

I kissed her forehead, damp and feather soft. She sighed.

I lifted my gaze and saw Angelique sitting in the chair across from us, her legs tucked beneath her, both hands holding a cup of coffee. Her hair hung over her shoulder in glimmering waves and she was wearing a black dress and boots. She smiled quietly.

There was something about the three of us together in that morning of golden light that felt right. Complete.

This doesn't belong to me, I reminded myself. Isabelle's not my daughter, Angelique will be gone in a few days. All of this is borrowed. Imagined.

Still. If all of eternity could reside in one moment, this was the moment I would choose. This was the single note that I would want to resonate in my heart.

I wished that it could have lasted one more minute.

But even as I acknowledged its perfection, it began to dissolve.

CHAPTER FORTY

Angelique:

Day faded into night and then back into day. I don't know
how long any of us slept. At some point, Isabelle came out
of her room and curled up on the sofa next to Chaz. I knew
my time here was limited, this false sense of safety would
expire. I just didn't know when. Russ was a ticking bomb
now. At any point in time he would turn me over to Neville, or worse: to Neville's Nine-Timer boss, some high-level
government official, and their interrogation would start. I
wouldn't be able to hold out. I didn't have their advantage. I
couldn't download into another clone when things got rough.

I got a few things together, and then realized how tired I
really was. I paused for a few minutes to drink another cup
of coffee, trying to clear the last bit of Newbie confusion
from my head. That was when Chaz woke up.

There was a split second when I wondered if I should tell
him everything. But my split second didn't last long enough.

Because that was when the war started inside me. A tor-
rent of voices trying to drown me out. All of a sudden I

couldn't think and my skull felt like it would crack down the middle, like I had been struck by lightning.

I moaned, or at least I think I did.

I could feel the struggle between my past personalities, all of my previous hopes and dreams, drowning in the deluge, washing out to sea.

You can't tell him what happened, he'll turn you in—

You have to run, now, before Russ comes—

You can't run, you won't survive without Chaz, you have to tell him—

He said my name then, my new name, and I felt an overwhelming peace, something I couldn't explain or define. The horrid internal battle began to subside. It was temporary, I knew. I still had to leave, even if it meant ripping my soul in half. Even if it meant part of me would be destroyed in the process.

But for now, this one moment was heavenly.

CHAPTER FORTY-ONE

∞

Chaz:

Some days have no right to be beautiful. The sky shouldn't be blue, the birds shouldn't sing. There shouldn't be white puffy clouds sailing like catamarans across a vellum sea. The air shouldn't be fragrant with daphne, honeysuckle and gardenia; there shouldn't be a sense of magnificence in each stolen breath.

Today was that day.

I got out of the car, two bodyguards piled out behind me. Three others led the way. We pushed through angry cattle-like crowds, all poised and ready to stampede. Fortunately Fresh Start had sent a citywide Verse-warning a few hours ago, just in case anybody decided to pull another gauntlet. If there was a disturbance today, all transgressors would lose their ticket into the next life.

Just then, a herd of reporters tried to shoulder their way through the mob, media bands around their foreheads recording everything they saw and heard, as if that somehow justified their presence here.

"How does it feel to be responsible for the worst tragedy in the past decade?"

"Can you explain why your niece survived, when sixteen other children were brutally murdered?"

"How do you sleep at night, Mr. Domingue?"

I pushed my way past the reporters, wondered why the sun was shining, why ragged clumps of wildflowers dared to grow between weathered crosses and skewed headstones, why life still smells sweet in the midst of decay.

Catcalls circled in my wake and some blockhead threw a handful of rocks. One of the guards surged forward, grabbed the culprit, wrestled him to the ground, started to perform an on-the-spot, down-and-dirty extraction of the man's Fresh Start chip.

"Let him go," I mumbled.

The sky hung, a brilliant blue, above the crumbling brick wall that skirted the cemetery perimeter, all of it guarded by a quiet sentinel, a gothic stone church.

Black clouds should have been assaulting the ground, tornadoes ripping through the firmament, dirt and dust searing our skin. The heavens should have been shouting a vehement protest. Bolts of lightning should have shot down like shards of celestial glass, striking every one of us through the chest and putting an end to this charade we called life.

Instead, every nation, tribe and tongue was converging on a tiny nineteenth-century cemetery just outside Metairie, Louisiana. Modern technology was colliding with ancient ritual. Off to the side, a crew of VR event coordinators frantically pressed buttons on a massive audio/visual board, alternately waving their hands and directing the proceedings like orchestra conductors.

And then a familiar face appeared in front of me—my mother. I hadn't seen her since her transmission shorted out last night. When the liquid light rolled into our lives.

"Hi, sweetheart. You doin' okay?" she asked.

I nodded. The crowd shambled around us, fists clenched, eyes swollen.

"I tried to get in to see you." She coughed, then paused for a moment. She looked tired. "But my VR suit's been on the blink."

"Are you okay?"

She grinned. We both knew she wasn't okay, and that she was never going to admit it. "How's Isabelle?"

"She's fine, Mom. I left her back at the hotel with Pete."

"Yeah. She's too young for this," she said. Then she coughed again. "All those kids were too young for this."

"Time for you to get into position," one of the ant-like VR coordinators interrupted. He pushed a remote-control button on his sleeve and she started to dissolve.

She disappeared, and at the same instant the ancient landscape around me began to magically transform as VR wizards practiced their dark technological sorcery. Row upon row of shimmering virtual patrons began to pop up in pre-paid positions—Mom was probably crammed in there somewhere, but I couldn't tell which one was her. Meanwhile, the brick wall that surrounded the cemetery morphed, blurred and then refocused, until it finally resembled the staggered seating in the Roman Colosseum. Within a few minutes the guests were stacked in six rows, one on top of another.

Spectators were coming from all around the world to see the funeral of the century.

Just then a crowd of bodyguards drifted past. And at their center, Russ and Marguerite.

I had a feeling none of them saw me, or if they did, they were ignoring me. Either way, it helped me decide which way to go. My guards joined theirs and we followed a few steps behind, close enough for me to listen in on their conversation.

"This is awful," my sister-in-law, Marguerite, whimpered as she held a handkerchief to her eyes. I wondered if she was crying or trying to hide from the press. Despite the heat, she wore a long-sleeved black dress. "I just hate this morbid fascination with death."

"Death is part of life," Russ mumbled as he shepherded her forward, threading their way through the throng of nearly five hundred people; a variegated hodgepodge of reporters, bodyguards, mugs and VR technicians mixed in with immediate family members and friends of the deceased children.

"Not anymore. Funerals are just outdated, superficial ceremonies—"

He grabbed her by the arm and she almost crumpled from the pain.

"Show some respect," he hissed as he pulled her closer. "They were children and they died in *our* house."

"Take your hand off my arm." Her voice was fading as they moved away. "I'm sick of this marriage and I'm really sick of you—"

Just then Lieutenant Skellar muscled his way through our private army until he stood between Russ and me. I gave Skellar a toothy grin, raised my left hand and waved, sporting newly grafted skin and a fresh tattoo on my palm. He pretended like I was invisible. Just the reaction I was hoping for.

Instead he focused on Marguerite, like a shark considering a between-meal snack.

"Trouble in paradise?" he asked. I had a feeling this guy planned on becoming our new best friend.

Russ swiveled around, noticed me for the first time. His eyes narrowed when they focused on Skellar. "This is the wrong time and the wrong place, Lieutenant."

"Just wanted to give the 'Mrs.' my card." The mug slipped a thin piece of plastic into Marguerite's hand. "That's got my contact info on it, Mrs. Domingue. Call me if you remember anything else about the other night."

She palmed the card silently.

"Where's your Newbie?" Skellar turned a laser-beam glare on me, then scanned the surrounding crowd. "Thought you two couldn't be parted without destroyin' the universe."

"We opted for a trial separation."

"Sounds like something your brother and his wife might want to consider."

"Shut up, Skellar," Russ growled. "You're out of your element here."

"I'm never out of my element," Skellar replied. But I noticed a tremor in his hands, just before he stuffed them back in his pockets.

"I heard that the latest shipment of jive-sweet was cut with strychnine," I said. "Saw a VR report that said some of your good old boys are in the hospital, hooked up to artificial respirators. Maybe that's why you're cranky today." I started humming a popular jive-sweet tune.

"You're goin' down, Domingue. You and your whole family."

"In your dreams, Skellar."

He sauntered away, stage left, through a sea of anonymous faces, most of them watching Russ and me.

"Where's Isabelle?" Russ asked.

Good to see you too. How'd your interrogation turn out? Anything you want to tell me, like what the hell is going on? "She's back at my place. With Angelique."

"You left my daughter with a Newbie? Are you crazy—"

"Guess you forgot. That Newbie saved your daughter's life." I could see his freak level had just about reached its limit, so I gave him a break. "Don't worry, Pete's there. And a team of guards. Hey, did you see Mom? She's here somewhere."

He glanced up at the surrounding VR stadium seating, then back at me. "I need to talk to you after this is over."

"I think we both have some stuff to discuss." I was thinking about that Newbie who downloaded on his front lawn. Her cryptic message about some dog and a girl named Ellen.

A thought burned behind guarded eyes. He lowered his voice. "I tried to get hold of Aditya Khan this morning, but couldn't get through. India's gone brown."

The Nine-Timer scenario. My pulse ratcheted up a notch. "What about Saudi Arabia?"

"Not yet. But they've got a number of Five- and Six-Timer hot pockets."

"This ain't good. Especially right now—"

Just then the crowd parted like the Red Sea. A stream of pallbearers marched past, carrying tiny caskets. A river of sixteen miniature coffins, close enough to touch. All sound vanished. No one spoke or moved. Then somewhere in the distance, one bird started to sing, a surreal off-key melody, discordant and unsettling. My fingers turned numb and I realized that I had been holding my breath. There was something unholy and unnatural about all of this, like watching the world being turned upside down.

I wished God or one of his angels would step forward and ask if we wanted any do-overs. How about you, Chaz? Would you like to relive the past three days? Absolutely, I'd answer. But this time, I'd stop those bloodsucking monsters, I'd eat that liquid light before I'd let it get inside Isabelle's room . . .

A ball of light rolls across the floor like a toy, then ignites and blasts, a heat so intense that it fries the kids from the inside out. Boils their blood, melts their brains, sizzles their skin.

One coffin was barely the length of my arm.

For a long moment the sky blotted out and turned dark.
All I could see were cinder-black bodies, sixteen scars on
the bedroom floor.

Sixteen children. Gone forever. Meanwhile, somewhere
on the other side of the world, the epileptic convulsions of
the Nine-Timer scenario were beginning.

The end of everything was about to begin.

PART V

"*An anonymous Fresh Start scientist
claims to have documented proof
that the DNA breaks down in Eighth and
Ninth Generation clones, a defect that causes sterility.
If true, this adds a new twist to the apocalyptic
Nine-Timer scenario. Not only would there
be an astronomical and unprecedented
worldwide death rate when
large groups of Nine-Timers die
within a short time period—but there
would also be no children to take their place.*"

—Robert Quinlan, reporter for the *Washington Post*

CHAPTER FORTY-TWO

Russell:

The funeral service began in all its horrible glory, black-cloaked man of God spouting empty words of comfort, a low-toned unintelligible drone. I wondered where he got his information. He safely skirted mention of any holy books, from the Bible to the Koran to the Bhagavad-Gita.

Then they lowered the much-too-small-to-be-real caskets into the ground. It started when the dirt was tossed in, earthen clumps that thudded, dark and dismal. A moan, heart-wrenching and pitiful, began to circle overhead like a flock of carrion birds. One of the mothers collapsed to her knees, her face buried in her hands. Then beside her, another woman began to cry, chest heaving, sobbing without pause. In a few moments it spread like a California brush fire, started in the valley where the parents stood and then swept up the mountainside, where the VR audience hovered above us. It felt like the whole world burned with sorrow.

We were being consumed by death. It was something we had ignored too long, and now, like a fire-breathing dragon, it raised its ugly head in our midst; it dared us to pretend we were anything more than mortal.

The fire burned and we couldn't put it out.

We were leaving. Numb. Broken.

I felt like someone had dragged me through a minefield of broken glass. Raw and bleeding, with a hundred invisible slivers that continued to cut.

Someone grabbed my sleeve. I ignored it at first, but they wouldn't let go.

"Please." A woman's voice.

I looked behind me and saw Mrs. Norris. I couldn't remember her first name. All I could see was a little girl's face superimposed on top of hers. Madeline Norris, eight years old. Dead.

"Please, can't you make an exception? Just this one time—" Her voice came out a ragged whisper as she pulled me closer. "Bring her back, bring my Madeline back. She was eight. That's old enough, isn't it? Resurrection would work on her, wouldn't it? Have you ever tried—"

I folded my hand over hers. Wished I could change my answer.

"No, Mrs. Norris. I can't. It doesn't work on children."

"But can't you try? Just this time, try it, *please.*"

"I'm sorry. I wish . . . I wish there was something, but . . ." My voice trailed off, my words stumbled over one another, helpless and ineffectual.

"I just don't understand." She stopped walking, stood still as the crowd rushed over her, a flood of black coats and lowered eyes. She just faded away as the mourners struggled to get out of the cemetery as quickly as they could.

I wanted to comfort her. In my mind I could hear Dad explain it and up until today I think I had always believed him.

"Resurrection doesn't work on anyone younger than twelve," he told me one cold winter afternoon.

I had argued with him, tried to figure out what we were doing wrong.

"It isn't what we're doing," he said. "It's us. It's the way we're made."

"I don't understand," I said.

"Children, they belong to God." He shrugged. "We just can't take what belongs to Him."

At that time it seemed to make sense.

But today, as the crowd rolled over Mrs. Norris like a tidal wave, I wanted to ask God why He didn't take better care of the things that belonged to Him.

CHAPTER FORTY-THREE

∞

Chaz:

There weren't many times when Russ asked for my opinion, when he even thought that I might have some idea worth listening to. I'm not sure when our "great divide" took place, when we drifted off into our separate universes and became more like rivals than friends. It was probably around the time our father died, although I think it had been brewing below the surface for a few years. You can't always put your finger right on the spot that hurts.

But there was one time, when I was about thirteen and he must have been fifteen, when Russ needed my help. I was someplace else in the plant when the accident happened, so I only heard stories that trickled down, whispers spoken when no one thought I was listening.

Dad was training Russ to perform the jumps, showing him how our satellites would transport the dead bodies, how we'd get the pre-ordered clones out of storage, then sort through the memories so the Stringers could keep the ones they wanted. But no matter how much we planned ahead, we always struggled with a nebulous potpourri of "what-ifs."

Things that could go monstrously wrong: what if the memories got mixed up; what if we used the wrong clone; what if the Stringer got lost somewhere in transit?

On this day, there was an unexpected Edgar Allan Poe-esque what-if.

What if the Stringer wasn't all the way dead when we started the jump?

Somebody along the way, some doctor or lab technician, made a wrong diagnosis, and this Stringer was still alive. Just barely. So when Russ started the download, it caused a horrible ripping inside the jumper. He flopped like a fish on the gurney, sparked back to a half-alive state, although most of the important stuff was already gone. He screamed and tried to break free. We didn't use restraints on the dead bodies, never needed them, so when he lunged forward he yanked off the connector wires and broke off the implant—a long, tube-like needle that we insert deep into the brain—that is, if the Stringer still has a brain.

Dad and some of his techno-wizards dashed into the room and tried to calm him, to hook him back up. Apparently everybody knew that this guy wasn't going to live, no way, no matter how valiantly he tried to fight death. I don't know all the medical details here, but he'd done some serious damage to his current body that couldn't be repaired. The bottom line is, Death was coming down the hallway and looking for this guy's room.

Meanwhile, Russ waited at the controls, like he'd been told. From where he stood, he could see this guy's clone, hooked up and already partially downloaded; he watched the clone move, saw it lift an arm at the same time as the Stringer. Saw it turn its head in the same direction.

But then the Stringer suddenly collapsed. Dead. Really dead this time.

At that same moment, the clone jumped off its gurney in

the other room. It went through all the same movements that the Stringer had done just a few minutes earlier, until finally it fell to the floor, silent.

All the guy's memories got fried in the process. And the soul—the Stringer's fragile, almost indefinable essence—escaped.

There was nothing left but an empty carcass and a damaged clone.

Dad tried to tell Russ that it wasn't his fault, but my brother didn't believe it. He went through an inner turmoil, quiet and self-destructive.

Over the following months, I saw darkness and fear rise to the surface in my brother's eyes at strange times, when he thought no one would notice. Until one night when I walked into his bedroom and found him alone at his desk, pretending to work on his journal.

One sleeve was rolled up and I saw a series of cuts on his arm. Self-inflicted and precise. As soon as he heard me behind him, he hid his arm.

He looked sick, like he had the flu.

"Whaddya want?" he asked, forcing a teen bravado that failed. He tried to mask the scared look in his eyes, but he was a second too late. I'd already seen it.

I don't remember why I went into his room. I probably had a question about my homework, but it vanished the moment I saw his arm.

I sat on his bed. Hoped he would say something. He didn't.

"It wasn't your fault," I said, wishing I could make the pain go away.

He laughed, a sardonic, twisted noise that sounded more like a sob. "Of course it wasn't. We're life-givers, not takers. I was just doin' my job."

But I knew it wasn't that simple. I knew that there was

something else going on, deep inside. I waited, quiet, hoping that he would tell me what it was. I never really expected him to open up the way he did. A hush fell over the room, thick as swamp water and just as dangerous. I imagined reptilian beasts hidden below the surface, waiting to bite, to pull one of us under. There came a point when I realized that I didn't want him to talk. I didn't want to know what was driving him mad anymore. I just wanted to leave and forget about it.

That was when he looked at me with hollow eyes. That was when he started to talk.

"I just . . . I just don't know how I can keep doing this crap," he confessed. "I feel like my soul got sucked out when that Stringer died." He stared at the floor, as if he could see invisible monsters swimming in black water. "I know it's not my fault, but I feel like I killed him. Like I pulled the switch too soon, or I hooked up the clone wrong. Or maybe I shoulda seen somethin' on his chart, some red flag, some misdiagnosis . . ."

Just then I saw a shadow move on the wall, like a long alligator snout raised above bayou water, ready to strike. I think that we both saw it, that we both knew something had always been there, just below the surface, stalking us. Hungry. Insatiable.

"I feel like I swallowed a rock," he said, "like my heart is missing and I got this damned rock in its place."

Russ had never opened up like this to me before. I didn't know what to say.

His eyes searched the room, as if the answer would be written on the walls and he would find a window of escape. "What should I do, Chaz? I don't know how to get rid of this rock, or this darkness that surrounds me. I don't know how to live when somebody else died because of me."

I didn't know the answer. And I didn't have the power to save him. I only had a vague memory of hope, something I'd heard over and over but never really put into practice.

"This thing, this guilt"—I paused, uncertain how to express what was in my heart, especially when I knew that a black monster was swimming through the room—"it isn't between you and that dead guy. Not really." I thought I heard the swish of a reptilian tail. "It's between you and God. He's the one that you need to talk to."

"Do you think I haven't tried?" There were tears on his face now, glimmering in the darkened room. His own personal river of pain. "I feel like He hung up the phone on me. Like He isn't taking my calls anymore."

"Then let's call Him together," I ventured. I expected him to laugh and tell me to leave, to go back to my pretty little childhood while he drifted off into dark, unfamiliar streets. I expected the black water to swell, to come to life, to swallow him whole right in front of me.

But that wasn't what happened.

Instead Russ lowered his head and wept. Then he got off his chair and knelt on the floor. I suddenly forgot about the monsters and knelt beside him.

For the first and only time in our lives, my brother and I prayed together.

My life changed after that. From that point on I knew God in a different way. It isn't something I can easily put into words and I don't even try very often. For the first time I realized that heaven was real and I wanted to go there. And I wanted to make sure I never saw that swimming black monster again.

I don't know what happened inside Russ. Because we never talked about it. A few days later he went back to work in the plant. But he never performed a jump again. Not even after he took over Fresh Start.

After we prayed together, the darkness that had surrounded him disappeared.

Until that day I stood in the cemetery and watched all those kids put to rest in the dirt.

And this time I had a feeling that it was after me.

CHAPTER FORTY-FOUR

Chaz:

The crowd began to move—somnambulistic—zombies walking through a desolate wilderness. I had reached my own ground zero. My lowest, darkest point. *After this, it gets better*, I decided. *Somehow.*

Russ and I hugged briefly, then parted ways. We were going to meet back over at the hotel suite on Bourbon Street; he was going to pick up Isabelle—him and a small army. I was going to try to forget about this, finish up my week with Angelique. We had an emergency board meeting scheduled for the next morning. A crew was trying to put together a makeshift VR connection with our plants in India, and we needed to do some damage control before the media could—

Someone brushed up against me, blocked my way. The crowd snaked past. Bodies without souls or purpose. I lifted my head to see who wanted a piece of me.

Skellar.

I was too tired to be surprised.

"Just what kind of game is your brother playin'?" he asked.

"What are you talking about?"

The crowd had thinned. Only a few stragglers remained and none of them were listening to us.

"Maybe you're just as bad as all the other 'sitters and maybe you're not, I don't really care," he said. Maybe that was his way of apologizing for letting one of his mugs fry my hand. It still didn't make up for his snake-pit interrogation tactics. "But your brother is in trouble with some nasty Uptown boys—"

"Look, we're not afraid of you or your mug buddies."

"I'm not talkin' 'bout mugs. These guys make us look like Girl Scouts."

I grinned. It was about time Skellar realized his team wasn't so tough.

"You ever seen this woman?" He spun a hologram in his palm. I watched as a dark-haired beauty in a lab coat checked her makeup, then glanced over her shoulder to talk to someone I couldn't see. I thought she looked familiar at first, something about the way she held her head, maybe a glimmer in the eyes. But I'd never seen her before. At least that was what I thought until I heard her voice when the audio kicked in.

Still, I couldn't quite place her.

I shook my head. "I don't know her," I said.

"Well, this girl, Ellen Witherspoon, she went missing 'bout three days ago. She was workin' on some pretty important stuff. These people are lookin' for her. Gotta lotta money too. They'll pay almost anything to find her. And your brother was the last one to see her."

"You think Russ is involved in this?"

"Maybe. Don't really matter what I think. It's what they think that matters."

I raised my eyebrows.

"The way I see it, she mighta jumped. And she's got

some mighty important information that this Uptown crowd needs." He paused. Looked around. "Word has it there's a new game in town."

"New game?"

"What you guys got down at Fresh Start is nothin' compared to what's comin'. You'll be outta business in less than a year when this stuff hits the streets."

He just walked away then. Didn't ask me any more questions. Didn't ask to look at our Stringer records to see who had jumped in the past two weeks. But it didn't really matter.

Because I suddenly knew the answer.

CHAPTER FORTY-FIVE

Chaz:

I think I always liked breaking the law. Even back before I got my magic Get-out-of-Jail-Free card, the tattoo that lets me break more laws than the mugs can invent. Sure, I wanted to be a musician, to spend my days and nights immersed in the jazz clubs that ring the city, to breathe in the smoke and the stench of liquor, to watch the world around me rot, even as it regenerates. I wanted to laugh and tell stories and philosophize about life with other burned-out, jive-sweet musicians on the street corners while the sun slid over the horizon. I wanted to watch the color bleed from society, drop by bloody drop, until there was nothing left.

Nothing left but the painful need for redemption.

But instead, the family wanted me to donate my musical ear, wanted me to sort through the myriad languages and dialects, from ancient to new, so I could converse with Newbies, until they adjusted to the newspeak of the day.

I wanted to run away, to live on dimes and nickels and drink in the pure music of jazz night and day. Instead I settled for a warm bed and a billion dollars and a saxophone that saw the light of day about once a month.

For all my tough talk, I sold out. I'm no rebel.

But that Get-out-of-Jail-Free card still comes in handy from time to time.

Like when I was twenty-three and my fiancé, Jeannie, died in that car wreck and jumped to some obscure, unknown life. I went after her. I broke every code in the Right to Privacy Act. I hunted down her files, hacked through the firewall into her personal records, found her new identity and her new life. If Skellar or one his buddies ever finds out what I did, they'll either cage me or kill me.

But I don't care. I'd do it again, if I had to.

In hindsight I guess you could say I stalked her. I found out where she lived, worked, shopped; who she hung out with; what she did in her free time. And then I found a way to meet her. It's not like I could just walk up to her and say, "Hi, remember me? That guy you were going to marry?" I had to be both discreet and romantic, I had to play it out like it was the first time.

It was great in the beginning. It had all the electricity of a first kiss, all the magic of falling in love at first sight. Almost.

But despite the faint promise of a renewed relationship, there was something missing. She had a strange, vacant look in her eyes. I kept thinking I would see some spark that said she remembered me. I mean, she loved me before, right? She had to remember. That's the way it works.

See, there are two memories we can't erase. Death is one. As ugly as it is, all the terror and pain and finality of dying becomes part of you and it refuses to let go.

Love is the other. You can pretend like it didn't exist, you can try to reprogram it or cover it up by attaching other memories, but the down-and-dirty resurrection bottom line is: if you've ever loved someone, that love will follow you. Like a stray dog you accidentally fed on a street corner, it will hunt you down. It will sleep with you, wake up with you, walk down a dark alley with you.

But Jeannie didn't remember. She had wiped me from her memory banks on purpose, and there was only one reason why she didn't remember me now.

She had never really loved me.

So I walked away.

It wasn't pretty and I don't regret it, even though I broke the law in the process. Believe it or not, there really are limits as to how far I'll go, what laws I'll break and which ones I won't. The list is pretty long for a Babysitter. Almost anything is permissible.

But something was hanging over me right now, a venomous cloud of suspicion and doubt, forcing me to reevaluate everything.

Murder.

Had my brother really gone that far? Had Russell stepped into that treacherous territory where the rules didn't matter anymore?

I didn't know for sure if what Skellar had said was true or not, but I didn't want my world to change. I didn't want my own brother to become the enemy. Because if it came down to it, I didn't know who would I choose. Russ or Angelique? Someone I had known all my life or someone I had known for only a few days?

The boundaries in my little kingdom were shifting, that well-worn safe map that guided me was gone, and I couldn't see where I was supposed to put the next step.

CHAPTER FORTY-SIX

∞

Omega:

Rain soaked the pavement. City sounds echoed through the forest of brick and stone. The smells were stronger now; the fragrance of food came with the wind, thick and sweet.

Omega climbed onto the hood of a car, lifted his nose, took several short sniffs. He could almost see the scent in the air, like gold dust. It seemed to float in front of him, then trailed off down the narrow street, around a corner and into a nearby alley. He turned toward the Others, let out a short bark—his command to follow. The pack watched him eagerly, backs bristled, tails curled, ears forward.

In a collective heartbeat, they were padding through a network of alleys, heads down, hunting. Dusk shadowed the city in morning half-light: a colorless world, a land that belonged to them.

He could almost taste it now, somewhere up ahead. A tiny stone city within a city; the wild dogs were weaving between stone sepulchers and mausoleums. The smell of death hung in the air, but it was old, musty. Another smell, strong and sweet, called.

Trinkets lay scattered in front of the whitewashed crypts. Shiny necklaces and flowers, candles and fetish bags. And baskets filled with sweet cakes.

Omega and the dominant female, his mate, ripped open the first basket together and then wolfed down the pastries drenched in icing. The other dogs began to tear open other baskets, and the cakes rolled out. Two of the males got into a fight, teeth shining in the murky light. Omega snapped a warning bark and growled. The brawling males stopped, hackles still up.

Then a noise sounded behind them, and two humans came out of the shadows.

The stench of fear surrounded them, metallic and sharp. The humans were looking at Omega's mate, a wild danger in their eyes.

Omega growled and tried to step between them and his female. But he was too late.

A crashing sound shot through the air and his female screamed, a high whine.

She fell to the ground. Blood. Her blood. Her life flowing out on dirty cement.

Omega leaped through the air, caught the first man by the throat and wrestled him to the ground. Sweet, dark blood. Bones cracking. The man yelled, fought, then finally fell still after a long shudder.

Another cracking boom shot out. A shock of pain struck Omega in the chest, then another caught him in the stomach. He tried to jump, to attack the second man, but the third shot got him right in the jaw.

Omega fell limp on the ground. Darkness was coming and with it, his old friend, Death. The dog looked at his mate, saw her feet twitching. She was going into shock. She was going to die. And then a wave of black washed over him, carried him away to the land of no tomorrows.

* * *

The second man panicked. Four more wild dogs growled, took a step closer. He dropped the gun when he ran away, dropped the knapsack filled with stolen cameras and wallets.

One of the video cameras fell out and switched on.

Red light focused. Lens open.

The recording started.

The Others chased the human until he vanished in the shadows. Then they returned, faithfully, to Omega and the female. They sniffed both bodies. One dead, the other dying. One of the males crouched down beside the dying female, pushed her with his nose, tried to make her get up.

But the dominant female wouldn't move.

Thunder sounded. A hundred miles away, somewhere on the other side of the Valley of Death. Lightning sparked across a black sky, then shot into his veins. Omega felt oxygen flooding into his lungs. Pain. The first breath always hurt. He didn't want to open his eyes.

He didn't want to see his mate. Dead.

Then he smelled it. Sunshine. Somewhere nearby.

He forced his eyes open.

There she was, his female. Still. Not moving. Not breathing.

He crawled to his feet, pain shooting through his muscles, fire in his veins. The Others cowered. They always did when he came back to life. He padded, soft and slow, over to her.

She was the only one who hadn't been afraid of what he was.

He lowered his head. Nuzzled her face. Licked her nose, her mouth. She was growing cold. He fought the pain that centered in his chest. Nudged her again. Saw a trickle of blood seep out from her side. He knelt beside her, laid his head on her chest, then licked her wound. Remembered a time when she had been brave enough to lick his wounds.

He licked her wound again.

Then he lifted his head to the heavens. And howled.

The video camera clicked and whirred, a mechanical beast that captured everything without emotion, without reaction. It watched, impassive, as the big, black German shepherd got up, resurrected from death. It hummed as he crouched beside the dead silver wolf, licked her wounds, then cried out in anguish.

It recorded everything—

The dead wolf jolted back to life, her body trembling and shaking. The convulsions grew stronger, then finally faded.

Then the wolf got to her feet, nuzzled her head against the shepherd, her mate.

A few moments later, the pack of wild dogs padded off, shadows against shadow, black shapes against pale gray.

And the camera lay on the ground, with a flash and a whir, staring into the gloom of another dawn.

CHAPTER FORTY-SEVEN

∞

Omega:

Twilight bled into morning. Sunlight whispered through the city canyons. The dog crouched, hidden behind the statue of an angel, a stone memento of forgotten faith. False light splashed through the forest of tombs. Humans. Voices called out to one another, seeking solace in their aloneness, in their confusion. They centered around the dead man, still sprawled on the ground, bloody and torn, his life spent in violence.

Omega hid from the humans. He was alone. His mate and his pack were safe, waiting back in a shadowed alley. He lifted his nose and sniffed the indigo sky. A few stars still colored the heavens, blinking, winking, fading. The coming day was only a promise, slow and hesitant to reveal itself.

And yet, he could smell it. Here. Somewhere. Sunshine.

He closed his eyes and took another deep breath. Fragrant. Beautiful.

The smell of love.

He opened his eyes, analyzed the breath-of-heaven perfume. She had been here, somewhere. The woman. The one human who loved him. The woman who had fed him, who had knelt beside him and stroked his fur through the cage bars. The woman who had tears in her eyes every time he shocked back to life. The woman who had set him free and told him to run and never come back.

She had been here. He needed to see her again. The desire flowed through him like hunger. He needed to find her. In some secret way she belonged to him. She was his. She was part of his pack.

But the other humans were here now. Cutting and slicing the dark morning with their beams of light and their frightened voices.

Just then a moment of silence descended. The humans all grew strangely quiet when one of them picked some whirring metallic toy off the ground. They all gathered together in an anxious huddle, murmuring, playing with the toy, then glancing over their shoulders.

Omega grew weary of the humans and their smell of fear. It hung like acid in the air, sharp and demanding. But he didn't want to respond. The only thing he wanted was to find the woman.

And she wasn't here right now.

So he rose from his hiding place and padded off.

Back into the velvet blue.

CHAPTER FORTY-EIGHT

∞

Chaz:

New Orleans used to be known for its jazz funerals, ceremonies where both sorrow and joy were packed into the soulful music of a brass band. A march would lead to the cemetery, with family and friends trailing behind. Hymns wailed from clarinets and saxophones and trumpets. But somewhere along the way we got lost. We no longer celebrated or honored the dead. Apparently, while we were busy dancing the resurrection shuffle, we forgot to pay our respects to those who got left behind.

The funeral broke up, black-shrouded parents stumbling away in a huddle. I climbed back in my car, gave my guards the rest of the day off, and in a few minutes the city was flying past in a blur of buildings.

It didn't hit me until I was almost back to the hotel. I don't know why I hadn't seen it sooner. If Russ got back to the hotel before me, there was a good chance he would try to cover his tracks. The only real proof anybody had about Ellen's death and disappearance was hidden deep inside Angelique.

He was going to try and neutralize her.

It's a process we don't perform very often, but every high-level exec at Fresh Start has the authority to take down a rogue Stringer. Ever since that bizarre series of events a couple years ago where a damaged Stringer got hold of a laser rifle and murdered a restaurant full of people. Then it had spread like a virus through all the Newbies who had used the same regeneration pod.

It took six other Babysitters and me almost a month to track down all the infected jumpers. We were able to save about four of them, and we managed to download them into their next life. But the jumpers that had committed capital crimes had to be neutralized.

I couldn't sleep for a week afterward.

I had to stop Russ before he did something stupid. That was when I suddenly realized that I didn't have to worry about whose side to be on.

Angelique was the one I really cared about.

I switched on my Verse and tried to call Pete. The ring echoed in my ear, tin and distant, a lonesome, desperate sound.

But he didn't answer.

I thought about calling Russ, but I hesitated, unsure.

Just then I rounded a corner and I could see the hotel. Russ's car was already out front. I don't know why, but I glanced up toward my suite, the one I shared with Angelique. I saw something flutter in the wind out of the corner of my eye, something black, ominous.

It was a body. Plummeting to the ground.

CHAPTER FORTY-NINE

Angelique:

A blanket covered me. A blanket of dark sky and bright stars. My skin prickled, every inch of it like needles carving stories on my flesh. My eyes were closed, but I could see Isabelle sitting in the corner, humming while she colored pictures of fairy tales. Snow White, I think. Or Sleeping Beauty.

Coloring pictures of me. Sleeping.

Chaz had put me to sleep, then left Isabelle and me here. With Pete.

Darkness descended, rolled over me in waves. Something dangerous was coming, I could feel it. I had to break free, had to wake up. I pushed my way through layers of gray and blue, layers of cotton and flesh. Voices swirled around me, sharp, staccato. Somebody was upset.

Wake up.

I shook off the dream, felt a cold chill wash over me and a surge of nausea. I leaned over, still fighting nightmarish tentacles, opened my eyes. I was alone in the bedroom. Isabelle stood in the doorway, looking out. Sucking her thumb.

Voices in the other room.

"Did you see that?"

"What the hell is going on?"

"Shuddup! Listen." The last voice was Pete.

Isabelle glanced at me and smiled. I held my finger to my lips as I crept toward the door. I heard the electronic echo of a VR screen. Pete and some of the guards were watching something, some news broadcast. I peeked around the corner. No one was looking in my direction. They all stared at the screen.

"We're going to play that video again," a woman newscaster said. "This time we'll explain what we think happened."

A gritty video began to play, electronically enhanced to compensate for the failing light.

"This is the City of the Dead," she said. "A man was found dead here this morning, apparently mauled to death by a pack of wild dogs. And this video camera captured what happened afterward. If you notice, right now, both of the dogs appear to be dead."

A massive black German shepherd sprawled on the ground, his body ripped and torn. It was Omega, it had to be. I fought the emotion that rushed over me, fought against what I saw. *He couldn't be dead.* Just then the camera wizards went in for a close-up. His face was shattered, his muzzle gone. I covered my mouth with my fist, fought against a sob.

"Watch this. Here."

But I couldn't watch. Instead I pulled Isabelle into my arms, turned her face away so she wouldn't see it either.

"Look. Do you see that?" the newscaster's voice continued, brazen, boasting. "His face is just . . . just rebuilding itself. And if you notice the gaping hole in his chest—"

I opened my eyes.

"Criminy! What the hell is goin' on with that dog?" one of the guards said.

Pete held up his hand to silence him.

The dog's face had almost completely reconstructed itself. And the wounds in his chest had disappeared. It looked like he was breathing. Low and shallow.

"Now look at his eyes," the newscaster said.

Omega opened his eyes. Moaned. Took a deep breath. He struggled to his feet, shaky at first.

The dog jogged over to the silver wolf, sat beside her, nudged her with his nose. She didn't move. He licked her face, licked her wounds, nudged her again. He lay beside her, his head on her chest, licked her wounds another time. After a few moments, he howled, a long heart-wrenching cry to the heavens.

And then the dead wolf came back to life.

"But that can't, it can't happen, boss—"

"That's not resurrection, that's not what we do, not the way that other dog—"

"I tolds y'all, shuddup!" Pete yelled.

Omega and his mate circled the area once before slipping away with their pack, before they became invisible in the morning shadows. One more time he trotted past the video camera, brushed his nose against the lens, testing it, probably attracted to the light.

But a shiver ran over my skin. It seemed as if the dog knew that I was on the other side of the lens, as if he was looking right at me. As if he wanted me to know . . .

Suddenly I remembered. I couldn't breathe for a couple of seconds as the last memory came back, the final missing piece.

I knew what I had done with the last dose of serum.

I glanced down at Isabelle as she leaned against my leg, her soft hair falling in curls over her shoulders, her soft life spilling all over the room like blood. I remembered the attack, how she had almost died from the liquid light. The monsters who broke into her bedroom would come back. They wouldn't stop until they got what they wanted.

I knelt beside her, pulled her away from the door so the others couldn't hear me.

"Isabelle, I have to go somewhere," I whispered. "Will you help me?"

She nodded, but her dark eyes said no. Some part of her didn't want me to leave.

"I'll come back," I said as I gave her a hug. "I promise."

Then I told her what to do, how to distract Pete and the guards so I could sneak out. All the while, hoping that I would be able to keep my promise and come back.

I was running again, just like the night I was killed. Down the hallway, away from the suite I shared with Chaz, my Babysitter. My protector.

I kept reminding myself why I was leaving. Every step got harder. I could feel my thoughts begin to scatter, voices on the nether wind. All of my lives seem to blend into a winding blacktop road that stretched out forever over unfamiliar hills.

The elevator snapped open up ahead.

I froze, suddenly afraid. I was too scared to get inside. Instead I slipped into a nearby shadowed doorway, clenched my knuckled fists to my chest, every muscle shaking. I forced myself to be still, to be calm. I was leaving my Baby-sitter. And it took all my strength to fight the need to go back. It was programmed so deep that I started to feel sick. I curled over.

I needed to get back to the City of the Dead. It's there. I had to go back.

Then I heard voices as a second elevator opened; people were coming toward me.

One of them was Russ.

I turned my face away from the hallway, tried to imagine that I was invisible. One of my hands slid over the door handle and instinctively pushed. The door opened. A stairway stretched before me.

I quickly slipped inside and started running down, running away. Russ couldn't find me, he just couldn't. Because if he did, he would kill me.

Again.

CHAPTER FIFTY

Neville:

Silent as an empty midnight mass, the silver-and-black chopper thumped to a velvet halt, descended like light from heaven, landed on the roof of the Carrington Hotel. A ragtag team of misfits climbed out, the one thing that united them a gen-spike stench, an odor of skin that had been stretched and pumped so many times that it began to decay from within.

"Follows me, boys," I said, leading the way toward the stairwell. "And makes sure yur darts is loaded. Like I says, ya might not needs them." I grinned over my shoulder at Seth, a lanky nineteen-year-old who still couldn't grow a beard. "But ya might wants to use them anyway."

Seth returned the smile, exposing crooked teeth, yellow from years of jive-sweet. His skinny arms were pockmarked from street-grade gen-spikes, something that had changed after he hooked up with my gutter brothers. Now he only got the best stuff. Jive-sweet was yesterday's candy. Today it was all about that euphoric high of genetic alteration.

A beam of sunlight glanced off the chopper, cascaded into a rainbow that turned everyone around me into faceless silhouettes. I felt an apprehensive shiver, crammed a handful of jive-sweet in my mouth. Something about the way the light sparked around us reminded me of that night in the bar, that 'sitter and his liquid light, the feeling I was being watched by something that transcended my understanding.

"Boss?" Seth hovered, uncertain, in the doorway, a shock of black hair falling across his forehead.

I lifted my chin and laughed. Pushed my way back to the front of the line, inside the door and down the stairs.

My laughter ricocheted and bounced throughout the narrow corridor. Like the fire of a machine gun. I pulled out a blowgun and slid it between my lips. Long and narrow, about the length of two cigarettes, it felt good as it rolled into place, a hollow slot between my first and second bicuspids.

I sucked in a deep breath through the tube, trembling slightly at the traces of bliss, the latest designer drug, that flowed into my lungs. Just enough to wipe away any lingering fear.

We all had our blowguns in place now; we all grinned as we jogged down the stairs.

I is light and freedom, I brings power to the people. Them that gots no hope.

I brings them what they needs.

Immortality.

CHAPTER FIFTY-ONE

Russell:

The world flowed past my window, like a river of color. The images smeared and blended. My eyes couldn't focus on anything. Not even Marguerite, although she sat beside me in the company car. But I hadn't been able to see her for years. She'd been a wisp of smoke, her emotions transparent and inconsequential. More of an irritant than an inspiration.

Ellen. Memories of Ellen clouded my vision.

I thought we had a chance together. Then she betrayed me. I glanced down at my lap, realized my hands were knotted in fists.

I had been a fool. But those days were over. I was tired of trying to fix the problems with the rest of the world. I only wanted to salvage what I could. The jet was ready. A villa hidden in the Andes waited. As soon as I was finished at the hotel, I was leaving. Taking Isabelle and Marguerite and flying off into the blue horizon.

After I got rid of Angelique. At this point I didn't care whether she was neutralized or given to Neville. I just wanted her and her Ellen-past gone.

The flow of color outside my window stopped. The world came back into focus. Sharp and immediate.

"We're here." Marguerite's voice. Already I was looking forward to the jet ride that would get us away from New Orleans.

One of the guards opened the car door and I stepped out. Took a shallow gulp of city air. Stared up at the towering hotel. Then I headed toward the lobby, unconsciously wiping my hands on my shirt.

As if that bloodstain splatter I had been dreading was already here.

"Where y'at, boss?" Pete stood in the door, a shallow husk of who he had been two weeks ago. He looked like he hadn't slept in days. Like something horrible haunted his dreams.

"Where y'at?" Marguerite answered him with a grin. She gave him a hug, then strolled inside Chaz's hotel suite. "Isabelle? Where are you, sugar?" she called out. "It's Mama."

Our daughter came dancing out of a bedroom, ran and jumped into my wife's arms. Her hair was neatly combed and she wore an oversized T-shirt that came down to her knees. But she was fine.

My heart skipped a beat. I hadn't realized until now just how terrified I'd been that something might happen to her.

"Mama, Daddy." She nuzzled her face in my wife's shoulder, then reached an arm out to me. We embraced as a trio for a long minute. For a crazy moment it felt like this was going to work out after all, the three of us together, us against the world.

"Boss?" Pete stood over by the VR screen. "I needs to show you somethin'."

I nodded. Kissed Isabelle on the cheek. "We'll be going home in a couple minutes, baby," I told her. Then I met Pete by the monitor.

"The news gots a video that's been runnin' all morning," he said as he hit a REWIND button.

"Where's the Newbie?" I asked, keeping my voice low. I didn't have much time. Chaz could be here in a few minutes. I needed to erase my past mistakes before he got back.

"Sleepin' in there." He pointed a thumb back toward the room where Isabelle had been. "Trust me, you gots to see this first." He hit the PLAY button.

The video began to run. For an instant I forgot about everything else. The dog we had experimented on was alive. But there was something going on that didn't make sense. "It's Omega," I said.

"Yeah."

"But that other dog, how did it come back to life?"

"See hows he licked her wounds?" Pete asked.

"But that shouldn't make any difference."

"There weren't never any tests like this, boss."

"Still—"

Just then Isabelle tugged at my shirt. "Daddy." She held her arms outstretched.

I picked her up and cradled her close. "Where was this taken?"

"They says it was the City of the Dead."

I thought I heard something, Marguerite talking to someone, probably a Verse call from one of her *sous-terrain société*. I shrugged it aside, tried to stay focused on the dog and the Newbie, tried to figure out what my next move should be on this complicated chessboard. But that was probably my biggest mistake. I had been focusing all of my attention on pawns and rooks.

In retrospect, I should have been guarding my queen.

CHAPTER FIFTY-TWO

Angelique:

My legs trembled as I ran down the stairs, as the map rolled out in my head again, the same map I'd seen that night in the car when Chaz handed me the marker. I could see the whole city of New Orleans laid out, street names, addresses. And a series of hot pockets—warehouses, buildings, houses, all marked in red.

It was all preprogrammed information. Embedded.

Dizzy, I paused to lean against the wall, tried to figure out what the location tags meant. Maybe they were places I had been in a previous life. The City of the Dead was there too, the brightest of the bunch.

Somebody put this map in my head for a reason. But who and why?

Nausea forced me to buckle over again, to catch my breath.

Pete. It had to be him. He must have been the other undercover agent in Fresh Start. Must have been the one who resurrected me, who told Neville where I was, who made the marker in my hand.

A thunder of footsteps charging down the stairs roused

me to attention. A few floors above me, sinister laughter. Gutterspeak. And one voice I recognized instantly. Like a jagged arrow, it ripped through my memories.

Neville.

He must have been waiting for my memories to resurface—

But none of that mattered anymore.

Because right now Neville and his bad boys were tromping down the stairs in my direction. And this wasn't some serendipitous coincidence. I was a big part of the puzzle here.

They were after me.

I forced myself to a standing position and started running down the stairs. As fast as I could.

CHAPTER FIFTY-THREE

Neville:

All around me the world thundered with laughter and energy. It felt like I had a thousand volts shooting through my veins, like me and my boys were all juiced up and ready for battle. Shadows sparked off the polished walls as we descended, luminous in our dark, pretty-pretty cocoons, ready to burst forth, ready to break through the paper-thin walls and earn eternal butterfly wings.

Two more flights and we would be there. Floor 33. The suite that 'sitter shared with his Newbie.

Legs pumping, feet stomping. Dusky, sweet laughter ringing. Soon the stench of decay would be wiped away.

"Heres it is, boss." Seth held the door open, a raw eagerness in his First-Timer eyes. The boy was a puppy, but he was well trained.

I rewarded him with a grin and a cuff to the head, which the boy easily dodged. Then Seth stopped, cocked his head to one side, lifted a finger to his lips.

I raised my hand for everyone to be silent.

We could all hear it now. Somebody was running down the stairs, a floor or two below us.

I nodded and pointed to Seth. "Go checks it out," I said. "Then meets us back up on the roof."

The boy took off, a hound after a fox, loping down the stairs, two at a time.

Then I slammed through the open door, led my boys over carpeted floors.

"Quiet now," I reminded them. "And loads yur darts. We's almost there."

CHAPTER FIFTY-FOUR

Chaz:

I slammed on my brakes and my car screamed in resistance; it jerked, skidded sideways, and then shuddered to a stop. Right in the middle of the intersection. I threw the door open and ran across the street. A crowd had already gathered on the sidewalk and I couldn't see what was going on. I tried to get past them, but almost immediately a popping and glittering band of virtual-reality crime-scene tape appeared, pushing all of us back.

"Babysitter! Let me through!" I yelled as I shoved my way through the stunned crowd.

It felt like we were covered in mud, like some gritty glue held all of us in place and we could only move in slow motion, one spare inch at a time. In my mind I screamed for everyone to get out of my way, but I don't think those words ever made it out. One part of me was moving faster than I ever had, while another part was stuck somewhere in the past, still back inside the car, overwhelmed with astonishment and terror.

I was a frozen blur, moving and stationary in the same

instant. Wishing that what I had seen wasn't true. Dreading what I would discover as soon as I pushed through this eternal moment of now that refused to bend.

Two mugs flashed into position in front of me, wearing a couple of those new experimental VR skinsuits, the ones with the more realistic faces—although all these faces looked the same.

"Hold it right there, Domingue." A hand sizzled in front of me, hit me square in the chest and held me in place. This was new for VR. Normally I would have been able to push my way through. Until now. I recognized the voice.

Skellar.

"Stay right where you are," he said, his voice fading in and out before it finally stabilized. Apparently the voice modulators on this skinjob weren't up to speed yet. "We have to scan for evidence before we can let you in."

I tried to see past him. Something fluttered on the ground, like the wing of a bird. Dark, torn fabric. Part of a dress.

A woman. The person lying dead on the ground, about ten feet in front of me, was a woman.

Please don't let it be Angelique, I prayed.

I looked up. Thought I saw someone standing on my balcony.

A team of VR mugs surrounded the body now. Behind me, somewhere in the distance, a siren sounded. The real goons would be here in a minute. For all I knew, one of them could be Skellar in the flesh. He could be wearing a VR suit in the back of a van, projecting himself here.

I was done waiting. I pushed my way back through the crowd. Whoever was on the ground was already dead.

And whoever was responsible was probably up in my suite.

CHAPTER FIFTY-FIVE

∞

Russell:

I watched that blasted dog video, over and over. Until it turned into a vintage *Twilight Zone* episode. Until both dogs trotted off into the dark night. Like a pair of invincible hounds of hell.

I think Marguerite may have said something, but whatever it was, it didn't register. It wasn't until I heard Pete cry out that I realized something was going on.

"Hey, don't opens that door—"

I glanced at Pete, saw a startled expression on his face. Then his knees buckled beneath him and he crumpled to the floor. The look of astonishment froze on his face.

"What the—" I swung around, instinctively shielding Isabelle.

The front door hung open, and a gang of gutter thugs had slithered into the room. They moved with strange, jerky movements, sometimes holding still, sometimes magically appearing halfway across the room. A veil of color slid between us, a glittery orange, and then an awful panic rolled over me, the realization that all this was beyond my control.

"Marguerite—" It was all I could say, every syllable exaggerated and stiff.

My skin prickled and I caught a whiff of something honey-sweet.

She was beside me then, taking Isabelle in her arms. "I'm sorry, Russ," she said.

Then I saw a yellow-feathered dart sticking out of my arm, felt my muscles melt like butter. I sagged to the floor, not as quick as Pete. Maybe they gave him something stronger.

"Puts him in a chair and ties his arms." An apocalyptic voice. Malevolent. Foreboding. Familiar.

An army of hands lashed me to a chair. Trails of light followed robotic creatures as they darted across my line of vision. Had we been invaded by humans or machines? I forced my thoughts to stay focused on Isabelle. Turned my head to follow her, saw her cradled in Marguerite's arms.

"Daddy, I wanna see Daddy!" she screamed, squirming to get down.

"Go aheads. Lets her down. Lets her say good-bye." That voice again. This time connected to a face. Murky green eyes, bald head covered with metal studs. Neville. My personal path of destruction. I wasn't surprised to see him. I had been dreading his arrival.

A glowing Isabelle scampered across the room, light flowing from the tips of her fingers and hair. "Daddy," her voice echoed as she burrowed her face in my chest.

"We needs to talk."

I glanced up, saw Neville guiding Marguerite to the balcony. The two of them were alone out there. He was telling her something and she was arguing with him, a look of bewilderment on her face—

No.

I couldn't say anything. My vocal cords wouldn't respond to the command I was screaming. Terror flooded my heart, a tidal wave that rolled over me, over Isabelle. Fear and anger filled the room, a crest that surged, that swallowed all hope.

No, Marguerite, don't go out there with him, don't trust him. I didn't mean it, I would never hurt you, I couldn't—

But they weren't arguing anymore. He glanced at me, lips creasing into a wicked grin. Then he turned back to Marguerite, lifted her in his arms.

And dropped her over the edge of the balcony.

CHAPTER FIFTY-SIX

Angelique:

One of Neville's gutter boys was after me, I could smell him. Still a floor above, but he was gaining. I could hear him jumping down the stairs, two and three at a time. I caught a glimpse of him when I glanced back. Tall and lanky, young, dressed in black, his face laced up with black stitches across the cheekbones. They all had to take the mark somewhere on their face. Usually across the forehead, something they could cover up with their signature black bangs. But this kid put his gutter mark up front for the world to see.

He had a point to make.

And I was probably part of it.

I wondered if Neville had taken the time to tell him that I should be kept alive. That I had information they needed. I saw a white stick hanging loose in the kid's mouth. Darts. This punk was loaded.

But what was he carrying? Sleep or death?

I ran, downward. Matching my pace with his. Jumping down steps, swinging around the corners. I knew how to escape, how to fight. My body was new and fresh and it responded to my training memories better than I had anticipated. Still, he was armed and I could tell that he was gaining on me.

I was going to have to do something unexpected.

Level 21.

I yanked the door open, raced over the carpeted hallway, felt him behind me, like he was my echo, like he was wearing my thoughts. I zigged back and forth, knowing that this would slow me down, but I couldn't take a chance on getting hit with a dart. I slammed my hand on the elevator button as I passed. Just then something shot past me, an invisible hiss. He'd taken a shot at me and missed. Exactly what I was hoping for. I collapsed in a tumble, fell into a clumsy half-rolled position on the ground, one arm slumped over my head, my face turned back toward him, one eye open just wide enough to see the startled look on his face as he slowed down. He approached cautiously.

Good. Keep coming.

I could tell he was looking for the dart.

Closer, almost here.

His right foot landed six inches from my face. Perfect.

I waited until he leaned forward, until he stretched his hand toward my still and crumpled body. I struck, in that moment when he was slightly off balance. I spun, tucked and rolled, swung one leg up, knocked him to the ground. Jumped to my feet, then kicked him in the chest. Heard the wind swoosh out of his lungs, saw his eyes flash closed in reflexive pain. Saw him curl like a spider on its back, legs folded inward.

Then I ran. Toward the open and waiting elevator. Toward the lobby and freedom.

I heard him groan behind me as I ran, thought I heard him struggle to his feet. He was stronger than I'd expected.

Something flashed in my brain as I almost made it through the doors. A familiar odor hung in the air.

The decay of gen-spike flesh.

I swung inside the elevator door, punched the DOWN button, crashed my back against the wall, chest heaving, mouth open. The doors started to close when I heard a horrid sound.

A high-pitched whispering whistle, air being pushed back as something shot forward, something flying so fast it was almost invisible.

It struck me in the thigh, the tuft of feathers shivering on impact.

I glanced up, saw his grinning face appear in the narrow space between the closing doors. Already I could feel it. Numb. Heavy. Like I was being plunged in icy-cold water.

My legs sagged beneath me, refused to bear my weight. The elevator plummeted downward and I collapsed, helpless, on the floor. One last comprehensible thought before a gossamer gray veil clouded everything.

Sleep or death?

CHAPTER FIFTY-SEVEN

Chaz:

The hotel lobby was a scramble of bodies; arms and legs and startled faces. It was as if everyone knew something horrible was coming and they didn't want it to get too close. They turned away as I ran past, as if that could protect them. As if I were the hurtling bullet, the fast-advancing plague.

As if I wore the mask of death.

Just like the crowd outside, I had to push my way through a slow-moving herd, human flesh the boundary between me and my goal.

The elevators. Across shining marble floors, between Grecian pillars. A pair of twin doors stood closed, yet expectant, like the lid on a wicked jack-in-the-box, ever ready to spring open and reveal some predatory monster within.

I ran. Skidded to a halt in front of the doors, punched the UP button with my palm. Glanced impatiently at the stairway door to the left.

Should I wait or should I run up the stairs?

There are times when your brain moves faster than your body, when you see your life five times quicker than it really happens, when you see the beginning and the end, almost simultaneously. Then it loops around again, this time with a different, and usually much worse, ending.

The loop kept playing through my head, and each time the stairs seemed more logical. I could scale those steps in a few seconds, I could be halfway there before the elevator doors opened, I was wasting time. And yet, some part of me knew this was a false conclusion. There was no way I could run up thirty-three flights and beat the elevator.

I had to wait.

And waiting was killing me.

I prayed it wasn't killing anyone else at the same time.

In that never-ending moment, as I stood waiting, my mind tumbled over all the safe words I had heard throughout my life: words like *love* and *hope* and *faith*. Every single one seemed to cause a sharp, jagged disconnect, to force me to continue to search for the perfect word, the one that would stop the tumble, the one that would stop the inward implosion that was going to drive me to madness if I had to wait another second.

Adrenaline slugged through my body; I leaned forward, willing time to push through the envelope, to reach the next second.

Waiting for the elevator doors to fly open.

Hoping that one word would finally win the lottery and stop the tumble.

CHAPTER FIFTY-EIGHT

Neville:

Marguerite flew over the edge of the balcony, a blackbird with dark wings that fluttered in the breeze. She was free now. Free to die and live again. Free to build another fake family from the broken bits and left-over pieces of the *sous-terrain société*. And this time I wouldn't be part of her genealogy. I was tired of pretending that I cared, tired of listening to her incessant whine.

As if the blue-blooded elite deserved to complain about anything.

She seemed to be looking up at me as she fell, her mouth a small circle, a silent yet expressive *O*.

I laughed, quietly, chest shaking from a recent gen-spike, thoughts focusing then unraveling slightly, like they always did whenever I reached that mountaintop high.

She was at the bottom now, so far away that she looked like a tiny doll. A crowd formed quickly around her, insects flocking to an open wound.

"Speeds it up, my puppies," I called to my team as I

walked back inside from the balcony. "The mugs will gets here in about two minutes." Bodies lay strewn throughout the suite, eyes open, not moving. Strapped to a chair, Russell tried to hold his head up, to keep his eyes focused while his daughter clung to him.

"Who gots the Newbie?" I asked.

Black-clad street warriors glanced at one another, then shrugged. "She ain't here," one ventured. "We hasn't seen—"

I struck the man down, glared at the others. "Where she at? Who gots her?"

"F'true, boss, we couldn't finds no Newbie here."

I latched onto Russell, yanked his head forward. "I only asks one more time."

"I haven't seen her," Russ answered, his words slurred.

"Yeah." I grinned, then let my hand slide down to Isabelle's shoulder. "Ya hasn't seen her." I lifted the little girl into my arms. "And maybe ya won't sees this little one again, neither."

"No, don't touch her!"

"Ya knows what I wants. The research and the dog. The key to immortality. I gots to has it."

"I told you, it's gone—"

I nodded toward the door. My dark troupe began to slip out, shadows melting. "And I tolds ya. 'Bout the things that would happen if ya didn't keeps yur end of the bargain."

Sirens whined in the distance. It was time to leave.

"Ya gots twenty-four hours, Domingue. Then the little princess here," I cradled Isabelle, kissed her forehead, "she gets painted to ride the flyin' horses."

I swung the child under my left arm, carried her around the waist, ignored her screams. I jogged out the door and down the hallway, toward the rooftop where the helicopter waited.

I sang as I ran. It was a dangerous song, usually heard in back alleys flooded with moonlight.

A song from the Underground Circus.

Wind from the roof whipped through the stairwell as soon as the door swung open. The chopper stood ready and waiting, blades slicing blue sky, energy pulsing. The team of gutter punks charged forward, heads down, a black running stitch across gravel tapestry.

A man stood at the edge of the open helicopter door, one hand pressed to his left ear, blind eyes searching. His right arm hung withered and useless. He was one of the many who could only afford black-market jumps; his clone body was slowly atrophying, pulling him back into the grave he had tried to escape.

I handed the child to one of the shadows inside the chopper.

"I hears somethin', boss," the blind man said. "That dog, I hears somethin' 'bout that dog on the news—"

"Gets inside," I ordered. "Where's Seth?"

Sightless eyes stared toward the empty stairway as he shook his head. "He runs with you, he ain't come back yet."

"Y'all gets inside!" I grabbed the other man, pushed him toward the open door as he climbed in. "Seth knows how to gets Backatown on his own. We gots to leave."

The door swung shut and the chopper lifted, like a yo-yo on the ascent.

I looked down at the shrinking rooftop, chuckling as I pointed.

Below us we all saw the shimmering materialization of a small team of VR mugs; they punched through, blazed in and out, then shorted out. Vanished.

The chopper filled with laughter as it swung over the city and away.

CHAPTER FIFTY-NINE

Russell:

The world faded and changed; all the color bled into one corner, all apricot sparkles. Sweet, like the orange huck-a-bucks that Isabelle ate in the summer. Frozen Kool-Aid in plastic cups. She gobbled them up until her mouth turned firework orange. Then she would stick out her tongue and we would both laugh.

But now words slammed through the orange fabric, silver and gray, words like bullets, sharp as knives, coarse razor-edged words that sliced through a velvet coral womb.

"Mr. Domingue! Can you hear us?"

When I first walked through the door, Marguerite was alive—she was laughing, joking with Pete. Then somebody messed with the dials in the universe, changed everything a sickening shade of mango orange. My wife sailed over the edge of the balcony and time stopped. Not long enough for me to say goodbye. Only long enough for me to wish that I could have saved her.

"What happened, Domingue?"

They flickered around me, all firefly light and electric current. Not real people. No one was real anymore. No one 'cept Isabelle.

"Isabelle?" My voice sounded like someone had stuffed cotton down my throat. I tried to lift my head, to see where she was. "Where y'at, baby girl?" My eyelids were stuck together, like somebody had poured glue over the lashes. I blinked.

"Where is your daughter, Domingue?"

My eyes met his, I saw a familiar glare. Even through the VR suit I knew who he was. Skellar. What was that monster doing here?

"Is anybody else alive in here?" he asked, looking back at one of his wavering shadow-bright detectives.

"We hasn't found nobody yet, Lieutenant."

"What do you mean?" I blinked again. "Pete, tell 'em you're okay." I couldn't hear Pete's answer, but I was too tired anyway. I took a long, deep breath, almost a sigh. My head sagged back and my eyes closed.

"Hey! He's goin' to sleep, somebody get that medic up here."

"He gots a dart—"

"I know he has a dart, you moron, that's why he needs a medic! Anybody here know what the yellow feather means?"

I could have told them. The yellow feather turns everything orange, it slows the world down, it paints everything with a melancholy brilliance, and it takes your breath away—

At that point somebody untied me and I fell off the chair, my mouth open. I slammed shoulder first, facedown, gasped like a fish dangling on a hook. My legs shook and my arms trembled. If I could have screamed, I would have.

But by now, the cotton was all the way down inside my lungs.

Oxygen was a distant memory. And in its place, a black ocean rolled in.

PART VI

"No reproduction without a valid death
certificate, that's what the
Worldwide Population and
Family Planning Law mandates.
As a result, there's a hunger that can't
be quenched, no matter how
many VR children you invent or
how many puppies you buy,
a hunger that can only be satisfied
by spending time with a real, live child ..."

—Underground Circus propaganda, sent via black-market
Verse to select customers

CHAPTER SIXTY

Chaz:

I have to confess there are things about this world, this time period, that are wonderful. Things that I would never want to live without. Virtual reality is one of them. The ability to go almost anywhere in the world, anywhere that the current VR signal reaches, anyplace you have the physical coordinates for. I could be in Singapore one minute and Paris the next. All of it is in real time, of course. That detail usually confuses first timers. You can go to Australia, just don't expect it to be the same time as it was back in San Francisco.

But even VR travel has it drawbacks. Just like deep-sea diving.

The frequent, shifting patterns of light can sometimes cause travelers to have hallucinations. So, like any other good thing, there are warnings, age limits, contraindications regarding certain drugs.

I'm not sure how people lived before we had virtual reality or accelerated learning techniques or Verse implants.

Before resurrection.

What was it like when everyone lived with the fear of

death peering over their shoulder? How did they get the courage to cross the ocean in primitive boats, to burrow tunnels beneath the earth in search of precious metal?

Sometimes I wonder what it was like before families were ripped to shreds, when holidays were spent with cousins, aunts and uncles—before the creation of the *sous-terrain société*. We've filled our empty spaces with fool's gold, taken false solace in the tumbling jesters and the flying horses and the carnival that never stops.

Our world ended the day the Underground Circus came to town.

Sometimes I think we pulled a window shade down to cover our dark night, to keep our safe light inside. Let the vampires wander the streets and only invite them in when we need company, when we've grown tired of looking in the mirror and seeing no reflection.

I wish I could undo the black-market flesh trade, that I could burn the hands off every pretend mother and father willing to pay for a few hours of family-time-and-then-some.

The Circus had three levels of hell. As if one wasn't enough.

It all began with a cast of kidnapped children, displayed in the black-market video bars and ordered like after-dinner desserts. The first level was trained, like pets, to perform at secret events for the wealthy. Sometimes these youngsters pretended to be members of the family, in a mock-celebration or holiday, kindling long-forgotten memories of a life when families gathered together, when a house echoed with the voices of brothers and sisters and cousins.

The second level was taught to dance and sing, a tiny cabaret on a candy-colored stage. Like nimble acrobats, they leaped across floors covered in expensive Persian carpets, tumbled between priceless antiques. Swift and lithe, their innocence erased with rouge and eyeliner, they acted out plays, entertained with rehearsed poetry.

But it was the third level that ripped out my heart, one swift wolf bite of flesh and blood and muscle, one devouring hunger that both maimed and killed. In the third level, prepubescent children were dressed in harlequin diamonds of black and white; they rode a carousel of flying horses. Here, the performance was dark and unrehearsed, the children were required to play adult roles . . .

Here, in a wassail feast of licentiousness, we destroyed the holy innocence of those we should have died to protect.

In my mind I can see the black market like a midnight bazaar in Marrakesh. Dark streets lined with open stalls, moon hidden behind the clouds. The air fills with the chatter of trained monkeys and the fragrance of exotic spice. Snake charmers linger in the shadows while someone offers to paint your body with henna tattoos. Colored lanterns flash within the stalls that you pass, revealing secret merchandise behind the counter. Illegal drugs, forged death certificates, clone bodies made to order. Anything you want, here and now, while you wait.

For a pound of flesh, the Underground Circus will come to town.

The horrors of the world, shimmering in veiled incandescence.

For a price, it can all be yours.

CHAPTER SIXTY-ONE

Chaz:

I waited forever, waited for the elevator doors to open. Outside, the sirens reached a fire-bright crescendo, an explosion of noise and light that demanded attention. The lobby filled with a cheap hothouse collection of real/not-real mugs, some dressed in VR skinsuits, some wearing actual flesh and blood.

Despite all the frenetic activity that pulsed around me, I stayed focused on the light above the door, the light that told me where the elevator was.

Third floor and descending.

Muscles tensed in my chest and arms.

Second floor. A pause.

I glanced again at the stairwell. Sweat on my brow, my neck.

First floor. A ringing sound. Gears grinding to a halt.

I heard the swoosh of the doors before they actually opened, I leaned forward, ready to push the inhabitants aside, to punch the elevator button and shoot up to the—

The doors were open now. A body lay crumpled in the

corner. Long white-blonde hair, slender figure in a black dress and boots.

A dart in her leg, the feathered plume tagging her like a prize.

Angelique.

My heart thundered out the rest of the world, pushed aside the sirens and the cacophony of voices. I rushed to her side, gently took her wrist, caught my breath when I felt a pulse.

She blinked her eyes, wearily, glanced up at me. Tried to smile. Whispered my name. Sounded more beautiful than I wanted to admit.

She was in my arms then. I was carrying her into the lobby; a medic with a big red cross on his white coat was running toward me; her head was on my shoulder and she whispered my name again.

I placed her, ever so gently, on a stretcher, my lips brushing her cheek as I did.

A kiss, I think. Unintentional perhaps.

But then again, maybe not.

Rules are meant to be broken sometimes, I think, when life and death collide on the street corner, when everything we value gets mangled in the wreckage.

At that point I decided that all the Babysitter rules didn't matter anymore.

The medic nodded at me. Angelique was wearing an oxygen mask and had an IV running in her arm. "She's gonna be okay," he said, "but I gotta get upstairs. Gutter punks shot darts up there too."

"Upstairs?"

Already his team was charging across the lobby toward the open elevator. I grabbed a nearby mug, shoved him beside Angelique. "You watch over her," I ordered, then showed him my tattoo. It was a command given by a superior. He nodded. "Make sure nobody touches her," I said.

Then I caught up with the paramedics, slid in behind them just before the elevator door slammed shut.

The moment I stepped off the elevator I saw the door to my suite hanging open. VR mugs shimmered in the hallway, then abruptly zapped away as they were each replaced by their real live incarnations. A couple of bodies lay on the carpet, like bits of hurricane debris ignored because the storm still raged. Wind swirling, howling, beast-like and voracious.

I could feel a chill on my skin as I drew nearer, a low-pressure zone that made the hair on the back of my neck stand up.

I rounded the corner, saw an instant replay of the scene in Isabelle's bedroom. I wanted to shove my fist through the fabric of the universe.

"God, no—"

Somebody was coming after the Domingue clan with a fierce determination, and now a hurricane vortex threatened to suck me in. I fought against it. Felt my muscles lock, turn to steel.

Fresh Start guards that I had personally trained lay scattered across the floor, some breathing, some not, all tagged with a variety of darts. Like this had been an experiment. Let's check out that new batch of blowguns, any darts will do, they all take down a man in less than two seconds. No matter if they get back up again.

"Took you long enough to get up here."

Skellar. The real thing this time, hands on his hips, he was surveying the room, stopped to focus on me.

A medic leaned over Pete, put an oxygen mask on his face. The guy gave a thumbs-up to someone across the room, then moved on to another prone body. Pete's eyes batted open, then closed again.

My brother lay on the floor a few feet away, a team of three white-coats surrounding him, all working furiously. It didn't look good.

"That was your sister-in-law on the ground outside," Skellar said.

"What the hell happened?" I looked at him like he was guilty. He shot the same look back at me. "Where's my niece?" I demanded.

He shook his head. "We haven't found her yet."

The dark cloud lowered, pressed heavy, squeezed all the oxygen from the room.

Without realizing it I grabbed something and threw it across the room. It broke with a loud crash. Startled heads looked up, then went back to work. This was not my reality, I was not going to accept this.

"Isabelle!" I called as I jogged toward my bedroom. "You can come out now. It's Uncle Chaz." I searched through the closet, looked under the bed, remembered games she used to play: hide-and-seek, tag. Little girls like to hide, please let her be hiding somewhere, let her be safe.

Let her be here.

I paused in the doorway, scanned the living room full of people, some working, some dying. None of them mattered. None of them had the answer I wanted. I kept seeing Isabelle's face as I sprinted to the VR room, then the bathroom, then Angelique's bedroom. I stopped again in the kitchen, glanced over the counter toward the living room, back where I had started.

Skellar was watching me. I could feel it, vicious heat on my skin. He moved closer, inside my danger zone.

"She ain't here, Domingue. I'm sorry," he said, something like pity in his eyes. The last expression I wanted to see on his face. "We're gonna have to work together from here on out."

I didn't want to listen to him, I'd rather he be my sacri-

ficial lamb, I'd rather toss him over the balcony like somebody had just done to Marguerite.

"This here's the work of gutter punks, nobody else in New
Orleans uses darts," he continued, as if he didn't notice that
I was about to explode. "But it doesn't make sense. Gutter
punks deal in illegal drugs and they use darts in gang wars,
not in a 'sitter's hotel suite. And I can't remember the last
time they kidnapped a little girl. Doesn't fit their code." He
paused. Maybe trying to see if I was paying attention, if he
was getting through. "Somebody led them to your doorstep.
Question is why."

I could smell it then, for the first time I recognized
something that I should have noticed the moment I walked
through the door. The sugary-sweet odor of flesh hovering
on the brink of decay. One of the medics had ripped Russ's
shirt open and an automated external defibrillator was slamming two hundred joules into his heart, trying to shock him
back to the land of the living. I could even see the bands of
muscle across his chest, rippling, expanding. I don't know
how he had hidden it from me or how I had been so blind.

My brother was a spike addict.

For an instant I was fifteen again, helpless in the dark
night, surrounded by a chanting mob, rocks flying.

My father dead on the ground.

And somebody had been standing just inches away, high
on spikes. I never saw him, but I knew he was there. Heard
his laugh, echoing hollow and cold.

The nightmare that wouldn't go away was alive and well.
Somebody was playing games with my family, knew all of
our weak spots. Even mine.

"Domingue, hey," Skellar called from the other side of the
room. "Take a look. They was watchin' this."

I snapped back to attention. He turned on a VR news video
of a dog. I watched a news clip, saw a black German shep-

herd rise from the dead, then somehow resurrect a second wild dog, a silver wolf hybrid. I watched the video, but in my mind I heard echoes of a previous conversation. Last night, that Newbie in Russ's front yard. "Where's the dog?" she asked, but I had been clueless. Never heard of a dog. Never heard about any of this, whatever it was.

"That must be the dog they're looking for," I murmured.

"Who's lookin' for it?"

I stared at him, didn't realize that I had spoken out loud. "The Newbie that self-destructed over at Russ's," I said. "She was asking about a dog. Right before she zapped herself to another clone."

He scratched the stubble on his chin, glanced around to see if anybody nearby was listening. They weren't. "Same thing happened down at the station last night," he said. Like he stood in a midnight confessional. "Somebody downloaded, usin' a handheld gizmo. He got in to see your brother, right before he was released. We found the body in the interrogation room, but all the video had been wiped clean."

"Somebody on your team is playin' both sides."

"It wouldn't be the first time." Skellar lifted his gaze toward the balcony, where several of his men were sampling for DNA residue, then he glanced back at me. "Look, whoever took your niece is gonna try to contact you. Or your brother, if he pulls through—"

The medics took the defibrillator pads off Russ, slipped an IV in his arm and strapped an oxygen mask over his face. He was breathing. He was alive. For now anyway.

"—and you're gonna let me know when they do. Got it?"

I nodded, wondering if I was willing to partner up with him. Didn't seem to matter what I wanted. All of a sudden, my options got pretty limited.

CHAPTER SIXTY-TWO

∞

Russell:

The orange light faded. In its place, dark water rolled over the horizon, poured into my lungs, black and brackish, pulling me down in a fierce undertow. A subsurface river crashed me against the rocks, thrashed me along the spiny ocean bottom until my chest ached. I fell limp and weary, wondered if in some other world I was still alive, still struggling to breathe.

Pain shot through my chest, white-hot fire and smoke. I arched my back; like a fish I flew out of the water, gasped a mouthful of air, then submerged again. Another shock wave jolted through my torso, my eyes flew open and I had a vision of the world the way it was before.

Isabelle laughing, hair in silken ringlets.

Marguerite dancing, red dress and silver earrings.

Dark water and a funeral barge, fire burning at the edges, me floating down the River Styx. I was breathing now, I think, but I was alone between worlds, heading for Hades.

Water lapping the sides of the boat, so close to immortality, if I could dip my hand over the side I would live forever—

Immortality. The dream that never belonged to me.

Voices. A multitude of whispering voices called me from rocky shores. Chaz. My mother. My father. They had questions for me and I tried to call back, but my throat was raw from that black, burning water. Still, my mouth moved and words came out, the dead speaking to the living, a séance that linked me one last time with the world of light.

All the while, the River Styx patiently lapped at the edge of my boat. Waiting for me to die.

If only I could dip my hand in the water.

CHAPTER SIXTY-THREE

∞

Chaz:

The hospital lights were turned down low and everyone spoke in hushed tones, as if that would make everything easier, like it could somehow soften the blow to the gut that was on its way.

He was dying. My brother was dying and I had to talk to him. Even if he didn't answer me. I asked Mom to give us a few minutes alone. She floated into the hallway, took holo Dad on some sort of glowing leash. I closed my eyes when he drifted past. Still can't bear to get too close to that thing.

We were alone now. Russ and I. He was breathing, ragged and rough. The doctor said he'd had some sort of allergic reaction to the dart. It wasn't a strong poison, but for some reason, maybe because of his weakened state from the spikes . . . there was no definitive answer for what was happening to him, but he probably wouldn't make it through the night.

He would never see his daughter again. Even if we could find Isabelle, right now, he wouldn't see her.

"Russ, it's Chaz."

His body lay still, arms tucked close to his sides. His eyes blinked open as he struggled against the darkness that surrounded him. "Isabelle," he whispered. Then a long minute later, "My baby girl—"

I held his hand. He was looking at me now, one of those brief coherent moments before the curtain comes crashing down and the lights go out. I could barely hear his words, so I moved closer, caught him in mid-sentence.

"—that monster took her," he murmured, "I couldn't move, I couldn't stop him—"

"Who was it, Russ? Tell me who took Isabelle—"

"—didn't you smell him that night?" He struggled to grab my shirt and pull me closer. "Didn't you smell him when everybody was chantin' and throwin' rocks? I can smell him, all the time—"

Rocks. Chanting. A stench wrapped around my intestines, soaked through my lungs. I could taste it in the back of my throat, heavy and sweet, like swallowing a mouthful of rotting honeysuckle. The night Dad was murdered. The nightmares. Somebody laughing in the darkness.

"Russ, are you saying that the guy who took Isabelle was there when Dad died?"

"—he's gonna put her on the flyin' horses—"

"Who? Tell me his name—"

He stared at me, as if he saw some dark terror in the distance, something approaching faster than he expected. He took one last jealous breath, then exhaled, long and slow. He fell still, all the answers I needed still locked inside.

There was a moment when all the lights in the room seemed to dim, when the darkness came on leather wings. It sat beside me, nameless and faceless, a beast all claws and teeth. I recognized the presence. Remembered a time when we met before.

Right now, more than anything I needed closure. And accountability.

"I'll get her back, Russ," I said, my words catching in my throat. I had to pause, had to ignore the gen-spike stench and the black slithering shadows. "No matter what it takes, I promise, I'll get Isabelle back."

CHAPTER SIXTY-FOUR

∞

October 14 • 4:59 A.M.

Chaz:

Midnight poured down into my gut, cold and stark. The monster that took Isabelle hadn't contacted us yet. I had a team of people searching the Grid for any clues. I hated to admit it, but my niece would probably turn up in the Underground Circus. I had to have people in place, watching for her.

All of them would be watching for a five-year-old, almost six-year-old, girl who would be sold in a few hours to the highest bidder.

Right now Angelique and Pete were sleeping off the venom that some punk had shot into their veins. In the morning, they'd help put together the disjointed pieces of this puzzle. Somehow they'd each played a part in this and it was time for them to confess.

Whether they wanted to or not.

But I didn't know if I would survive that long. Isabelle was out there somewhere, scared and alone. Waiting for someone to rescue her.

I stood on a wrought-iron balcony, overlooking the French

Quarter. The day had been sliced neatly in half, divided down the middle into dark and light and I was poised on the edge of both, wondering what would happen next. I felt like I had been in this position all of my life. Waiting for a bolt of lightning to shoot down from heaven. Hoping that someone would expose the evil that had taken up residence all around me.

It was finally time for me to make a decision—to fight, to die if I had to, risk everything to stop this madness. I didn't even know what the kidnappers wanted or who they were.

But I knew what I wanted. I could feel it boiling in my blood like a virus.

Revenge.

I wanted to see some monster's head on a pike, hear the beast drowning in the moat just outside the castle walls, and then bring the princess home, safe.

When had I turned into a warrior with barbed-wire flesh? I never asked to play this part. This was my Gethsemane, my rocky garden crucible. And I could tell a sacrifice was coming.

It was an hour before dawn.

Below me the streets flowed heavy with fog, a river of hazy gauze, a mist that stalked the city every night on panther paws. A cotton-like silence filled the sky. It ate sounds and spit them back out, half-born. Streetlights curved overhead; they winked and then went off. Suddenly the whole world narrowed down to the single street, covered with cobblestones and lined with double gallery houses, stunningly beautiful in their decay.

A phantom light danced through the mists. A precursor to the sun.

The City That Care Forgot began to reveal itself when a man on the street started to play a trumpet, the soft, haunting melody stirring ghosts from the mists. Shrouds and skeleton-like creatures emerged from the vaporous mists; they danced and swayed. People dressed for Carnival, high on life, high on black-market alcohol, high on whatever illegal drug they could afford. Like sinuous snakes they followed the music, hips swinging, arms lifted high in mock worship.

I watched as they shifted through white shadows, until finally they disappeared through a doorway.

And then I was alone.

Is this what purgatory used to be like, back before God emptied it of the dead, before there were no more souls left? No one prayed for the dead anymore. The Pope forbade it twenty years ago.

Pray for the living, that was what he said we should do.

But nobody listened. Instead we all forgot how to pray.

I fell to my knees then as the damp, dark fog swirled around me; I lifted my hands to the heavens that I could no longer see.

In the dark night of the soul, faith feels as dry and brittle as autumn leaves.

Spare Isabelle, I prayed. *Please. If there must be a sacrifice here, then let it be mine.*

This time, let it be mine.

CHAPTER SIXTY-FIVE

∞

Neville:

My boss stood bathed in his own circle of light in the center of the room. As always, he wore one of those vintage virtual reality suits, the kind that masks your face and garbles your voice. A couple of gutter punks lay on the floor, feet twitching like they were having puppy dreams. The room was littered with empty bottles that once had held a homemade concoction of bliss and jive-sweet and black-market rum. Strips of century-old wallpaper sagged in the corners of the room, revealing water-stained battle wounds from a war this shotgun cottage fought and lost, long ago.

I waited for the argument I knew was coming. I didn't have to wait long.

"This isn't going to work," my boss said.

I grinned. "Trusts me," I said. "This here will works just fine. All pretty-pretty, likes I told ya."

"No, it won't, you idiot. Russell Domingue is dead! I told you not to kill anybody—"

"I didn't kills nobody, that Domingue was pumped up with spikes—"

"Then how are you going to get the serum now?"

"I works magic, I always does. I gots voodoo in my blood—"

"You're high." The VR image fluttered and sizzled, transmission fuzzy.

"Still, I knows what to do."

"What? Tell me, how are you going to fix this mess?"

I picked up a tray filled with jars of cosmetics: powder, rouge, lipstick. I balanced it in one hand and gestured with the other. "I's gonna paints the little girl. Just like I plans all along. Gets her ready for the flyin' horses."

"But her father's dead and he's the one who knew where the—"

"The uncle's the one we wants now. Him and his Newbie. They'll gets us the stuff."

"How can you be so sure you can manipulate the uncle as easily as the father?"

I set down the tray, then flicked on a VR screen on the far wall. "Remember them surveillance tapes from the night we breaks into their house? Just watch and you'll sees."

Like a vintage film noir, a gritty sequence of images flashed across the screen. It was a copy of a copy and all the color had been washed out. Black-and-white digital photography had been shot in the little girl's bedroom, the sound muffled. According to the digital clock readout in the lower right corner, it started when three people walked into the bedroom at 5:56 P.M. Isabelle, Chaz, and the Newbie. The Newbie sat in a corner, silent, looking almost like a mannequin. Chaz played with his niece, talked to her, helped her decide what to wear.

I glanced at my boss. He wasn't convinced. Yet.

The video jumped ahead to 7:08 P.M. A blinding flash washed out the screen and erased everything. The liquid light. The tape had been tampered with, a scene removed—

the scene that showed me breaking through the window, tossing in a ball that rolled across the floor, then ignited. The light faded.

The room was now filled with blackened bodies, all children.

My boss looked away for a moment.

I's not afraids to look. I's never afraids of what comes next. I stands with open eyes and I waits, always I waits for what needs to happen . . .

"Watch it!" I commanded.

He turned back, VR head facing the screen.

Chaz was in the room now, frantic. Looking for something, weaving his way through the puzzle of dead children. Then he turned toward the bathroom door. "Isabelle!" he cried, his voice echoing on the recording, "Isabelle, are you in there?"

"Uncle Chaz—" The little girl's voice was almost lost beneath the roar of the crackling fire.

"Watch his face," I said.

The video skipped again. To the part where the broken door was peeled away. Russell and Chaz glanced at each other for a brief moment.

Here the video had been enhanced to show a close-up.

Something blazed in Chaz's eyes, settled on his brow, almost as if he thought about pushing his brother aside, going in and rescuing the little girl himself. Then Russell shouldered his way through the door and picked the child up, carried her out to safety.

I paused the video.

And there, frozen on the screen, was a close-up of Chaz's face. He could no longer hold it in, tears spilled down his cheeks, revealing the secret he had tried for years to conceal.

"Do ya sees it?" I asked.

My boss nodded.

"Then tells me, what does ya see?"

"The uncle, Chaz, he . . ." He paused for a moment, stared into the black-and-white face as if he recognized the emotion, as if he could relate to the hidden longing. "He wishes that the little girl was his."

"Exactly."

I is the silver wind that rushes through the night trees, the invisible river that changes the course of life and death. I is the bright star that burns forever.

I is the one that brings immortality to the gutter.

Where it belongs.

CHAPTER SIXTY-SIX

Angelique:

The dart shot poison through my system. My flesh burned. A virus rushed through my veins, my blood turned into blistering, smoldering magma. I felt like I would melt, my skin was wax and it was peeling off my bones in layers. I fell on the floor of the elevator and I was on fire.

I lost consciousness.

I woke up for a brief moment. Chaz was holding me. I felt safe then. For one instant, I felt safe.

Then I slipped away again. And the nightmares began.

It felt like I was going mad, my life became one long lucid dream and I couldn't break free. Sometimes I was aware of what was going on around me, sometimes I was sure that I was dreaming, but at other times reality seemed to take on a new meaning.

I was in a hospital and Chaz was with me. I couldn't see him, but I could sense his thoughts, pushing through the membrane of my mind.

I was falling in love with him.

But I couldn't.

I was standing in the hills of Scotland, beside William, his dark hair laced with silver, the lines on his face deeper than when we first married. He laughed, a thick, rich, boisterous sound, and he took me in his arms. We danced in the long grass while our herd of sheep watched. He kissed me and I leaned against him, hungry for his touch.

"It's been so long, Will," I said.

"Long, my love?" He laughed again. "Have you already forgotten this morning?"

I couldn't remember anything but this moment on this hill, this now. I wanted to stay with him forever, then I remembered. The dark cloud. My rebellion.

I had taken the Fresh Start chip.

He pulled away from me then, his touch cold, as if he had just remembered it too.

"You shouldn't have done that," he said. "You've damned yourself now."

"That's not true," I argued. "The Pope said—"

"And now, Miss High And Mighty herself believes everything the Pope says."

"No, that's not what I meant."

"It isn't too late," he whispered, now from a distant mountaintop. He was growing smaller and smaller, traveling farther away by the second.

"Too late for what?"

"To pay a penance for your sin."

Don't go, don't leave me alone, I don't want to be damned. But he faded away and I was alone in the dark, in this horrid unending hallucination.

And I knew there would be a reckoning soon.

CHAPTER SIXTY-SEVEN

∞

Chaz:

The hospital came alive with a clatter and a rumble, like a trolley car rolling down broken tracks. Gurneys and medicine carts wheeled through once empty corridors, the stench of antiseptic ratcheted up a notch. White shoes and white coats and a herd of would-be saviors jostled for placement in a morning rush hour.

Skellar and I each held a cup of strong coffee as we huddled together in Angelique's room. Our voices collided with each other, sometimes hushed when we remembered the danger involved, sometimes close to shouting when we tried to focus on what needed to be done.

"We caught one of them gutter punks last night, hidin' in the stairwell," Skellar said. Steam rose from the coffee as he leaned nearer and took a sip.

"Did you find out who took Isabelle?" I asked.

"Eventually." A crooked grin slid over rugged territory, creased one side of his face. "After I gave that punk one of those 'spill-your-guts' cocktails that you liked so much."

Angelique blinked and rubbed her forehead. She was waking up.

"And?" I prodded him.

"And suddenly he remembered a lot more. Like who took your niece." He pulled a photo from his pocket. "You know this guy?"

I stared at the picture. Icy fingers slid down into my gut.

It was that joker from the bar, the one who'd tried to take Angelique.

Skellar seemed to enjoy my reaction. "After talkin' to that gutter rat, I ran a background check on this goon and found out he was in Marguerite's *sous-terrain société*," he said. "This guy was one of her surrogate brothers. He has been for over five years. Maybe that's why he got called in for this job. Or maybe this is a setup that's been planned for a long time."

"You're sayin' this maggot had been crawling around my family for five years? Why?"

"That's Neville Saturno," Angelique said, her voice raspy and low.

I reached one hand out, touched her cheek. It still felt hot. "You okay?"

"I think so." She gave me slow smile, one that made my heart skip a beat. Made me feel alive again.

"You're pretty lucky you got to a medic so quick last night," Skellar said. "Your friend Pete got the same dart as you and he ain't doin' so great."

"What happened?" She pulled herself into a sitting position, sluggishly ran her fingers through her hair.

"Gutter punks broke into our hotel suite." I frowned. "They shot darts—"

"But Isabelle's okay, right?"

I glanced down at the tile beneath my feet, tried to imagine where my niece was right now, felt the surge of pain return like a cannonball through my chest.

She was holding my hand. "Chaz, she's okay, isn't she?"

"We don't know." Skellar spoke the words that I couldn't bring myself to say. He tossed the photo in her lap. "What's your connection with this guy?"

"I—I've known him a long time," she said, a dark expression in her eyes. "Since my last life." She looked hesitant to say more in front of Skellar.

"He's the one that has Isabelle," Skellar said.

Angelique stared into space for a moment, a terrified look on her face. "Has he contacted you or Russ yet? Did he tell you—did he say what he wants?"

"Russ is dead." My voice cracked when I said it, the words made it more final, more real. "And nobody's contacted us yet. What do you know about all this, Angelique?"

She glanced at Skellar like he was contagious. "Are you sure we can trust this guy? Odds are he's on the same payroll as Neville and all the other mugs—"

"Hey, sister, I ain't on nobody's payroll. Would my teeth look like this if I could afford somethin' better than jive-sweet?" Skellar grinned wide, showed us yellow teeth stained brown on the edges. "And believe it or not, there's some things I refuse to do. Kidnappin' little girls is one of them."

"I don't like mugs any more than you do," I admitted. "But we haven't got a choice here. Those gutter punks knocked out everybody I trust. There isn't anyone else."

"Okay, okay." She pulled her knees to her chest and her eyes turned the color of a stormy sky. "I don't care who ends up with the key to immortality, not anymore, not as long as we can get Isabelle back . . ."

She kept talking but I didn't hear what she was saying. I glanced at Skellar and I could tell he was having the same reaction I was. I felt like somebody had just rammed a steel pipe against my back.

"Are you tellin' me somebody figured out how to make resurrection work more than nine times?" I asked. My mouth felt dry. What sick jerk would want to hang around here that long? "But the DNA breaks down after six times. On the ninth cycle, everything is—"

She met my gaze. "We weren't using clones. This isn't like technological resurrection. This is something else. One injection. That's it." She paused, a pained expression on her face, as if she just remembered something. When she spoke again her voice lowered, became almost inaudible. "One dose, and then every time you die, your body just repairs itself. You just get back up."

"Like the dog," Skellar said. He was leaning forward.

"Yeah." A tear was running down her cheek. "Just like the friggin' dog."

I crossed my arms and settled back in my chair. Skeptical.

"You do the research?" Skellar asked.

"Me and Russ." She was watching me. "And Pete."

"You're sayin' Pete knew about this and he didn't tell me?" I pushed myself out of my chair, stood over her. "I can see Russ pulling something like this, he always wanted to be a hero, wanted everybody to bow down and make him king, but Pete? I don't believe it."

"Pete did my jump. After Russ . . . after . . ." Her hands clenched the blanket, then released.

"You're that Ellen they been lookin' for." Skellar connected the Domingue dots. "Russell killed you, didn't he?"

I blinked. All of a sudden it felt like I was playing solo, but the notes were coming out all wrong.

Angelique looked away, didn't answer his question. "Pete helped us with the research, you know he's a computer whiz. But Neville must have got his hooks in him somehow, got him to turn in reports on what we were doing. I always knew there was somebody else working both sides." She paused.

"But there came a point when I just—I couldn't do it anymore, so I destroyed all our files and let the dog go."

"You destroyed the research?" Skellar looked at Angelique like she was nuts.

She ignored him, continued to talk to me like he wasn't there. "Chaz, the mugs can't help us. They're in on it. The U.S. government is in on it too. This is bigger than Fresh Start, than any of us."

"Thanks for that vote of reassurance, sister. I'm lookin' forward to workin' with you too." Skellar glanced down into an empty paper cup, crumpled it, and then tossed it into a nearby waste can.

"You really don't get it, do you?" she said, a puzzled expression on her face. "Russ never told you. About your father's death, about your mom."

I watched the light in her eyes change. "He never told me what?"

"This guy, he killed your father. And he infected your mother."

I put the world on pause, began to pace the room, forced my lungs to keep working. The same guy who murdered my father had just kidnapped Isabelle. He killed Russ and Marguerite, tried to kill Angelique and Pete. And he gave my mother the life of a leper.

"Chaz?"

I could hear the music of my life turning sour, felt an emptiness in the pit of my stomach.

"Chaz." Angelique stood before me, the blanket wrapped around her. "It's going to be all right. I know how to get your niece back."

I saw her mouth move, heard the words, but somehow the chord progression was still all wrong, every note off-key.

"I've got what Neville wants." Eyes the color of summer

rain, refreshing and pure, met mine, forced me to pay attention.

"But you said you destroyed the research."

"Not the serum," she said. "That's where I was going when you found me in the elevator. I hid enough for one, maybe two doses. We can trade it for Isabelle."

Suddenly I knew I was the only one who could hear it, the only one who had it all figured out. I laughed. It was a song of madness, a song of dark depression and despair, a song that had been playing throughout my life. But it didn't matter anymore. We were going to win.

I sat in the chair and laughed until I started to cry.

I knew Angelique and Skellar thought that I was losing my mind, but I didn't care.

We were going to get Isabelle back. All I had to do was give eternal life to the monster that had haunted my dreams since I was a kid.

CHAPTER SIXTY-EIGHT

∞

Chaz:

He wasn't going to make it. I had to go rescue my niece from a Nazi wannabe, I would have to hold eternal life in my hand for a nanosecond and then turn it over to some gutter punk sociopath. But right now my best friend was dying and I had to say good-bye. Even if he had betrayed me.

Pete would always be my best friend.

Long pauses divided each breath. It sounded like he had barbed wire tangled in his lungs and they were filling with blood, like his insides were being sliced up by a miniature army wielding tiny razor blades.

He coughed. Blood speckled his lips. One eye danced open.

I think he saw me, but I wasn't sure.

"Pete, it's Chaz."

A whisper, hoarse and raw. "Where y'at, bruh." A thin smile. His skin was too pale, the circles under his eyes even darker than usual. He looked at me, death clouding his gaze. "Hey, I wants . . . to keep it . . . all," he said, each word wet and heavy like a shovelful of dirt on a grave. "Don't erases nothin'."

"I won't."

"And we never talks 'bout it, but yur gonna . . ."

I finished his sentence. "Be your 'sitter." I forced a laugh. "You think I'd let anybody else mess with you? I'll be right there, from Day One."

He closed his eyes, still smiling. Pain twisted his grin, turned it into a grimace.

I should have let him go in peace, but I couldn't.

"Pete, why didn't you tell me? Did Neville threaten somebody in your family?"

His eyes opened halfway. "Yeah." A look of torment flashed. "You." He coughed. He was using his last bit of energy for this. "He was gonna . . . gives ya what he gave yur mom . . . he was gonna takes yur life away, bruh, and ya only gots the one, I couldn't—"

I don't know what I expected. Maybe that Pete had gone soft for his own kind, that he finally realized that the view from the gutter overshadowed anything else. But I know I didn't expect this. That Pete had been standing in the gap for me, without my even knowing it.

"I'll see you on the other side," I said.

"Yeah." His last grin. In this lifetime.

And then he jumped. My best friend died and within an hour he would be downloaded into a clone somewhere back at the factory. Already somebody was starting the process. I made a quick call, told them to let Pete keep everything, all his memories. Meanwhile, a Fresh Start attendant bustled into the room; he ran a few tests, then whisked the body away.

I stood up and straightened my shirt, glanced at the clock on the wall. Stopped in the bathroom to comb my hair. I had to look presentable.

We were going live in twenty minutes. On the ten-o'clock news.

CHAPTER SIXTY-NINE

Chaz:

They dressed her in harlequin diamonds of black and white, painted her face and curled her hair. She drank something—some kiddie cocktail laced with drugs—and then she posed on a carousel horse amidst colored lights and calliope music. With a laugh and a giggle, her eyes half closed, she sang a song to a hidden camera.

And the bidding began.

I got the call one minute before Angelique and I went on the news.

"Yur little darlin, she gonna brings in a good price. She somethin' special, oh yeah. Wish ya could sees her right now, the way she flirts with those bidders when they asks their questions."

I put one hand over my ear, turned away from the makeup girl that was trying to take the shine off my nose. "You better end your auction," I said. "Right now, Neville, or all deals are off."

"What deals? You and me, we gots no deals."

"Turn on the news, you monster, and if anybody touches

my niece, I'll send you to hell myself." A light flashed and I switched off my Verse, then turned back toward the camera. The newscaster watched me with a puzzled expression, but as soon as the cameras came on, she was all liquid silver and sparkling teeth.

"Mr. Domingue," she began. I think her name was Judy. Or Jane. Or Janet.

"Chaz, call me Chaz." I flashed a smile of my own.

"Yes, Chaz, I understand you have some information about that miraculous dog we saw earlier today." She gave a subtle cue and the City of the Dead video ran while we talked. I watched Omega on the monitor, saw him die and then get back up. "Is this some sort of experimental prototype? Some new form of resurrection?"

I laughed. "Not exactly. Ms. Baptiste, why don't you explain, in layman's terms, what we see here?"

Angelique nodded. "Of course. My team and I were working on a breakthrough medical discovery—similar to the technological resurrection we're all familiar with—but actually—"

Judy-Jane interrupted. "You were trying to find an answer to the Nine-Timer dilemma, weren't you?"

"Well, it's like Chaz said, not exactly. We weren't working with clones, so as you can see the dog didn't need anyone to download him into a new body when he died. So it's not exactly resurrection—"

It was my turn to deliver the punch line. "It's immortality."

The newscaster stared at both of us. Dead air.

I grinned at the camera, knew that Neville was watching.

"Immortality . . ." Judy-Jane finally found her voice again. "So that dog? He's—he's immortal?"

Angelique and I nodded.

"There's just one problem," Angelique said apologetically. "We had an accident in the lab and all of our research was destroyed. And of course, we never did get a chance to try it out on a human, so we don't know for sure if it would have worked on people."

"But . . . but . . . if you created this once, surely you can do it again."

"I wish it were that simple." I was really enjoying the tormented look on the newscaster's face. Wished I could see Neville's. "You see, we based everything on the research done by my grandfather. If we hadn't had his research to begin with, we never would have gotten as far as we did. Unfortunately, his work was destroyed as well."

"But whoever worked on this project should be able to remember some of it."

"That would be my brother." I stared into the camera, a level gaze. "But he just died, a few hours ago."

Our interviewer glanced down at her notes, tried to figure out what to say next.

"There is one bright spot in all of this," Angelique offered.

"What's that?" Judy-Jane asked without lifting her head.

"We have one dose of the serum left."

She was looking at us now, open-mouthed. "Just one?"

Again we both nodded.

"Do you mind if I ask, what—what do you plan to do with it?"

"We're going to put it up for auction," I said. "And sell it to the highest bidder."

The offers started coming in before we even left the studio. We had a site set up on the Grid for a silent auction, any bid was allowed, and we made it clear that we would consider barter as an option. After all, we weren't looking for money. I put a block on my Verse to shut out interruptions, and I saved the number from my most recent caller. Neville.

His gravel-edged voice had carved runes in my brain, like

an ancient alphabet, spelling words I didn't dare speak out loud.

Memories of sleepless nights. My father, dead on the ground.

The fear within me turning to something cold and hard over the years.

A part of me was dead because of that man. He didn't know it yet, but I was the hunter now and he was the prey. Like a jackal, he ran over open fields, my niece in his iron jaws. But soon he would tire, his grip would loosen.

And that was when I would strike.

CHAPTER SEVENTY

Chaz:

A VR video was waiting for us when we got back to Fresh Start, my headquarters for the auction. A beacon pulsed, red and orange, at the top of the list of bids. I glanced at Angelique and Skellar. This one was a live feed. I told Skellar to get out of sight. I waited until he walked around the corner, then I flicked the system on.

"Messages."

The Grid sizzled and crackled, then with a jolt the live feed shot through.

Somebody was standing in front of Angelique and me, wearing an antique VR suit, face concealed. Clever. When the voice came through, it was impossible to tell whether it was male or female.

"Domingue." He paused. I was convinced it was a man, even though I had no evidence to prove it. "I have what you want."

"Really? You have two billion dollars?"

He laughed. "You don't want money." His transmission

sputtered, like it was corrupting the system, like it might crash at any moment.

"I don't know," I answered. "Money sounds pretty damn sweet right now. Lots of it. But since you're the genius here, what do I want?"

For a second he held still, like a mountain lake on a mid-summer eve.

"Revenge."

This guy was smart. I nodded, glanced at Angelique, then shrugged. "Yeah, revenge sounds good too. Just exactly what kind of revenge are we talkin' about here?"

"Revenge for your father's death."

"You tellin' me you were responsible?"

"Not exactly," the VR creature said. His voice went up in pitch, the transmission faded out, then snapped back in place. "But I can give you the guy that set it up."

"We already know who that was," Angelique said. "Neville Saturno."

"But you don't have any evidence. And you probably don't know what he did to your mother."

"What are you talking about?"

"I knew that would get your attention." I couldn't tell if our VR visitor was laughing or if the transmission was crackling. "He gave her that virus she has now. Made her live in quarantine, took her away from the rest of the family. I guess you could say he's not a very nice man."

"Or I could say that he does everything you tell him to."

He shrugged. "Did you know that he was also the one that broke into your brother's house the other night?" He shook his masked head as if mourning what had happened. "That beast killed all those kids with liquid light. I warned him, told him to use a lower dose, but he's like a wild horse. Impossible to tame. You know there's only one thing that can stop him." There was a long pause. "He needs to be exterminated."

We agreed on that point.

"Are you making me an offer for the immortality serum, or are you just wasting my time?" I asked. I wondered what Skellar was doing right now. He'd had plenty of time to run a trace on this transmission. As far as I knew, his men might already have this VR monster's house surrounded. But I kept up the facade. Besides, I still needed more information. "Because I have two hundred other bids clogging up my system and I need to—"

"You want to see your niece, alive and unharmed?"

"If you hurt Isabelle, you can forget about eternal life. You might not even live to see tomorrow."

His transmission crackled and hissed again, this time I was sure he was laughing. Nice to know I amused him. I imagined Skellar giving me five minutes alone with this cockroach, thought about how much damage I could do in that amount of time.

Just then an image appeared beside him, the auction video of Isabelle, the one that was still running. I hadn't seen it yet, we'd been too busy setting up our own auction. But as soon as I saw it, I wanted to erase it from my mind. I wanted to reach into the nether world of virtual reality and yank her out. She was tired, the rouge on her cheeks and lips had smeared, but she still sat on that painted pony. Superimposed on the bottom of the video was a list of questions that the bidders had asked, along with her answers; above her head, like a thorny crown, was the current high bid.

"Neville's running that auction," the human beast wearing the ancient VR suit said. "And he has your niece."

I didn't realize I was trembling until Angelique took my hand. Blood-hot rage coursed through my veins, forced its way into my chest. I felt like a pressure cooker ready to explode, ready to burst into metallic shrapnel. But I had to hold it in, I had to complete this deal.

All the way or not at all.

"Send me your evidence on Neville," I said, a slight tremor in my voice. "Immediately." I couldn't let him know our plans, I had to ask for more. "And give me his coordinates, give me info on the layout of his hideout. Once you send that, we'll make arrangements for you to get the serum."

"Risky. But fair." He turned and spoke to some invisible companion behind him. He was facing me again. "Okay, you should have it now."

I scrolled through my in-box. Found a message titled "For Your Eyes Only: Neville Saturno." Opened it and read. It was worth the trade. Too bad this guy wasn't going to get what he asked for.

"Did you get it?" a voice said in my ear. Skellar.

"Yes, this is exactly what I wanted," I said.

"Good," Skellar continued in a voice only I could hear. "'Cause my boys got this guy's place surrounded. They're gonna cut off all his communications in a second. Can't have him tippin' off old Neville. Keep him on the line for another minute or two."

"This is good," I said. "You're sure Neville has my niece and that he hasn't hurt her?"

The VR creature nodded. Silent.

"Just remember, if you're lying, immortality won't protect you from me. I can still make you wish you were never born—"

Just then his transmission sputtered. He looked over his shoulder as if startled. He didn't have time to say anything, his VR just zapped out. Gone.

A moment later Skellar walked back around the corner.

"We got him." He was chuckling. "He's not happy, I can tell you that much. Good catch, Domingue. This guy just happens to be a U.S. senator. Raffaele Greco from New York—looks like the government is involved in this somehow. He's gonna be fun to interrogate. I had to tell my boys to wait for me. Don't want to miss this one."

"I'd like to be in on that."

"It can be arranged," he answered. Then his face turned serious again, must have just gotten some update from his bust. "Yeah, I figured as much," he said to one of his boys. Then he glanced up at me. "Your niece ain't there. At least he was tellin' ya the truth about that, so there's a good chance Neville really does have her."

Angelique was rubbing her forehead. She leaned against the wall.

"You okay?" I asked. "Are you sure you're up for what we have to do?"

"You won't find the serum without me." Her eyes were closed and beads of perspiration glistened on her face. The poison was still working its way out of her system.

"I told you we could use a placebo—"

"Do you really want to take a chance with Isabelle's life?" She unbuttoned her collar and pulled her hair back. Her skin was flushed, like she still had a low-grade fever.

I walked over to her and cupped her face in mine. She felt like she was on fire. "No," I answered. "But I don't want to take a chance with yours either."

"I'll make you a deal," she said, licking her lips. "You do what you have to and I'll go to the lab and give myself a shot of antibiotics."

"You'll be ready in about half an hour?"

She nodded.

I glanced at Skellar. He grinned. I still couldn't believe that I trusted him. I think he probably felt the same way.

"I'll already be there, waiting," he said. "You won't see me, but I'll be able to see you. And keep your Verse on, that way I'll be able to hear everything."

Pete's clone lay on the gurney, quiet, waiting for life. Within a few minutes his download would be complete. His new body didn't look much like the old one, but I wasn't surprised. Everybody wanted to upgrade. One-Timers stick out in a crowd, with all their pores and pimples and childhood scars. The room filled with a soft glow as the transfer of his memories completed. He was breathing now, slow and rhythmic, peaceful. I almost hated to bring him back here.

"Wake up. It's Day One," I said. I could see Angelique outside the Plexiglas wall. She and Skellar were arguing about something, and it looked like he was winning.

Pete's eyes flicked open. Brown eyes, dark hair, skin the color of weathered oak. He looked he could have been my brother. He smiled. It felt strange to have someone recognize me immediately.

"How you feel?" I asked.

"Sleepy. Excited." His voice was different, a shade deeper than before. "Like ten things is goin' on inside my head at once. Did ya finds Isabelle?"

"Not yet."

He tried to sit up, but I put a hand on his shoulder. "You're not ready yet, bruh. I need you to stay here and rest."

He yawned.

"You might not like it," I told him, "but right now you're goin' back to sleep."

"Yur not supposed to uses those Master Keys on me," he said, yawning again. Then he lay back down and closed his eyes. In less than a minute he fell back to sleep.

I sighed, wished he was able to come with me. I glanced back through the window. Angelique and Skellar were both gone. It was obvious that they didn't want to work together, that we were all stretched past our limits. Our chances for success were pretty low, although I refused to admit it, even to myself.

I glanced at my watch. We had to get in position, fast.

Isabelle's auction ended in an hour.

CHAPTER SEVENTY-ONE

Angelique:

Sometimes you die all at once. It's over before you even see it coming. And then sometimes you die a little bit at a time, a tiny sliver every day. It's like watching a door close, knowing that outside everybody else is still at the party, the lights are sparkling, the fountain of life is flowing. But inside, it's growing a little darker by the second.

That was how I felt right now. Ever since I got shot with that dart.

Heat flowed through me, my chest tightened. I left Chaz and headed toward the lab, walking on stiff, unresponsive legs. Stopped to lean against a wall, felt my eyes close. I thought I was alone, but I wasn't.

"You're not up to this."

My favorite man in blue. Skellar.

"Maybe none of us are up to it," I answered, my voice weaker than I expected. "But that doesn't matter, does it?"

"You're a liability. You're not even fully cooked. What day are ya on?"

I frowned. "Is that was this is about? The fact that I'm a

Newbie?" I realized that we were right outside the resurrection chamber, I could see Chaz and Pete through the Plexiglas. I turned my back to the window. "Or maybe you're just
trying to find out where I put the key to eternal life. So you
can slink over there and take it for yourself."

Skellar grinned, a nightmarish sight as we stood alone in
shadowy halls. "You don't trust me, do ya?"

The fever felt like it was rising, my throat was dry. "For
some reason, Chaz trusts you," I said finally, "and he's the
quarterback on our little team, so—"

He pushed his face closer to mine, lowered his voice to a
threatening whisper. "You wouldn't be doin' all this to get
back at Russ, now, would ya? Cause there's a little girl out
there that needs some help. If I find out that ya'll are just
playin' some double-cross trick, you won't get no next life. I
got my own connections, sister, I'll make sure ya jump into
an infected clone."

I felt a chill wash over me. I wished I could credit Skellar
and his feeble threat, but I knew it was the fever, moving on
to the next level. I closed my eyes again.

"You better go get your meds," he said, almost as a con-
cession when I didn't reply. "But just remember, I'm gonna
be watchin' ya. If I see you do anything suspicious, I'll take
ya down myself. You won't need to worry 'bout your old pal
Neville."

"Glad you're on my team, Lieutenant," I said.

And I walked away.

I stood in the doorway, squinting when the fluorescent lights
flashed on, bathing the room in a garish brilliance. The
desks were in the same place, the computer monitors dark.
The left side of the room was still lined with empty cages.

I forced my body to move, to obey my commands. It
wanted to stay out in the hall, it wanted to run away. A

scream lodged in my throat, deep inside, like it was caught and couldn't get out. I passed the spot where I fell, four days ago.

Where Russ pinned me to the ground and strangled me.

A dark shadow seemed to move through the room, following me. At times I felt a chill, like it touched me, draped a black hand on my shoulder. Memories of my own death haunted me. I could almost hear the screams—my own—the lungful of air that I should have bellowed when he attacked me. But I didn't cry out. At least I don't remember if I did.

I flung a drawer open and grabbed a syringe, rifled through a bank of refrigerated cabinets until I found some antibiotics. I hastily filled the syringe and gave myself a shot. Then I grabbed an extra syringe, stuffed it in my pocket.

Might as well be prepared to introduce Neville to eternity.

I paused beside the cages; one door hung open. Omega's cage.

I knelt beside it, imagined that I could see his chestnut-brown eyes peering at me through the bars. He always watched me with hope in his eyes. Maybe he had known that I wanted to help him. And that I loved him.

Maybe he felt the same way.

I stood, my legs wobbly, my head spinning. I wondered if Omega and his pack were still roaming around the City of the Dead.

Dear God, I hope not. Please, let him be back in the bayou, or in some dark alley. Don't let him get anywhere near Neville and his Backatown demons. Not today. Not ever.

CHAPTER SEVENTY-TWO

∞

Omega:

A sea of broken-down cars glistened in the noonday sun; overhead, a competition of hazy blue and gold, underneath, a metallic accordion of rusted fenders, broken taillights and shattered windshields. Patches of dry grass bristled between flat tires; hoods and trunks hung open like lizards yawning in a sun-dappled swamp.

Omega and his pack lounged in the shade of three ancient Cadillacs, the cars piled on top of one another like the tiers of a chrome wedding cake. The dogs lay panting, mouths open, ears back. People didn't wander through the junkyard very often. They didn't seem interested in the old cars. Occasionally a rabbit or a squirrel had the misfortune to come scurrying past. But they never made it back it out again.

A gentle breeze sifted through the canyon of automobile carcasses. Omega lifted his nose, sniffed.

Something was coming. He'd felt it all day, like a tremor in the earth's skin. He could feel it in his paws, could almost taste it, sharp, on the back of his tongue.

A taste like blood.

It made him hungry and cautious.

He trotted over to a puddle and drank, water falling from his muzzle when he finally lifted his head. The air blew cold and brisk. He glanced at the Others. Two of the males and one female were sleeping. His mate met his gaze. She watched him almost all the time now, ever since she'd died and he brought her back.

Since he stole her from Death.

She rested her head on her front paws, but her eyes continued to follow his movements. He lifted his snout and took another deep breath. The river of air was changing, currents shifting, he could almost see a dark pattern taking shape overhead. Swirling, sinuous. Dangerous. His muscles tensed and his hackles rose. He raised his head to the sky and howled, long, mournful.

The Others were awake now, standing up, watching him. They all began to howl.

It was coming, whatever it was, and it would be here soon.

Omega padded off, following the currents. The Others tried to follow him, but he turned and barked, teeth bared. They all backed up, sat down at the edge of the junkyard. Only his mate refused. She stayed far enough away that he couldn't see her.

He continued to follow the river of air, knew where it would lead him.

And as long as his mate stayed far enough behind him, where no one else would see her, then she would be safe. The taste of blood was strong in his mouth now.

And on top of it, he could smell her. The woman who had given him eternal life.

She was coming back to the City of the Dead.

CHAPTER SEVENTY-THREE

∞

Chaz:

Light fell like sparks from heaven; it grazed sun-bleached tombs, cast staccato shadows through rusted gates. It fell in radiant beams between the vaults built to look like tiny houses replete with iron fences. It exposed narrow paths that stretched through this village of the dead, twists and turns hidden from view, where murderers and muggers often lurked. But the faithful and the curious still came. Even in the daylight, votive candles burned a quiet testimonial. They glimmered between cloth bags filled with dried herbs, chicken bones and hoodoo money.

The fragrance of death hung in the air, a scent old and fragile, like papery flesh.

"Over here."

Angelique walked ahead of me through the maze of stone monuments. Her long silvery-blonde hair caught in the breeze, seemed to float around her like she was a mermaid swimming through a coral reef. An ache centered in my chest when I watched her pause at a turn in the path. Despite all the confidence I had allowed myself up to this point, I knew now that this still might not work. Neville might refuse to make the trade. Maybe he never really cared about immortality. Maybe he was just doing what his boss told him to do, and now that we had his boss in custody, the parameters of this game were going to change.

Angelique glanced back at me, her face flushed, her cheeks a deep pink. The fever never really left. She should be back in the hospital.

I scanned the surrounding rooftops and wondered where Skellar was hiding. Was he watching us? Had he seen her stumble and almost fall a minute ago?

She was kneeling now, before a tomb littered with tokens.

"Here, this one," she said, pulling on a necklace that hung around the neck of a stone angel.

I looked at it, nodded. It didn't look special. A simple glass vial strung on a leather cord. It didn't look like something that would turn the world upside down.

"This is where we were the other night," I said, noting the landmarks. "Where you collapsed."

"Yes. I was looking for something, but couldn't remember what. I guess I was on autopilot." She tried to smile as she looked up at me. I could see the pain in her eyes. "Here, you take it." She started to untangle the cord from the other necklaces woven around the statue's neck.

"No." I changed my mind. We were going to do this differently than we planned. "Leave it there. For now." I helped her to her feet, then we headed back toward the cemetery entrance, shadows drifting as we passed ancient tombs that belonged to pirates, politicians and voodoo queens.

Somehow it seemed fitting that the secret to eternal life would be hidden here.

In the last City of the Dead.

Throughout the centuries, death couldn't be hidden in this city that pulsed with exotic blood. Because of the high water table, grave plots filled with water before we could bury our dead and coffins often floated away. Our early settlers had tried lining the caskets with stones or drilling them with holes, but it didn't matter.

In this delta land, the earth didn't want our dead.

And neither did we.

The wind picked up and turned cold, like it suddenly carried slivers of ice. Clouds were forming overhead and a shower of darkness descended as I called Neville. It was as if the heavens were rebelling against what I was about to do.

But they couldn't stop me.

I was supposed to go to his house, we were going to surround him with a perimeter of glittering VR mugs, like shining sentinels. But I realized that I couldn't trust this to a team of mugs. Angelique was right. Too many of them were on some hidden payroll. I wasn't even convinced that they were going to be able to keep that senator in jail long enough for us to pull this off.

High noon.

Isabelle's auction would end in twenty minutes.

"What does ya wants, Domingue?" Neville answered the call immediately, an unexpected slur in his words. He'd probably just jammed another gen-spike in his arm. "I hasn't heards nothin' bout ya makin' no deals. Do ya thinks ya can just toss some jive-sweet words at me and I's gonna hands over yur little princess?"

"Your boss turned you in, Neville," I said.

He laughed. "What the hell is ya talkin' bout?"

"Your senator friend Greco, he gave us enough evidence to fry you and stop you from jumping. He even told me where you're at right now. End of the line, bruh."

"I doesn't really works for him," he answered. I could

almost hear the gears shifting inside his head, as if he were looking for a way to still come out on top.

"The deal is between you and me now."

"It always was."

"Then put me down as the winning bidder in Isabelle's auction," I said. "I'll give you whatever you want."

"I wants the serum."

I grinned. *Good answer.* "Bring Isabelle and meet me at the City of the Dead. Be here in fifteen minutes or the deal is off. And don't bring your gutter-punk friends, unless you want me to kill every last one of them."

Neville laughed, a brutal and broken rattle, a scar of sound that reminded me of everything he had stolen from me. "Ya thinks yur tough, Domingue, but it's likes I said before, yur just a puppy."

Yeah, I'm the puppy that's going to end your life, I'm going to see you twisted on the ground just like my father.

I hung up the Verse.

Soon, and very soon. All wicked things were going to come to an end.

CHAPTER SEVENTY-FOUR

Chaz:

I'm supposed to be a big-picture guy, supposed to see all the angles from front to back, inside and out. Details, they're supposed to come later. I'm supposed to keep both eyes focused on how Fresh Start relates to everybody else, watch as the angst of the world pours into a silver bowl, drips over the edges. Fire, brimstone, ash. Watch it all catch fire, people turn to pillars of salt. Dead. Unmoving.

Nine-Timers, frozen in their footsteps, right in the middle of their last life.

Watch, complacent while the Hindus use resurrection in their unending search for Nirvana, for better placement in the caste-system directory. Watch as the Muslims seek a greater piece of Paradise, more virgins, a greater reward; turn my head when terrorism goes up and One-Timer razzle-dazzle redemption goes down.

Turn the other cheek whenever somebody asks the million-dollar question.

Why don't born-agains want to be born again?

Like a stone dropped in a pond of water, concentric circles

were going to widen and grow, until we were faced with a tidal wave of cause and effect that would erode the economic and spiritual shoreline of our country, of the entire world, if we didn't do something soon.

But it was really too late to save the world.

That's what my big-picture vision told me right now. At best, I might be able to salvage a tiny piece.

A little dark-haired girl. Five, almost six years old.

One child, if I could save one—this one—then that was all that mattered.

The rest of it could burn. In fact, it was probably already on fire.

I could taste revenge in the back of my throat as I waited for Neville. Like water in the desert, it both satisfied and made me thirst for more.

"What're you doin', Domingue?"

Part of me was wondering that myself.

Skellar's voice sizzled through my brain, he was waiting for my answer.

"I already have guys lined up, ready to surround Neville's hideout. Why'd ya go and change the plan?"

Because I don't trust your boys. Because I think somebody on your side isn't really on your side.

"Can you hear me, or do I need to come down there and—"

"Stay right where you are, Skellar," I answered. Angelique was leaning against a tomb, arms wrapped around herself from the chill that had come on us suddenly. Overhead the clouds moved and darkened, swirled tempestuously. The wind swept leaves from nearby trees, cast them at us like funeral prayer cards, like there was a message somebody was trying to tell us.

But I refused to listen to anything but the thundering rage in my heart.

CHAPTER SEVENTY-FIVE

Angelique:

The sun disappeared and a chill wind blew, and an eerie sense of desperation fell over everything. I was shivering in the midst of a skeleton silence. No longer guardians left to protect those sleeping, the myriad stone angels stood frozen in place, as if they too had been condemned and cast down. The heavens hung heavy, like stone, pressing against my chest. Each breath came as a struggle, like somebody had shoved tiny knives inside my lungs.

I coughed, almost expecting to see drops of blood when I wiped my mouth.

I leaned against a stone temple, wondered vaguely who was inside and if they had ever craved immortality, if they now tossed and turned in some dark torment and wanted to be set free. Even if it meant walking the earth. Forever.

I wanted to sleep. I wished I could lie down on one of those stone slabs and forget about all of this. Only one thing kept me alert. Isabelle.

Beautiful face, sparkling eyes.

Eyes like my Joshua. Gone now. I finally remembered

what had happened. He had decided to become a One-Timer. He left me and this spinning ball of green and blue. I wondered where he was, what was on the other side of all of this. Were his feet on streets of gold? Did he know my William? Were they friends?

Would I ever see either of them again?

I closed my eyes. Neville would be here soon. A wave of fever rolled over me, then another chill. Leaves cascaded through the cemetery, crackling and rustling, like dry scratchy paws. It almost sounded like claws, digging—

My eyes flashed open and I saw him, a short distance away. Padding between the tombs, still hidden in the shadows.

Omega.

I almost cried out when I saw him, but I held it in, glanced back. Chaz was facing the street, waiting for Neville. He didn't see the dog. I pushed myself away from the tomb, into the shadows, crouched and held my arms outstretched.

Omega bounded toward me then, almost knocked me over, covered my face with dog kisses, sniffed my hair, finally laid his head in my lap. I wrapped my arms around his thick neck, kissed the top of his head. In another life he would have been my dog, we would have walked through green fields together, he would have helped me herd the sheep. He would have slept on the floor at night, before the fire. In the morning he would have greeted me with a wide grin and a wagging tail.

Instead we met each other for a few fleeting moments in a cemetery of stone, him standing on one side of eternity and me on the other.

"Omega," I whispered his name as I delicately ran my fingers over his face, remembering the news video. There were no scars, nothing that testified to his recent death and resurrection. He looked up into my eyes. Almost as if he wanted to say something, like he had been hoping to find me here.

Then he pulled back. Suddenly cautious, he lifted his nose

and sniffed the air. A low growl sounded in his throat as he stared over my shoulder.

I looked behind me and saw Neville walking through the cemetery gates. I could smell his stench even from this distance. The sweet decay of gen-spike flesh.

"Stay," I said softly, in a voice only Omega could hear.

Then I turned and headed toward the demon that had set all this in motion.

CHAPTER SEVENTY-SIX

Omega:

The woman turned away. Overhead the sky howled, mournful and heartbroken, as if the heavens already knew what was going to happen. Omega crouched behind one of the stone tombs, watching her. She was sick. He could feel it in her touch. She needed to come with him, away from this place. He had tried to tell her, to get her to come with him, back to his pack. She would have been safe there.

But it was too late now.

It was coming, that thing he had been waiting for, walking through the cemetery gates. Sometimes it looked like a man, and sometimes it didn't. It stood upright, but it moved, wrapped in shadow, darkness trailing behind it, a swirling gossamer pattern that spun out in corkscrew curls. The darkness flowed and fluttered like a cape in the wind.

Omega felt a growl, deep inside. He wanted to lunge, to strike this man-beast, to attack him.

The man walked with the stench of death and he needed to be destroyed.

Omega stamped the ground with his front paw. He tried to get the woman to look at him, to turn and come.

But she kept her eyes fixed on the approaching demon, and on the vehicle that rumbled at the curb.

CHAPTER SEVENTY-SEVEN

∞

Chaz:

Clouds covered the sky, turned all the bright, hard edges into something shadowy, something obscure. I felt lost. In one moment my reason and my command of the approaching situation dissolved. Like sand castles worn away by one swift wave. Angelique retreated into a narrow crevice between the tombs, she knelt, her back to me.

Despair raged in my heart, stronger than any emotion I had ever known.

Isabelle's face appeared before me, transposed on the darkening sky, like a transparent piece of film: full of color and expression, yet distant. She might not come back to me, for all my plans. She might always appear this way, a memory, beautiful and fragile.

Oh, God, this ache was more than I could bear.

Then I heard the rumbling growl of a car, wide tires ripping gravel, saw steel and aluminum sparking in the dull light. It stopped in front of the gates, some hybrid monster that bridged the gap between a Hummer and an oversized SUV. A door breezed open and he stepped out.

The man I never wanted to see again. Not alive anyway.

Dressed in gutter-punk black, his muscles rippled through his clothes, like his body had a life of its own. His bald head was covered with metal studs, his lizard eyes hidden behind mirrored sunglasses. A lazy grin snaked up his left cheek, carved a dimple.

The door closed behind him and I wondered, was Isabelle inside? Was she safe?

The wrought-iron gate creaked as he pushed it open.

"Takes off yur jacket and shirt, Domingue. Throws 'em on the ground." He stopped about ten feet away from me. "And empties yur pockets. Slow and easy, now. Don't be tossin' no liquid light, neither."

I kept my eyes on him as I pulled off my jacket. I was unbuttoning my shirt when I saw a movement, faster than anything I could have reacted to. One of his hands lifted something.

"Chaz!" Angelique cried out, but we both knew it was too late.

The sting of a dart. A tufted yellow feather blowing in the wind. I yanked it out of my arm, saw an orange haze descend before the dart landed on the ground by my feet.

"Ya'll won't be no causing me no problems now, wills ya?"

Neville laughed as my knees buckled beneath me, as I crumpled into a crouching position. Orange light colored everything, clouds rolled into my chest. It felt like I was trying to breathe with a pillow over my head.

"Is she in the car?" I asked. I pushed myself back up to a standing position, felt my legs wobble, kept my eyes focused on his.

He nodded.

"Get her out, let me see her or no deal."

"It ain't gonna works like that. Yur Newbie, she's gonna

go inside and brings yur little princess out. All safe and pretty-pretty, just like I promises."

I shot a glance at Angelique, her skin moist, her eyes dull. She was too weak; if anything happened—

"Okay," she said, moving toward the vehicle on unsteady feet. "But if anything happens to me or the little girl, you might not like the consequences."

"Angelique, don't go—" I tried to stop her, but I don't know if my words even left my mouth. The door to the Hummer opened, then she stepped into a dark, fathomless chasm and disappeared.

And at the same moment, Neville kicked me in the gut.

I rolled forward, gasping for air, and discovered that a one-sided fight had just begun.

CHAPTER SEVENTY-EIGHT

∞

Chaz:

Orange tombs swayed and tossed, an angry sea, a melancholy parade. The wind blew, cold, the sky hung low, and the ground sparkled with flecks of red. My blood, I think. One of my teeth was missing, but I wasn't sure, underneath the pain.

One punch followed another, a rapid downbeat rhythm of knuckle against flesh—Neville's fists, my flesh, the tempo fueled by his gen-spike madness. At some point I thought that he would go on like this all day, until his halo high dissipated and I was a pile of brain-dead hamburger, ready for full VR life support.

But then, for some reason he stopped. Maybe because he realized that if he continued, he'd never get what he wanted. If I was dead or unconscious, his deal wouldn't go through. There'd be nobody at the counter to take his order.

One serving of immortality, ready and waiting. Yes, sir.

I pushed myself back into a sitting position. I needed some semblance of life, had to make him see that I wasn't broken. Not really. Damaged, yes. Defeated, no.

I thought I saw something move in the shadows between the crypts. Something black, watching me. I blinked. It was a dog, I think, but it pulled back into the darkness and disappeared. Just as well.

One mongrel was enough to fight right now.

The door to the Hummer breezed open. Both Isabelle and Angelique stepped out.

They looked okay, they both looked fine. Angelique seemed a bit weaker, she stumbled as she moved forward and Neville watched her with a sly, crooked grin.

But Isabelle broke away and ran. Still wearing the black-and-white diamonds, her face smeared with rouge, she ran toward me, her arms out, tears on her cheeks.

"Uncle Chaz! Uncle Chaz!" She flew into my arms like a baby bird and I held her close, felt her tremble and heard her weep. She was safe, my little girl was safe. Now that Russ and her mom were gone she was mine to protect, love and shelter.

And I wasn't going to make any of the same mistakes my brother had.

"She's leaving now," I said, my voice coming out like a growl. "Did you hear me?"

Skellar's voice echoed in my ear. "On my way. Immediately."

The lieutenant's car screamed down from a nearby rooftop, hovered a few feet over the tombs to my left. The passenger door opened and a stairway slid down to the ground.

Neville didn't react. He just watched. Almost as if he had expected this.

"I keeps my part of the bargain," he said.

"Go up the stairs," I told Isabelle. She didn't want to leave, she cried and argued for a moment, then realized that she had to go, that I wasn't going to change my mind. "I'll see you soon, sweetheart."

She paused halfway up the stairs and looked back at me. "You promise?"

"I promise."

Skellar reached out and took her by the arm, helped her inside the car. Then they took off, zipped out of sight. Almost like neither one of them had really been here. It was just us now, Neville, Angelique and me. And that dog, somewhere in the shadows. He was watching Angelique.

It had to be Omega. That dog she had experimented on. The one she and Russ had killed over and over again.

I just prayed that he wasn't here looking for revenge.

CHAPTER SEVENTY-NINE

∞

Chaz:

Sometimes life can be measured in small miracles. A string of diamond-bright supernatural interventions. Right now he stood over me, the monster that wanted to end the world, one person at a time. He had invaded my family gates and then waited years for this moment. Right now, he was winning. I was still on the ground, unable to stand, his poison in my veins. My life was his, and as far as I was concerned, that was just fine.

Because Isabelle was safe. Skellar came through. I never knew for sure if he would hold up his end of our agreement, if he would come down from the sky at just the right moment and carry her away. But he did.

That was my miracle. My reason for living and dying.

I guess I forgot that there might be more to the story.

"Gives it to me," Neville said. His lips were pale and cracked, the stench of decay overwhelming. That was when the scales of Providence tipped. No more interventions for me and mine. With lightning reflexes, Neville grabbed Angelique by the hair and pulled her toward him. She winced in pain.

I tried to stand up, swung a feeble arm in his direction.

"Let her go!" I cried.

He ignored me, grinned down at Angelique. "We forgots to mention something, didn't we? Tells yur boyfriend here yur little secret. Tells him what happened inside the car."

I instinctively ran my gaze over her body, tried to figure out what could have happened in twenty minutes.

"It doesn't matter," she said, her voice weak.

"She doesn't sounds so brave, does she?" He paused to laugh, raw and guttural. "Ya knows why? 'Cause we takes out her Fresh Start chip. She's a One-Timer now. Just likes you."

She lifted her chin. "I was done jumping."

Just then a blade flashed in the dying light, silver and sharp. It caught the sun on its tip, held it captive for a blinding moment then slid into position. Against Angelique's throat. Neville watched me as he pressed the handle of the knife. A trickle of blood flowed down, began to stain her dress. The look in her eyes made me want to cry out—she looked like a fawn, knowing it's about to be slaughtered. She was struggling to fight the fear but it rose to the surface, clouded her eyes.

"Ya tries anything and she's done," he said, then whispered loudly in her ear. "Whadya thinks 'bout that, sugah? Ya ready to steps into the Great Beyond?"

"The serum's over here," I said, forcing myself to my feet, ignoring the pain that made me want to double over. I staggered a few steps and gestured weakly for him to follow.

He pulled Angelique with him, one hand wrapped in her hair, the other pressing the knife. I kept glancing back as I moved forward. One misstep, one stumble and he could accidentally slice through her skin, the blade would find her jugular and take her away forever.

Just then the wind picked up, howled through the surrounding trees, caught dead leaves and forced them to dance around us, like lifeless marionettes spinning in a macabre pirouette.

Behind us Omega lifted his nose, sniffed the air, watched Angelique as she shuffled away from him. He took a cautious step, following us.

Not now, dog, if you jump now, she's dead. I shot him a warning glance.

Neville paused, then looked behind him as if he sensed something.

Omega melted into the shadows. Only I could see him now.

Neville's grip tightened on Angelique and a soft cry of pain shot from her lips. I had to get his attention away from the hidden dog, needed to make him face me and lift his pressure from the knife.

"Here!" I called. "It's just past this crypt."

He was facing me again, stumbling in my direction, pushing Angelique forward step by step. Her eyes met mine and she forced a smile.

"Come on," I said as I rounded a corner.

Then I knelt before one of the crumbling tombs, ran my fingers through the tokens that lay draped around the neck of a stone angel. Mixed in amidst weathered rosaries and strings of Mardi Gras beads I found it, the simple leather cord with a glass vial on the end. I held it delicately between my thumb and forefinger as I untangled it and pulled it free.

"What's this?" He came around the corner just as I was clasping it in my fist. "This ain't no time for prayin', Domingue. Off yur knees."

I clamped my fingers tight. "Let her go."

"What ya gots in yur hand?" He leaned forward, curious.

I opened my palm to reveal the vial. The serum caught a ray of sunlight and seemed to glow with a phosphorescent light, like a jewel from another world. I was just outside his reach. He'd have to take another step forward and release Angelique if he wanted the vial.

"Immortality," I said. "Eternity. There's one injection left."

Neville chuckled. It looked like he was going to do what I wanted. His pressure on the knife lessened slightly. He took a step forward and leaned toward me, reaching out with his other hand. Only a few more inches and she'd be free. I stretched my hand toward his, ready for this exchange to be over.

Just then a wild growl sounded from the shadows.

Neville turned his head slightly, frowning. "What the hell is—"

Before either of us could react, Omega bounded out from a crevice between the tombs. He had been stalking Neville, had worked his way closer through the maze of tombs and now he was flying through the air, teeth bared, claws like talons, a rumbling snarl deep in his throat.

"No!" Angelique cried out, her voice strangely muffled.

In an instant, the dog struck Neville in the back, the force of Omega's weight pushing Angelique away. But in that same moment, Neville instinctively dug his knife deeper.

A widening pool of blood spread beneath her.

She slumped to the ground, uttered a long moan and then fell quiet.

Neville still clasped the knife and now he lunged toward me, propelled by the momentum of the dog. His left hand grabbed mine and we both clenched the vial, pressed inside our palms.

With his right hand he drove the blade into my gut. Six inches of steel honed in on that sweet spot between my ribs.

Meanwhile, dagger-like teeth latched onto Neville's throat. The dog buried his muzzle in flesh and bone; he snapped and tore and thrashed until bones crunched and blood sprayed out.

Then all three of us tumbled backward in an endless arc of pain until finally my spine slammed against the cement, an agony of torn muscle and broken vertebrae. A second later, our fists hammered the ground in unison. I felt the bones in my wrist shatter and then a hundred tiny knives sliced into my palm.

Somewhere beyond horror and pain I realized what was happening.

But I was helpless to stop it.

Neville's body thumped on top of me and he cried out with his last breath. He struggled to break free from the dog's relentless attack, but his strength waned as his blood continued to flow. The force of his fall drove the blade even deeper into my chest until it found the ultimate prize.

My heart.

But that was when the real nightmare began, when he finally stopped flailing, for his left hand was still clasped with mine.

We were dying, both of us.

Our hands were locked together. And inside our palms, the shards of broken glass cut like a thousand needles, ripping through flesh and cartilage, intersecting blood vessels and capillaries.

And now the serum was flowing into both of our bodies.

CHAPTER EIGHTY

In Between

Chaz:

Once, centuries ago, we thought the world ended at the horizon, thought the world was flat. Oceans spilled over the tabletop edge and mountain ranges crumbled to dust. The sky burned black; the sun faded away. At the edge of our understanding, the universe ended. All reason converged to a flat plane, became something we could never traverse.

This imaginary vista tormented adventurers, kept them sleepless in cradled beds as they bobbed across surging oceans, as they were propelled into the unknown.

And then once we had crossed the Great Unknown Beyond, we lost all memories of that flat vista, we decided it was imaginary, something made of dreams and visions.

But now I know it was made of nightmares. And it was real.

Because that was where I stood right now.

The battle for life faded away as Neville's knife plunged deeper, found my heart, stopped me from going forward into Year Number 39. For a moment I flashed back and forth.

One second, I was lying on the cement, pain in my back, my chest, my right hand. Then I was standing on a foreign horizon, unable to comprehend, my mind too small to grasp where I was. Another broken breath and I was back in the City of Dead, fighting a dying man to possess the key to immortal life.

I became transparent, invisible, two places at once.

Part of me felt like I was being ripped in half; the other part felt more complete than I had ever been.

Then the flashing stopped. I found myself standing on a flat plane that seemed to stretch forever, shrouded in all directions by a foggy mist. And the battle wasn't over.

"Lets me go!" Neville growled. "Gives it to me."

My right hand clasped his left, almost like we were glued together.

Then he cried out in pain and I realized that this place wasn't what I thought it was. There was a division down the middle. I stood on one side, he on the other. Suddenly the mist cleared, as if a great solar wind surged it away, and I saw flames moving around him. No. People. Or what had once been people. Now engulfed in sulfuric fire, they writhed in torment, an unending holocaust.

Hell. He was standing a foot inside hell.

"Lets me out of here!" he cried. He stumbled, yanked me toward him. I felt the searing breath of hell sweep across my face, the stench of eternal damnation filled my nostrils. I fought and wrenched away, leaned back into a peace that surpassed anything I had ever experienced. Golden light bathed my skin, washed away the horror. I couldn't see them, but I could sense them behind me.

A heavenly host. More than I could count. I heard the sweet thunder of angel wings, inhaled the incense of ancient prayers.

And he was there, somewhere behind me. I was never allowed to look square into the face of heaven, but I knew that he was there, waiting for me.

My father.

Meanwhile, Neville and I stood, fighting for freedom, each of us looking into the eternity that could have been ours, if we had made different choices along the way.

Curses rolled from his lips as he struggled to break free from my grip, venomous words that fell to his feet like spiders, then scurried away. Overhead the sky hung black and red, scorched and barren of moon or stars; mountains loomed in the nether distance, too great to cross. They stood like a massive prison fence. And on the edge of the mountains I saw it, an orange-red lake of fire, more like an ocean really, with waves and whirlpools. It roared in the distance, like a hungry lion, waiting to be fed.

Waiting to surge, endlessly, dining on the souls that wandered across the hopeless horizon.

I wanted to let Neville go, to turn and enter the land that beckoned behind me, but I couldn't. We were bonded together, born like Siamese twins into this land of eternity.

Then lightning flashed across the sky. It tore the world in two, and a voice sounded like thunder, speaking words I couldn't understand. I trembled when it spoke and fell to my knees. When I looked up, I saw that Neville was on his knees too, that every creature near and far had fallen prostrate when the voice spoke.

The hellish vista faded.

We were back in the City of the Dead. Alive, clothed in flesh and blood. On our knees, facing each other, our hands still clasped together. His knife lay on the ground, and behind us Omega crouched over Angelique, as if protecting her.

Neville blinked, wordless, then he pulled his hand from mine. He swept up the knife instinctively, brandished it in my direction, then, as if realizing what could happen if we fought again, he held it low as he staggered to his feet.

I didn't react. My mind was still scorched with images of hell, a part of me felt as if I had been dead for a thousand years. I struggled to breathe, felt the muscles in my heart still mending, sensed fresh blood flowing through my veins, life returning.

I heard him running away then, footsteps that echoed through dusty temple-lined corridors, and I didn't care. I knew where he would end up eventually. I lifted my hand, glanced at the scars in my palm, scars that weren't healed, that would never heal, slashes from the fragments of glass. One shard had pushed all the way through the bones and flesh, left a hole in my right hand.

I stood on shaky legs, stole one complete mouthful of oxygen, sent it plunging on knife-sharp wings through my lungs. Turned toward what really mattered, more than anything, more than the demon that had been set free from hell, more than the thunderous applause of angel wings.

Angelique. My bright piece of heaven on earth.

She lay in a widening pool of blood, Omega, her snarling guardian, at her side. He growled and snapped as I approached, then seemed to sense the sorrow in my heart. He turned back toward her, licked her wound, slid a rough tongue over her neck and then lifted his head to hollow skies and howled.

But it had no effect. She didn't move, she didn't breathe.

Whatever power this dog had to bring his own mate back to life didn't work here.

CHAPTER EIGHTY-ONE

Chaz:

There was a point, at the beginning of all this, when the earth rolled out beneath turquoise skies, when heaven touched our horizon. Some say that back then, the first man and the first woman gave up eternal life, sacrificed it on some unknown altar. Maybe it was so they could stay together. She went alone, along a path of death and enlightenment, deceived perhaps. But then he followed, willingly. To be with her.

In that moment, when I held Angelique in my arms, I understood all of it.

Sometimes love propels you to do something you would never do otherwise. Like stand on the edge of eternity and fight a demon, to free a little girl from a life of hell. Like hold the woman you love and beg God not to take her.

Please not this. Not eternal life alone.

Please don't let me stand with heaven forever at my back, staring into torment.

I don't know how prayer works, don't think any of us will ever really know how spoken words can change the world we live in, how or why God would choose to stop the uni-

verse and listen. Like I said, I don't know how it works. I
only know it does. I only know that someone stands on the
other side of an invisible curtain and nods his head.

I held Angelique in my arms and wept. I knelt beside her
and remembered seeing the sky of heaven rip in two because
I didn't belong there. But I didn't belong here either. Already
I could feel the earth fading away, as if time no longer mattered; as if I stood still long enough I would see the city
crumble to dust around me, I would watch another generation rise up. And they would be just as hungry for immortality as the one before them.

Don't take her, please.

Words tumbled from my lips, tokens of the emotions that
raged inside. I found myself saying all the things I wished I
had spoken—before all this happened. But every word hung
hollow in the air, seemed to fall flat on the cement and crash
against worn tombstones.

She didn't move. Didn't breathe.

Omega continued to watch over her, a restlessness in his
eyes. He howled again and paced around both of us, then
finally he lay down beside me, his dark fur pressed against
my leg, his head in her lap.

Overhead, the lowering sun sparked through a bank of
trees. It dragged a host of shifting shadows through the cemetery. They stood in the empty spaces between the tombs
and then lingered there, as if watching me. Tall and slender,
the dark wavering shapes always stayed just out of my line
of sight, moving whenever I turned my head.

My throat was sore and her body was cold.

I knew that the empire my family built would collapse
soon, tumble over like a house of straw. The Number Nines
would rule the world for one brief moment and then it would
all burst into flame. Soon there would be no need for Babysitters. I would wander through eternity alone, like some sort

of unclean spirit, chasing down back alleys in search of Neville. I would catch him eventually. There might even come a point when the two of us would be the only two people left, our journey across a charred landscape forever destined to cross paths—at the intersection of heaven and hell.

My tears continued to fall and I shuddered, pulled Angelique's body closer.

Throughout it all, the dog stayed at her side, faithful. Perhaps he was unable to understand Death since it had no power over him. A chill wind whisked around us, ruffling the dog's fur, whispering Angelique's hair. And at the same time, the shadows moved nearer, no longer hiding—they surrounded me now and the City of the Dead seemed to pulse with a strange, rugged energy, something primitive, almost supernatural. I could feel the presence of that eerie horizon, the border between heaven and hell. Maybe it never left me. Maybe part of me was still there and I had pulled these spectral shadows back with me. I didn't know and I didn't care.

Light danced across Angelique's hand, almost made it look like her fingers moved, like some part of her was still alive.

I leaned forward and cradled her face in my hands. Every touch left a stain of her blood behind, a smear on her cheek, fingerprints on her forehead. My hands were red with it now.

I wished I could see the sparkle in her eyes once more.

I pressed my lips to hers, my heart crying.

One kiss. To say good-bye. It was our first kiss, really.

Imagination and hope can be cruel partners. In that moment, they worked together to create a lifetime of what could have been: Angelique and I together, laughing, finding some existence apart from my family's empire. I even thought that I felt warmth, that some part of her responded to my touch and I couldn't bear to let her go.

Then the dog howled again, long and plaintive and mournful, the sort of cry that breaks your heart because it's so wild and raw and alone. I wanted to howl along with him, wanted to rip this bad dream apart with claws and fangs. But it was time to let Angelique go. My arms were still wrapped around her and I knew Skellar would be sending a medical team soon. They would be too late, but still, they would take her from me, get her body ready for the grave.

Please don't take her away from me, I begged one last time.

Then the shadows moved even closer until they engulfed both of us, and that was when I realized that they weren't made of darkness. They were like holes in the fabric of the universe, each one of them filled with pinpricks of light, each one whispering and calling her name.

Calling Angelique to return.

That was when I felt it, when her chest was pressed against mine. It was so faint, so fragile. Almost like a distant echo, deep inside her.

A heartbeat. But only one.

I pulled away. As I stared at her, the ragged slash across her neck began to disappear, the wound closing. And then a moment later, a pulse centered at the base of her throat. Warmth began to return to her limbs and a pale color returned to her skin. Her cheeks and lips darkened to a soft rose and then, finally, her mouth opened a fraction of an inch and I heard her take a shallow breath.

"Angelique—" I whispered.

Omega lifted his head, his ears up, his tail wagging.

Another breath. I could tell it was painful, I could almost feel the sharp bite of knives deep inside, I wished I could take away the pain. Then the shadows moved away from us, dissolving in the autumn sun.

In that instant, her eyes fluttered open and she stared into the sky for a moment, as if saying good-bye to something. Then she looked at me and I saw it.

The sparkle in her eyes that said she loved me, that she wanted to be here with me. That maybe immortality wasn't such a bad thing after all.

And I knew then that I wouldn't have to spend eternity alone.

EPILOGUE

Chaz:

"Promise me, Uncle Chaz. Promise me that when I'm gone you'll burn it. All of it. Promise me that you'll get rid of me, and that the Nine-Timers will never be able to bring me back."

Her voice echoed across the years and I kept my vow.

We raised Isabelle as our daughter, Angelique and I, in that hidden South American villa Russ had stashed away. My niece lived a long, beautiful life, got married and had children of her own. After the Nine-Timer scenario began, there were no more rules about how many children you could have, so Isabelle had five. Two boys, three girls. I loved all of them like they were my own.

But the Nine-Timers didn't stop, just because their plan to live forever had failed.

Their DNA had broken down. So they went on a scavenger hunt for more. Hunting through the graves and medical storehouses, they began resurrecting One-Timers, people who had died hundreds of years ago, people who had died yesterday. They treated them like lab rats, using them to create fresh clones, desperate for a way to make resurrection work beyond Number Nine.

And they succeeded.

So now Angelique and I travel around the world, performing Freedom Ceremonies, secretly teaching others our methods.

When Isabelle passed away, we gathered every trace of her DNA, every sample of blood and tissue, every scrap of hair, and we burned it. In a way, her Freedom Ceremony resembled a pagan funeral, her body on a pyre, all the DNA samples in earthen jars beside her. Her oldest son lighting the fire with a torch. The flames scorching the heavens.

Ashes to ashes, dust to dust.

The world is fading, just like I knew it would, color bleeding away as each person I love dies. I will blink my eyes and Isabelle's children will pass away, I will turn around and then her grandchildren will be gone.

But the amazing thing is, with each generation, this family of mine grows.

We live in the mountains, hidden from the world. Omega and his mate, Alpha, are with us. He brings her back every time she falls, with a kiss. The wolf prefers to roam through the jungles, but Omega always comes back to be with Angelique.

From time to time, Neville pulls me back to the edge of eternity. Every time he dies. We are linked, 'til Judgment Day. Our hands clasped as we stand on the edge of heaven and hell, we fight, we struggle to be set free from each other, from this horrid destiny.

I have tried to turn my head around, to see that which is behind me. Streets of gold, chariots of fire, angels with skin like brass. My father, my mother, and now, Isabelle.

I saw Russ once, on the other side. His face had melted into something almost unrecognizable, but I'm certain it was him. He still carries the stench of gen-spike addiction. He looked at me, anguish in his gaze, and I wished I could do something. I wish I could've done something back when it really mattered.

"Isabelle's safe," I told him. It was all I could think to say.

"I know," he answered. "I can see her behind you." He tried to smile, but I guess joy isn't possible on his side of the Great Divide. He turned and walked away. I never saw him again.

Civilizations turn to dust around me, buildings seem to crumble the same day they are built. Time no longer has meaning, and yet, it continues to reign over the lives of those around me. It won't stand still but it has become transparent, almost like a mist without beginning or end.

Angelique is my wife, my Eve, my mate for eternity.

She died, a few days ago. Once she struggled with cancer, once she died from pneumonia. This time it was a heart attack. I found her several hours later.

Her body was cold, her face pale. I held her to my chest, whispered that I love her, that I will always love her. Kissed her lips. Felt the warmth return, slowly. Listened for that first gasp, that precious shallow breath, watched her wince from the pain. Felt the pain like it was my own.

Then she opened her eyes and stared up at the sky, like always, catching slivers of turquoise and sapphire. Another breath, more steady this time.

"How many times is it now?" she asked, still looking up. I always wonder what she sees, but we don't talk about it.

"I lost count," I answered. "Seventeen? Twenty?"

She smiled, soft, the grin that makes my heart skip a beat. Then she looked at me and I saw the love that I need to keep going one more day. And something else. A gift that I've come to need almost as much.

For a few sweet moments I can see what I have never been allowed to see.

In her eyes, I see the reflection of heaven.

And it reminds me that one day I might see it for myself.

THE NIGHT HUNTRESS NOVELS FROM

JEANIENE FROST

✠ HALFWAY TO THE GRAVE ✠

978-0-06-124508-4

Kick-ass demon hunter and half-vampire Cat Crawfield and her sexy mentor, Bones, are being pursued by a group of killers. Now Cat will have to choose a side...and Bones is turning out to be as tempting as any man with a heartbeat.

✠ ONE FOOT IN THE GRAVE ✠

978-0-06-124509-1

Cat Crawfield is now a special agent working to rid the world of the rogue undead. But when she's targeted for assassination she turns to her ex, the sexy and dangerous vampire Bones, to help her.

✠ AT GRAVE'S END ✠

978-0-06-158307-0

Caught in the crosshairs of a vengeful vamp, Cat's about to learn the true meaning of bad blood—just as she and Bones need to stop a lethal magic from being unleashed.

✠ DESTINED FOR AN EARLY GRAVE ✠

978-0-06-158321-6

Cat is having terrifying visions in her dreams of a vampire named Gregor who's more powerful than Bones.

✠ FIRST DROP OF CRIMSON ✠

978-0-06-158322-3

Spade, a powerful, mysterious vampire, is duty-bound to protect Denise MacGregor—even if it means destroying his own kind.

JFR 0510